CONGLOMEROS

jesse browner

CONGLOMEROS

RANDOM HOUSE 🏠 *NEW YORK*

Library of Congress Cataloging-in-Publication Data

Browner, Jesse.
Conglomeros / Jesse Browner.
p.   cm.
ISBN 0-679-40879-7
I. Title.
PS3552.R774C66   1992
813'.54—dc20   92-16365

Book design by Collin Leech

Manufactured in the United States of America
2   3   4   5   6   7   8   9
First Edition

To Jacky Baudot

CONGLOMEROS

No,
it's not the end of the world—it's only spring.

I have said that once before, a year ago, in very different circumstances; but this is a very different spring, and I was then a very different person. A lot can happen in a year to change a man, and has, in my case; and a long winter of isolation and meditation can bring him to certain conclusions about himself and the world in which he is supposed to live. Not happy, perhaps, but having exorcised the darkest of the tempting shadows, I am prepared. It is early evening late in March; the sun sinks below a wooded ridge, a ragged shadow climbs the stone walls of my hermitage, up past the window, past the gutters, past the chimney, and into the forest beyond; all is in shadow, though not yet dark. It is time for me to write my story.

It is true, I doubt my capacity to tell that story; I doubt its capacity to be understood; and mostly, I doubt its capacity to be believed. But if I were Jonah, or Job, or Odysseus, or even Germanicus, whose death caused mothers to disavow their newborn babies and barbarian princes to shave their wives' heads in grief, I would be plagued by similar doubts. And yet, theirs are stories that are believed and on occasion even understood. Well, I am neither Jonah nor Job nor Odysseus nor Germanicus—I am just an ordinary man whose ordinary weaknesses were tested by extraordinary circumstances—but I must tell my story doubts notwithstanding. And, taking my lesson from history, in order to tell my story right and to allay any suspicion intendant upon all claims of autobiographical objectivity, I should like to tell it as a parable.

Why a parable? Because a parable requires the reader's trust, because no one need believe in plagues of boils, sheltering whales, supermen, or evil empires in order to accept the truths that they embody, and because my story, all truthful as it is, makes similar demands upon credulity. An artist, perhaps, would rise to the challenge of making his story "believable," with all that that entails, but I am not an artist, either. I am compelled, like any writer of parable, to lull the mind with fantasy in order to attack the heart with truth. That is what trust is, and trust is what I ask of anybody who reads my story.

Picture me, then, as a great bearded Grandpa by the fire, dressed in downiest flannel, all redolent of Pinaud and hickory chips, and you sitting on my lap or at my feet, a child again. You'll believe me, won't you, if for the sake of a story I tell you the moon is made of cheese? And if I say, "This is the story of a little boy and a little girl and how they grew up together in a magic kingdom . . . ," you'd never dream of interrupting me, would you, or of questioning the fact that I am talking about all little boys and all little girls, of which you are one?

Well, then, though I am neither bearded nor old, and

though it is a lot to ask, let me be your Grandpa, sit on my lap, inhale my breath—trust me. And when I say, "This story is a parable," curl up a little, take the load off your feet, nestle down in the warmth of my belly, and cast the cares and burdens of the day from your heart, for you are going to hear a story, and you know you can trust the storyteller to tell you the truth. And when you're nice and relaxed, a little languid even; and when you're ready to hear a story that actually happened to me not so long ago; and when you're ready to believe me before I have even begun; and when you're ready for a little spell to let me tell you how to think; and when you hear the words: "Once upon a time an evil, ugly thing was born on Earth, and that thing was Man"—then you'll know that the parable is about to begin.

Aaron X.
Stone Ridge, New York
March, 198–

To get to the heart of the matter, I shall simply say that people I love have died, leaving me things. My grandfather died, leaving me his diaries; my father died, leaving me in a foreign land with a sick mother to care for; and my wife died, leaving me a wealthy man. That is everything, I think, that any reader need know about me, back when my life was normal and not worth retelling.

Well, perhaps not quite everything, since I have heard it said that familiarity with a narrator's background is supposed to enrich the quality of his narrative. What, for instance, do I mean by "normal"? To some people, my having been married since the age of nineteen to an English heiress might not seem "normal." The "background" that makes such facts normal is that I married a heroin addict, that we had been separated for some time, and that she died ignominiously at the age of twenty-five. I had tried very hard to help her, and when I failed had sent her back to her parents, who thought they could do better. Obviously, they did not. In the meantime, I found myself a lover who was different from her in every way, but something of my wife's alienated self-involvement remained with me and I in turn failed to readjust to the new, optimistic, constructive life my lover foresaw for me. Thus, cruel as it may seem and as it undoubtedly was, when my wife died about a year after our separation, and we were still legally married, I jumped at the opportunity my inheritance offered to resume, in her name and her memory, the fatuous ways we had pursued together.

The two years after Sarah's death were spent in a whirlwind of activity and globe-trotting as I endeavored to dissipate the wealth that destiny had bestowed upon me like an oil spill on a pristine shore. I gave up my lover, my freelance proofreading, my volunteer work at a city shelter, my correspondence Bible course, and any remaining association with bohemia. From my base in New York City, I scoured the four corners of the Earth in the pursuit of edification and distraction. Indeed, looking back upon it now, I see that the uses to which I put my wealth showed a lack of imagination worthy only of the rich to whom such things are not merely the analecta of privilege but the very substance of their spiritual diet. I bought my suits in England, my shoes in Italy, my salmon in Scotland, and my love in Bangkok. I paid the sun to follow me south in winter and north in summer. I paid the tides to rock and the winds to sing me to sleep at night. I paid the clouds to snow and the rains to cease. I loved not safely but too well. Lions in Kenya and starlets in Hollywood ate from my hand. I transformed myself into a variety of animals and natural phenomena to seduce, fertilizing the continents and their seas with my seed, which fell into the waters and gave birth to new islands, new fish, new heroes. I gave battle to poisonous serpents and vicious harpies, and emerged ever victorious. I became a Patron of the Arts and led the chosen people to the Promised Land.

Need I say, in this day and age, that I had no idea what I was looking for, and that I didn't find it? Or need I conclude that most people, given freedom such as was mine, would squander it as I did on wild-goose chases? Such musing may be timeworn and threadbare from the vainglorious abuse of philosophers and demagogues, but that is probably not without good reason.

Need I go on? I believe my point is made, and the purpose of my narrative lies elsewhere. I simply wish to convey the sense that my life was as devoid of satisfaction as anyone else's, but that my wealth had put me in a better position to appreciate that fact. True, it is an old story, perhaps the oldest, but if a person has any moral stamina or the stomach for unpleasant truths, he will be able to understand it less as moral mythology than as moral history, keeping in mind, of course, that no one has ever denied the slim possibility of learning lessons from history. Indeed, what sort of storyteller would I be were I to devalue the currency of truth and so impoverish the reader as to make hardship of the purchase of its lessons? No, like baboons in the zoo, the rich seem vapid and happy to us because they are conspicuous, that's all, and I am in a position to know. But in fact they are as empty and as lonely and as miserable as the rest of humanity, and sometimes they even know it.

That is the state of mind I had achieved after two years of plundering a selection of Western and Oriental civilizations. As I strolled along the rue Saint-Honoré in Paris one afternoon, I happened to glance into the window of a boutique, where a hairdresser in a white robe was manipulating the head of a seated customer. Suddenly, the realization that my life was without meaning fell upon me and swept me away like a tsunami upon an unsuspecting seaside village. I kept walking, but in a trancelike state of emotional shock. The weight of iniquity on my shoulders soon grew burdensome, but I somehow managed to reach the Museum of Modern Art, where I hoped to check it in at the cloakroom.

I wandered forlornly through the echoing halls, feeling sorry not so much for myself as for the world that had bred a man like me. It occurred to me that my wife—who, unlike me, had been a parasite since birth—had probably been set on the path to self-destruction by just such a sentiment, and I was compelled to wonder whether I wouldn't end my days as she had. I had never thought of suicide before I was rich, and lately it had come to mind with alarming frequency. Oh, for something to do! I feel certain that many suicides might be averted by having something to do—as mine was.

Entering a large exhibition room, I was distracted from these thoughts by a minor altercation going on in the corner. A tourist was arguing in French with a guard. The tourist was somewhat improbably dressed in a homburg and mackintosh, and though he was very old and very small, he stamped his feet and argued with the tenacity of a pit bull. It wasn't particularly interesting to watch, so I turned away to examine the pieces in the exhibition while the men pursued their heated discussion behind me. A few moments later, the guard, having been bested, walked past me muttering and shaking his head, while the tourist adjusted his hat and turned to examine a large sculpture nearby, though not before throwing a generically malevolent look in my direction, since I was the only person in the room. He had one eye covered by a black patch, like a pirate.

I followed the paintings along the perimeter of the wall. The exhibition was a retrospective of a little-known surrealist painter, one whom I, in any case, had never heard of. As far as I could tell, the paintings for the most part represented the artist's ongoing battle with his own ego, which was figuratively reproduced as a variety of symbolic and archetypal animals, demiurges, high priests, or demons. Finding little in his work to interest me, and being somewhat taken up with my own unhappiness, I moved rapidly around the circumference of the room, half-heartedly perusing a few sculptures on display around the floor. The last piece, and evidently the keystone to the exhibition, was the sculpture in the corner, which the tourist was still examining in its minutest detail. As I approached, I heard the tourist grumbling under his breath. He stood very close to the sculpture, in a proprietary stance, but as it was over six feet tall and standing on a pedestal, and as he was really very small, I had a fairly unobstructed view of it. At first, just to annoy the sour little man, I lingered motionless at his shoulder for several minutes. But presently I realized with surprise that I found the statue very disturbing, though I was at a loss to fathom the reason for my agitation.

By any standards, it was a rather frivolous construction. It represented a sort of anthropomorphic monster, cast in some sort of plaster. The monster had a large, slightly elongated human head, with great gentle doe eyes in relief. In this, it resembled a great many of the symbolic figures in the paintings—somewhat schematic, almost embryonic in the smoothness of its features and the prominence of its eyes. But it differed in two enormous respects: first in that, instead of ears, two small arms protruded from either side of the head, like little tentacles, long enough perhaps to reach around and cover the eyes, though in the statue they were extended forward, palms upward, in a gesture of vague supplication; second in that, beneath the head was not one but three bodies, a female sandwiched between two males. Each body had a graceful, arching neck that connected it to the head, the female's at the nape, the males' slightly higher, at the occiput. The bodies, faithful in every respect to the human model, were apparently pubescent: The female body had small, pear-shaped breasts with prominent areolae, and a well-rounded mons veneris; the male bodies, slim though not without a certain adolescent vigor, displayed the hairless and semideveloped organs of fourteen-year-old boys. They were positioned so that the female faced outward, and the males on either side faced toward her and one another, their arms entwined as if they were all three dancing together. And indeed, though hardly human, the smiling creature exuded a soft, hebetic sensuality, and one could almost feel the glowing resilience of its flesh beneath the downy skin of its supple limbs. It differed so greatly in emotional intensity from the other works in the room that, if it weren't for the eyes, one might have thought it the creation of a different artist.

The tourist had finally skulked off, and I approached the pedestal to read the legend. The sculpture was named "Conglomeros," and was completed in 1941 by Victor Brauner. As with the other pieces, the facts provided in the legend were accompanied by a small explanatory quotation by the artist. Of "Conglomeros," Brauner had written in French:

> Once upon a time, an evil, ugly thing was born on Earth, and that thing was Man. But before Man was the Conglomeros, and after Man will be the Conglomeros, for in Man is the Conglomeros.

The name, the artist, the quotation—they all meant nothing to me, less than nothing, the cryptic babblings of some talentless neophyte. And yet they had a powerful effect on me, the source of which I was unable to locate, the sort of effect one sees in a movie hero who, suffering from amnesia, comes across some artifact of his former life. I returned to my hotel strangely troubled, vainly focusing my powers of concentration on this enigma. After a light supper, I crossed over to the Left Bank to browse through the bookstores for anything on the artist Brauner, but that, too, proved futile. A cognac at Flore capped off my evening, and I hailed a cab and went home to bed.

I awoke with a start in the middle of the night, the sweat popping on my brow, my heart racing. A dream had shown me what, all unknowing, I had been looking for, and the revelation was such as to shake me violently from my seat of self-pity. I was on a plane to New York by noon the next day, and that evening found me rereading my grandfather's diaries.

▲▲▲▲

It is a curious anomaly that my wife, who lived such a short, self-indulgent life most untragically cut short by an overdose of heroin, should have left behind enough to make me a man of leisure, whereas my maternal grandfather, whose life had been rich and adventurous and productive, had left nothing but a few photographs, a small savings account, and a box of diaries. But stranger still is the fact that the diaries were to be at least as responsible for changing my life as the money. If I had known that at the time, I might have thrown the box unopened into the incinerator. But this occurred when I was only sixteen or so, and while my father, the historian of the family as well as the family historian, was still alive. It was only natural, then, that he should have eagerly volunteered to be the safekeeper of the diaries, which were dispatched forthwith to our London apartment.

I remember well the day they arrived in an unassuming cardboard box. I watched my father, trembling with excitement as if he were unsealing the Ark of the Covenant itself, slice with infinite patience through the tape with a razor blade and open the box, releasing a strong smell of mildew into the room. The box contained four tightly packed stacks of notebooks and a letter from my grandfather's lawyer requesting acknowledgment of receipt. My father removed the notebooks cautiously, leaving a thin layer of dust and paper fragments at the bottom of the box, and examined each of them in turn. They were all written in Yiddish, the oldest ones in a cramped, feverish hand that, with the passing years marked off from diary to diary, gradually evolved into a rounder, more fulsome style. The last entry was dated a week before my grandmother's death, some fifteen years before my grandfather's. What had ever possessed my grandfather, whom I had always admired as a simple man of simple pleasures, to keep a diary was beyond our understanding of human complexity, but my father nonetheless set to translating, editing, and codifying the enormous *oeuvre*. When he had completed his task about a year later, he presented me with a clean, typewritten manuscript of some twelve hundred pages. Recalling the fireside evenings spent on my grandpa's lap, listening in rapt oblivion to his tales of an adventurous youth, I found myself a quiet corner and read.

I soon found that my grandfather had pulled off quite a remarkable tour de force—he had taken a life so replete with danger and adventure in its early days as to fulfill any boy's dreams, and later crowned with a large family, robust health, and relative affluence, and had turned it into a twelve-hundred-page catalog of deadening banality. Of course, I had always known him to be a man of sober tastes and mundane philosophies, but somehow the mere existence of these diaries had led me to hope that he had harbored a secret and more passionate nature than the one he presented to the world. Instead, the reverse was true: He had used the diaries as a repository for all his blandest insights, the way some people hide their home movies in the attic, hoping they will be forgotten. I was even horrified to find, on one of the very first pages, the old joke that he had trotted out at every family reunion in my experience: "How do you make a Romanian omelette? First, steal three

eggs . . ." The fact that this joke was told him by a cossack
just before the cossack's horse trampled him underhoof
failed, in my mind, to lessen the shock of seeing the joke in
print. And it degenerated steadily from there—endless trea-
tises on knot-tying and saddle-waxing filled its pages, conversations with syphilitic inn wenches, drawn-out musings
on the fluctuating price of various breeds of Balkan leaf, de-
tailed analyses of the respective advantages of this mountain pass over that, or that over this, and so on with relentless
tedium. Here and there the narrative was broken by an
amusing anecdote or the relation of an egregious event
(such as the castration of a Macedonian pasha), but these
were so lacking in conventional "folk wisdom" and wit as to
be dismally appalling. In fact, if ever there was a document
demonstrating irrefutably that the concept of "folk wisdom"
was a myth invented by the rich as a palliative to their conscience, this was it. It was clear that in his youth my grandfather had been a man of eminent material practicality, and
that, like many of us, he came to regard consistency as a
virtue as he grew older. If I briefly relate the chronicle of his
life, it is only to emphasize the disparity between the things
that happened to him and the effect they had on the quality
of his imagination.

The son of a bootmaker, he was raised among his own
people in a Moldavian shtetl. During the pogroms of the
1880s, the shtetl was wiped out and his parents were slain,
but he managed to escape with his little brother Jakob to
Piatra Neamt, a village in the Carpathian Mountains across
the Moldova. The boys were adopted by a kindly Austrian
tanner and grew up concealing their Jewish origins. Eventually, though, growing scarcity and the increasing presence
of press-gangs caused them to flee once more: The tanner
gave them enough money to make it to Sfintu Gheorghe,
and from there they were to find their own way to Constanti-
nople and, finally, to America. But the boys were somehow

separated in Bucharest, and my grandfather never saw Jakob again. He roamed the streets of Bucharest searching for his brother, and was picked up by a press-gang, from which he soon escaped. A deserter now, and liable to be shot on sight, he tried to make his way back to Piatra Neamt, and instead fell in with a gang of Jewish smugglers whom he met in the Carpathian forests. He stayed with them for many years, smuggling soap, tobacco, leather, and other commodities from the Ukraine. It was only at this time, when he was seventeen or eighteen years old, that he began to keep a diary to while away the long evenings in their forest encampments, since he did not share his companions' taste for wine and rape. And it was that same restraint and sobriety that enabled him in the long run to save enough money to renew his journey, this time in style. He arrived in New York in 1902, and within a year was making a handsome living as a moneylender to Jews raising funds to bring their families from the old countries. That is how he met my grandmother, when her family invited him to celebrate her escape from Kishinev. They prospered over the next twenty-five years, bringing six sons and a daughter (my mother) into the world. Then they were hit by the Depression, immigration quotas were changed, my grandfather's fortunes suffered, and when he died in his mid-nineties he was still trying, unsuccessfully, to recoup them.

Either explicitly or through allusion, the diaries provided most of this information, which might reasonably be expected to sustain a fairly lively chronicle. And yet, whatever historical or cultural value it might have been said to possess was more than offset by the stolid lack of curiosity with which the diaries were written—the only enigma being why they had been written at all. I can remember feeling sadly and profoundly disappointed that all that remained of my grandfather was this twelve-hundred-page testament to human—human what? ambition? apathy? I asked myself at the

time—and continue to do so in relation to my own experience—how ambition and apathy are liable to be so ineffably
fused in one human saga. Perhaps the reader has given
more thought to such dilemmas than I; in which case, I leave
the question in his or her capable hands. In all events, it was
not long before I had forgotten both my disappointment and
the diaries in the excess of self-indulgence that was to follow upon my early marriage and widowhood.

But it was a sudden and violent recollection of those diaries that jolted me awake in my bed at the Georges V that
night, and that had me scurrying back to New York in tremulous excitement the next day. It did not take me long to find
the passage I was looking for, as it was very near the beginning. In retrospect, one might wonder why this passage did
not jump out at me from the start, being as unusual as it was,
or remain indelibly etched in my memory. But, of course,
twelve years is a long time to remember one paragraph; furthermore, at the time I had read it, it had struck me as unusual merely because it exhibited an imagination with
which I had not credited my grandfather; and whereas,
quoted here out of all context, it may appear to have the
playful ingenuousness of the truly legendary "folk tale," in
the body of the text it melds with ineluctable blandness into
the great gray landscape of the ongoing narrative so as to be
practically indistinguishable from the rest, like the shadow
of a flying bird on the bottom of a riverbed.

Here, then, is the passage. The year is 1899. My grandfather's band was being relentlessly pursued by a special de-
tachment of imperial cavalrymen that, like a horseback
posse in the Old West, ignored all political boundaries in its
determination to snare the smugglers. The band was driven
so far to the west that they were forced to ford the Moldova
and take refuge in the Carpathians, where they successfully
secreted themselves while the troops scoured the valley below. The gravity of their plight was such that they were com-

pelled to remain hidden for several weeks, during which my grandfather took part in a number of hunting expeditions in the upper reaches of the range, particularly on the massif of Ceahlau, above Piatra Neamt. It is the account of one such hunting party that I now quote verbatim from the translation (my father having edited out grammatical, punctuation, and orthographical errors):

... We got to the top of the ridge. Tudor pointed down into the hollow. "The doe is in there, I'm sure," he said. "You, Joshua," he said to me, "follow the ridge to the other side there, and Nico, you go down this [illegible] ... Whistle when you get there, and I'll whistle twice, as a signal. Then make for the center and we'll have her trapped. Be quiet as you go." Then I left, and made off. I got to the opposite side of the hollow and whistled, but I couldn't see Tudor or Nico. Then I heard the double whistle and started down the slope, creeping with no noise, which I am skilled at doing due to my many years of practice and my [illegible] ... I didn't see the doe but I kept going. Then I heard a noise, branches snapping. I thought it was the doe and I got my gun ready. I crawled to the edge of a small clearing, where the noise was coming from, and there was a lot of it. "It must be a very clumsy doe, to be making so much noise," I thought. But it wasn't a doe and I don't [illegible] ... in the clearing a boy, all naked, picking berries. But then I looked closer and saw it was a woman, a girl, with breasts. But then it was a boy again, with arms growing out of his head like antlers where ears should be. It had oval eyes, like a deer's. And I looked again and it was all of these at once. It had three naked bodies, two boys' and a girl's, all growing from the same head, and these arms from its ears, eight arms all in all. But it was hard to tell, because one body was leaning over the other which was crouching and the other man's body was kneeling, and they were all picking berries and stuffing them into its mouth. The bodies were all thin and didn't look very strong, but the skin was tan and smooth all over. This is what I saw and for sure I didn't really, I was tired and hungry and the mountains do strange things to men like that, but that was what I saw in the clearing. Then I made a noise and [illegible] . . . away, all of its bodies in a line like school-children or a centipede, and it disappeared into the woods. I couldn't believe it, this thing, and I didn't tell the others about it. But it was strange and I'm glad we left the mountains two days later.

I went over this passage several times, unable or unwilling fully to accept its import. My head reeled, and the full weight of my intellect, like a speeding locomotive coming into an impossibly tight turn, screamed against the confining rails of logic and experience. We all know what happens to a mind compelled to rebel against the evidence of its senses, and yet there sometimes comes a moment when the irrefutable imposes itself: Brauner's statue and the creature my grandfather described were one and the same! There could be no doubt about it! The number of bodies, the many limbs, the great oval eyes, the smooth young skin—all matched and gave dimension to the other, like the two plates of a stereopticon. What was I to make of it? What would you have made of it?

There, in the air-conditioned cloister of my bedroom, I strained for the meaning of the riddle, and, after giving it a great deal of tortured thought, I arrived at a number of possible explanations. Coincidence, though highly improbable, could not be ruled out by logical process, since the very soul of coincidence is its improbability; I ruled it out nevertheless. Another possibility was that the creature formed some part of Romanian folklore that had insinuated itself into my grandfather's psyche, to reemerge as a hallucination in a moment of weakness, pressure, or drunkenness. If Brauner had somehow heard of this legend, he might well have been prompted to give it form. A further option, again unlikely, was that Brauner and my grandfather had known each other, or that somehow Brauner had read my grandfather's diary; yet another was that, for some reason, my grandfather had taken great pains to forge the entry into his diary after seeing Brauner's sculpture, or that both men had copied the idea from a third, unknown source. Farfetched I knew each alternative to be, but how far more so was the evidence that had prompted me to concoct it! Nevertheless, none of these explanations was sufficient in and of itself to take a firm hold on the imagination. They all lacked a certain quality necessary to elicit the visceral reaction prompted by an unassailable truth. There came to mind only one explanation that was adequate in that regard, that truly conformed to the vast, contorted shape of the enigma, but it was one which I hardly dared to consider, let alone to believe. Yet even so, with a foreboding prescience that shook my very soul, I knew from the moment it came to me (and perhaps, unconsciously, from the moment I first laid eyes on Brauner's sculpture) that it was the only explanation possible, that its very implausibility recommended it perversely for acceptance, and that it must be the truth. It was the hypothesis that the creature actually existed, and that Brauner and my grandfather may well have been the only two men ever to have seen it!

All reason, all experience, all skepticism cried out against such a belief. With limp argument I sought to highlight the apparent tautology of this conclusion. I told myself that the only creatures remaining unknown to science are obscure subspecies of tropical aspidiscidae or tiny blind crustaceans living five miles below the ocean's surface; that no quirk of evolutionary mutation could ever produce such an animal; that monsters exist only in fairy tales and natural history museums; and other flaccid objections of that ilk. And yet, rather than dismiss it as pure deluded fancy, as every fiber of my being called upon me to do, the more I pondered the question, the more I was inclined to accept it. Consider the likelihood, for instance, that there is intelligent life other than ours in the universe—it is great, given the statistics; but thanks to the machinations of cranks and yellow journalism, few educated people give it much credence, whereas their erudition should, in fact, lead them to accept it. So it is with ghosts, living dinosaurs, telekinesis, heavier-than-air flying machines, the splitting of the atom, travel in outer space—is that clear? One's education, in expanding the mind, must also expand the imagination which outstrips and often second-guesses it, rather than preclude beliefs that foreshadow undiscovered or undiscoverable phenomena. All I mean to say is that, when one considers the things and beings that seem to exist in this world, the existence of a creature such as the Conglomeros is not as unlikely as it might at first appear to be. It has been on the slimmest foundation of circumstantial evidence—such as, for instance, the market economy or the resurrection of Christ—that many of our greatest institutions have been founded. And so it was with the immediacy and immutability of my preposterous conviction that the Conglomeros was alive in Romania. I did not want to believe, I did not dare to believe, but believe I must and believe I did.

I spent the next few weeks hunting down information on Brauner and Romanian folklore. I exhausted entire days visiting secondhand bookshops, galleries, museums, libraries private and public. I called the Museum of Modern Art in Paris and interviewed administrators of MOMA in New York. I wrote letters to eminent art historians and mined extensively through microfiche indexes and catalogs. I even placed a query in *The New York Times Book Review*: "For a biography on the surrealist painter Victor Brauner, I would appreciate any correspondence, published information, and anecdotal material from anyone who knew him."

Of course, basic biographical references were easy to

come by, and gave my theory its first, all-important vindication: Brauner had been born and raised in Piatra Neamt. While I was elated by this discovery, my faith in the veracity of my hypothesis had matured so quickly that it was barely cause for surprise. But every day, as my file on Brauner thickened, I saw the pieces of a puzzle come together in a way that was dazzling, awesome, vertiginous in the light of my singular secret. For it should be understood that none of my information was new or revealing in and of itself: There are historians who know far more details of Brauner's work and his place in art than I; and likewise, members of his family who know far more about his private life. But as I studied, I became further and ever more deeply convinced that none of them—neither his parents, his wife, his friends, his biographers, nor his devotees—was aware of the one element in his history that cast its shadow over everything he was and had done, that entirely altered the complexion of everything he ever said and the relationships with everyone he knew, intimates and acolytes alike. As in the Rue Morgue murders, the clues could not be divined without a radical shift of perspective—indeed, would not be seen as clues to anything at all—and such a shift only I, of every human soul living or dead, was able to execute. With the information at my disposal, and the secret that was the key to unlocking it, I brewed deductive brainstorms, wove spiderwebs of inference, influence, and connection, reasoned away the dark clouds of mystery that shrouded his life like a pall, repatterned, reconstructed, and re-created the artist's biography until it reemerged, glistening with the sweat of my labors, a monument to the timeless ingenuity of the human mind, a jewel reflecting the innermost crimson recesses of the human heart, and irrefutable proof of the existence of the Conglomeros. And when my biography was complete, I was able to reexamine the nature of Brauner's works, explaining what had hitherto been unexplainable, and deciphering the entire vocabulary of his enigmatic cryptography. Their hidden emotional intensity revealed in turn for the first time, the decoded works informed the biography with an unsuspected pathos, a lyric transcendence, and, ultimately, a deeply tragic undercurrent that was Brauner's eventual undoing.

What I present here are highly abbreviated versions of the works that grew out of my study. There is a biography, and an interpretation of the secret autobiography that the biography reveals Brauner's entire *oeuvre* to be. I have provided outlines only because the originals are too long and too analytical to be of interest to the casual reader, and because, within the scope of my narrative, they are no more than vehicles to an entirely different end.

As I have said, Victor Brauner was born in Piatra Neamt, Romania, in 1903. His birthplace is but a few miles from the woods described in my grandfather's diary. His father, a Jew, was deeply involved in spiritualism, and the séances that Victor attended in his childhood—séances during which tables were said to revolve, furniture to groan, and the medium to levitate—were to color his view of the world ever after. In 1914 he made his "grand tour" of the Danube, and it was in 1916, I believe, that he saw the Conglomeros for the first time. A short trip or a day's hike may have afforded the opportunity for this first encounter, and though such a journey remains undocumented, a strange shift noted in his behavioral pattern at that time seems to certify it. For he began his first experiments in painting immediately afterward, almost invariably choosing as his locus operandi the Belu cemetery in Bucharest. It may be that, given his upbringing, he believed that what he had seen in the woods of Ceahlau was an apparition, a demon or an angel, some excrescence of an alternate universe. Furthermore, it was at this time that he developed a passion for zoology, which such a sighting might plausibly have provoked and which seems to indicate a certain confusion over whether the creature was a natural or a supernatural being. That confusion would certainly have been exacerbated by the fact—which I shall corroborate later—that he spoke or communicated in some way with the Conglomeros, and that the Conglomeros vouchsafed the prophecy that was to change his life. Whether Victor ever tried to repeat this meeting thereafter, we shall never know. But it is certain that he did not see the Conglomeros again for another twenty years.

The following decade, in my biography, holds little interest. He developed a quiet Cézannesque style, which he abandoned for the Dada approach—propounded through his own review, *75 H.P.*—on his introduction into the Romanian avant-garde. In 1925 he went to Paris for the first time. As we shall see later, it was in Paris in 1927 that he first manifested a knowledge of his own future. Why he waited over ten years to express this knowledge is unknown and a point of controversy, but I believe that he had been severely traumatized by his encounter with the Conglomeros and had repressed the memory of it. It was not until he arrived in Paris, the site of the event that had been foretold, that he was able to recall with any degree of clarity the meeting and the prophecy. This theory is bolstered by the fact that his first painting in Paris was entitled "Ville Mediumnique." He returned the same year to Bucharest, where he was to remain until 1930. It is possible that one reason for his return was to search for the creature whose memory was beginning to haunt him daily. If that was the case, the search was in vain, at least for the moment.

In 1930, he settled in Paris, where over the next few years his friend and compatriot Constantin Brancusi introduced him to Tanguy, Giacometti, Breton, and the other surrealists, whose cause he fervently adopted. He had his first one-man exhibition in 1934, the critical failure of which prompted him in 1935 to return once more to Bucharest, where he joined the clandestine Communist Party in its fight against the insurgent fascism then overcoming his homeland. This journey, as far as I am concerned, was a great turning point in his life, because (I am convinced of it) it was during this time that he came to know the Conglomeros well. Whether he actively sought the creature out, or whether it came to him, I do not know. But it is certain that some sort of friendship or understanding developed between them, and that, in Victor's case at least, this relationship had deepened into love—what was, in fact, implausibly to become the greatest love of his life.

In 1938, at the time of the Moscow Trials, he was forced to flee Romania and return to France, a desperately unhappy man. In any case, like the servant fleeing to Damascus, he was compelled to return to Paris for the prophecy to be fulfilled, for in that same year his left eye was put out by shards of flying glass while he was endeavoring to come between two quarreling friends. This was the event foretold in 1916, the one he had been explicitly predicting in his painting (as we shall see later) for the past many years. All the greatest Brauner scholars—Mabille, Alexandrian, Jouffroy—as well as his closest friends, seem to concur on one point, namely that, in the words of Pierre Mabille, "the whole of Brauner's life converged toward that mutilation." With the ill-omened event behind him, Brauner was liberated, at least artistically—the disaster initiated the dawn of his "Twilight" period, which most critics agree to be his best. Nevertheless, in his heart he remained miserable, separated as he was from the object of his *amour fou.*

During the German occupation, he fled to the south, closely watched by the Vichy Government. However, and I state it confidently, the surveillance was not close enough. Harried and flayed by his heart's torment, and taking advantage of the reigning confusion, he undertook the long and arduous trek across Europe (on foot? by sea? by train?), eventually to regain his Carpathian woods and the creature he loved so dearly. It was a desperate act, and one that was to cost him his health, which never fully recovered; the more so since, I suspect, he was either cruelly rebuffed or deceived, in some way tragically disappointed by the Conglomeros. He returned to France and was immediately hospitalized, though none knew the true reason for the failure of his health. His recovery was a slow and painful one, as recovery tends to be for those who have lost the will to live.

He tried to enlist the help of several influential friends, including Max Ernst and Peggy Guggenheim, in securing a passage to America, with no success. For the remainder of the war, he installed himself as a quasi hermit in the Basses-Alpes, devoting himself to weirdly hermetic artworks in wax. What kept him alive at this time was a deep inward-turning, a defensive hardening of the heart. Indeed, a French art encyclopedia recognizes the various stages of Victor's recovery after this last trip to Romania: Beginning with an "exacerbated subjectivity" in 1941, it moves through "interior turmoil" in 1948 and a "period of retraction" in 1951 to a sort of "serenity" by 1965. What is remarkable, as we shall see, is the degree to which such critics so often correctly diagnosed the symptoms of his heartsickness without possessing the least awareness of its cause, a testimony to the eloquence of Brauner's works.

He eventually broke from the surrealist cabal in 1949, and was in continual decline—morally, if not artistically—until his death in 1966, a broken man whose only dream of love remained unfulfilled.

As I have intimated, this biography was in part painstak-ingly willed from a close perusal of Brauner's artwork, with-out which many of the required leaps of logic could not have been made. His paintings, sculptures, drawings, and pro-nouncements abound with veiled reference to his secret, as we shall see; indeed, after his final journey, they seem to be nothing but one continuous account of his struggle to overcome his misery—one vast, monolithic obsession. One might be tempted to conclude thereby that Brauner was taunting the public and secretly mocking the shallow efforts of the exegetes. But I believe that he was too unhappy to revel in his plight, and that he gave form and substance to his anguish merely so as to be better able to expel it, just as savages anthropomorphize their own emotions. The fact of the matter is, Victor could not help himself: He painted the progress of his sorrow the way people in love thoughtlessly doodle the name of their loved one, over and over again. And he does seem to have succeeded to a certain degree in objectifying his pain, but at a terrible cost to his human heart. But once interpreted, the works speak eloquently for themselves, so I will say no more.

1903–1930 As I have said, this is mainly Brauner's period of maturation, and his first meeting with the Conglomeros in 1916 may be regarded as its catalyst, though there appears to be no direct reference to it in his work. During this period, there are two manifestations of Brauner's foreknowledge of his 1938 accident. The one, already mentioned, is the painting "Ville Mediumnique" (1925). The second is a photograph taken in 1927 on a walk through Paris. The photograph shows acrobats performing on the sidewalk directly in front of the building where the accident will occur eleven years later.

1930–1935 "Self-portrait." An expressionist exercise, the painting shows the artist with his right eye enucleated and blood dripping down his cheek. At the time, Brauner obstinately insisted that he did not understand his own reasons for painting it so, and of course it would seem to signify nothing but morbid obsession for the next eight years, after which the popular consensus would favor the recognition of

Brauner's premonitory powers. There are other works which, at the time of execution, seemed to be carved from the same *idée fixe,* and which later also turned out to be prophecy. Such are his "Mediterranean Landscape" (1932) and "Magic of the Seashore" (1935), in which the artist is portrayed with his right eye pierced by a prong or instrument to which is appended the letter *D.* It was, in fact, the artist Dominguez who would put out his eye. None can question the involvement of a mystery at work in the case, but whereas critics and historians assume the forces of prophecy or psychology at work, I see the hand of a sibyl—the Conglomeros.

1935–1936 "Anatomy of Desire" series. These drawings provide the indices for Brauner's prolonged sojourn with the Conglomeros. Several sketches in pen and china ink depict the deformed woman perfectly adapted for male sexual gratification, including pectoral vulvae, gripping handles on the hips, three-inch nipples, tails for wrapping around a partner's legs or waist, dorsal breasts, foot rests on the calves, and fleshy holes in the hands. We see through these drawings a man unaccountably obsessed and frustrated by the sexuality of the monstrous.

1936–1937 "The Phantom of Departure," pen and china ink.

"The Last Journey." The meaning of this painting, like that of many others, was indecipherable without a prior understanding of those that came much later. The canvas contains three figures in a desert landscape under a gloomy sky, with one straight road leading to the flat horizon. In the foreground is a type of monster, or organic robot, human in shape but with curved horns sprouting from the eye sockets—a symbol, according to Mabille, of male virility. In its hand it holds an eyeball, which it seems to be perusing wistfully. Behind it walks a pair of legs without head or torso, but with an eye placed at the top of the truncated hips. Behind this, a weeping man sits forlornly on a giant eyeball at the side of the road. A smokestack belching steam on the far right horizon completes the ensemble.

When one remembers that at this time Brauner was in perhaps daily contact with the Conglomeros, which by now he had grown to love (cf. 1941–), the meaning of this painting becomes clear. He has lost the political struggle in his homeland and must leave, staying only at the peril of his life; this may indeed be his "last journey," which accounts for the weeping man: All he can take with him as a memento is the prophecy of doom upon which he sits; he leaves blindly, "headless." He knows, too, that his eye is not long for this world, and so regards it wistfully, as if for the last time. The smokestack is the ominous and inescapable presence of industrialized Western Europe, to which he must now return, leaving his loved one behind.

1939   Paintings of the "Twilight" period. Inspired by melancholy, not for his lost eye but for his lost love. It is quite clear in retrospect that these are labors of love, a fact which Alain Jouffroy seems to recognize by calling "Nude and Spectral Still Life" a reference to "prereality and postreality." The seductive sorceress of "The Philosopher's Stone" (1940), and its glowing, haloed diamond; the dark, reflective sadness of "The Inner Life"; the searing torsion of "Departure I": All show a man pining, torn apart by love, and seem almost to suggest the impulse of sexual desire.

1941   It is not until this year that the characteristic head structure of the Conglomeros (enormous oval eyes, Roman nose, Slavic cheekbones, and sweeping jawline) begins to appear in Brauner's work, and then with alarming frequency.

The "Conglomeros" series. This includes a dozen studies of the monster, one canvas, and the sculpture mentioned above, all executed between July 25 and September 13, immediately after Brauner's discharge from the hospital in Marseille. These were the works that finally convinced me not only of the creature's existence, but also of the clandestine 1940 visit. It seemed a strange coincidence to me that Victor, with no history of ill health, should have fallen gravely ill at precisely the moment when it was discovered that his whereabouts had been unknown for some time (the reader will remember that, with France but newly fallen, communication was rather haphazard and unreliable). And then, to embark on a frenzy of creativity, all with the same subject, as if he had only been waiting for his health to return in order to discharge this heavy burden of obsession— all of this seemed highly unusual unless one assumed a third visit, in which case it fit snugly into the overall scheme of things.

1942–1945 With painting materials unavailable, Brauner uses his candle rations to create strange pieces out of molten wax on wood panels. Secluded in his cabin, high on the Alpine slopes that remind him of his Carpathian idyll, Brauner darkly broods.

1946 From this time begins his transition into what critics have variously labeled "effigial painting," "painting-writing," or "figurative abstraction." Strange effigies appear, shrouded in mystical and hermetic symbols, icons to an unclarified vision of mythology, in which the sharp graphism "seems deliberately to confuse the meaning and corporality of beings." Clearly, they are the products of a deeply disturbed mind: Victor has already understood that he will never see his beloved again, and these paintings represent his inner dialectic, his coming-to-terms on the one hand with his overpowering attachment, and on the other with the realization of its inevitable frustration. Take, for instance, the work "Mythotomie": ". . . the body of a naked woman is topped by four heads in profile; to one side through a window one sees a dark mountainscape, a blindfolded priestess holding an Egyptian tau and a snake, her ceremonial robes draped so as to reveal her breasts and sex. Her head is crowned by a double-face whose one frontal eye is encompassed by flames." This seems to be yet another enigmatic depiction of the inner turmoil which Brauner was experiencing over his confused sexuality. The naked woman is the Conglomeros, deliberately disguised by the artist in what may be a clumsy attempt to defuse his own image of it/her. The priestess is Brauner himself, blinded, unsure of his own sex, dominated by the opposing forces of life and sin. It was this painting that gave me the idea that Brauner had been rebuffed, since a mutually reciprocated love, even if thwarted by fate, would not have given rise to such confusion. As one critic puts it, "a slice of mythology, mythic anatomy, one cannot tell." In any case, the rest of his life will be devoted to reconciling himself to cruel destiny, and to the overthrow of the haunting memory of his love.

"The Meeting at 2 bis rue Perrel" (Brauner's then-current address). This painting, a deliberate reference to Rousseau, cleared up many points of uncertainty for me. On a background of moonlit woods, a two-bodied Conglomeros reaches out its hands, palms upwards, to a dark, voluptuous young woman with a snake draped over her shoulders. A pink flamingo watches what might be a seduction scene and is certainly a dreamscape. Studying this painting, I realized that it represented *the* dream, the one hope of Victor's poor life. The monster is incomplete, unwhole, and must absorb the third body (Brauner) in order to achieve wholeness. This is Victor's dream—the Conglomeros needs him if it is ever to be whole again. It is the only glimmer of hope in all those dreary years behind and ahead. To my mind there are two interpretations possible. The first is that Victor feels himself to be the injured party, the "innocent one," and the monster's upturned hands are in token of atonement or apology, which jibes with the rejection theory. The second is that Victor is the guilty one, the party at fault in the dispute, and that it is properly *his* impurity which prevents the reconciliations; the hands in this case are begging for *his* apology, the atonement of *his* guilt, without which a reconciliation cannot be effected, the creature itself being pure. Could it be that, somehow, Brauner had developed some sort of perverse sexual desire for the creature? Poor, desperate Victor, how well you understood the hopelessness of the situation!

"The Triumph of Doubt."

1948   "Totem of Wounded Subjectivity." He is building the subjective strength necessary to bear his burden; it is a painful process, but not without rewards in regard to his agony.

"Victor Victorios Crushing the Caster of Spells." An unwitting critic has aptly commented on this painting: "The ego has opted for the strength of real subjectivity, and violently pulverizes those who impede its triumphal march ..." It would be easy to congratulate Victor on the defeat of his torment. But what has the victory cost him? The wall of self-immolation is almost complete, and love has been shut out as we see in:

1951   "A Being Retracted, Refracted, Spied on by His Own Conscience." Oh, miserable, wretched Victor! Of himself, he can only say: "I cry and I make rain, it rains and the rain flows from my eyes."

1952 "Depolarization of the Conscience." Brauner comments: "Lost beings in search of a bond of love . . . in spite of being together find themselves definitely isolated in their subjective yearning."

1957 "Realization of the Couple." In an incandescent coffin the couple reaches out to touch and is finally united for the first time—in death. This is Victor's ultimate resignation: He has hit bottom.

1964 In a commentary on his painting "The Silent Light," Brauner shows to what extent his love is now but a slight, onerous memory, and himself an island of solipsism: "I am the humanized-dehumanized assemblage, and beyond the circumstantial tumult, I am inorganic peace."

1965 "The Mother of Myths." A year before Brauner's death, the Conglomeros no longer bears its own form, it has become a primitive woman dancing in the belly of a jungle proto-mammal; it has been entirely synthesized into myth, etherealized, "inorganic," the atavistic memory of the primordial. Whose single eye stares over her left shoulder? Perhaps, in his decline, that is how Victor saw himself all those years—staring at life over the shoulder of a myth.

1966 Death comes to Victor Brauner. In tribute, Guido Ballo will write: "Brauner himself considered art and life to be the same thing." He might have added, "And so too with love and death."

▲▲▲▲

The unabridged versions of these studies run to hundreds of pages, completed in the space of a few weeks. Having finished them, I collapsed from exhaustion and stress, and took to my bed. My convalescence gave me time to think, and my thoughts soon turned to terrifying pursuits. Anyone who has understood the significance of my studies can well imagine what I am about to say.

I had discovered, beyond any shadow of a doubt and any limit of credulity, the existence of a real, living mythical creature on the planet, such as has been sought over the millennia and found only by the ancients. Of course, the last documented sightings had taken place over forty years earlier, and I had to accept the fact that anything could have happened to the creature since then. Nevertheless, I felt in my heart that it was still alive. Was I mad, do you think? If I sound mad, it is because of the difficulty inherent in describing my certainty about the creature's existence. On the other hand, perhaps I was mad; perhaps one *must* be mad to admit of the possibility of such things, even if—or perhaps because—they do exist. Indeed, subsequent events were to prove that one can be mad and correct at the same time.

And what sort of monster was it? In that regard alone, my studies had raised more questions than they had answered: Deductive speculation had been my only guide. All my insights led me to believe that it was gentle, endowed with some manner of intelligence, capable of communication with humans, somehow graced with prescience, and improbably possessing human emotion and sexuality; in short, either a mutant species of *homo sapiens,* a freak of nature, or the descendant of an all-but-extinct family of hominids. But what could I know for sure, other than that it existed? Could it speak, think, reproduce? Was it alone, or were there others of its kind? Did it, in fact, possess any capacity for intelligent thought, or was it merely a dumb brute? For all I knew, Brauner might have been insane and infatuated with a creature that was no more intellectual, no more prescient, no more humanly sexual than a fallow deer. And if he were not? What sort of creature could be both as hideous as a spider

and as seductive as a siren? As gentle as a lamb and as ruthless as a wolf? As loving as a mother and as cruel as a cour-
tesan? As generous with its knowledge as God and as
parsimonious of its sympathy as the Devil? Could such a
creature exist? And yet it did!

Of all the men or women in this world, I was the only one
in a position to answer these questions, and there was only
one way in which they could be answered. Was I wrong to go
to Romania, to meddle where I had no business? Quite probably. All I know is that the call to go was strident and irre-
sistible within me, as strong as any instinct and as livid as
any wound, and I defy anyone who finds himself in such
unique circumstances to claim that he would act differently.
Yes, the purity of my gothic quest may have been perverted
by dreams of grandeur, recognition, conquest, a place in history—a purpose!—but whose wouldn't be? Here was the opportunity to do what had never been done. Who would not
defile a grave to exhume the bones of Adam? Who would not
pollute the sanctity of Ararat for one plank of Noah's ark?
Who would not shatter the temple for one string of David's
lyre? I am a man, with a man's weaknesses and a man's
insatiable hunger for knowledge, and these I offer as my
only excuse. I will assert, however, that my primary goals
and instincts were good ones, and that I meant no harm. I
wanted only to *know*. Who can blame me for that? And yet
. . . and yet, things might have turned out so differently . . .

When my strength and mental stability had been fully recovered, I began preparations for my great journey.

Every great adventure, if it is to have the least hope of success, requires careful planning for every contingency. In bitter retrospect, I now recognize that it is in the nature of important contingencies to be unforeseeable to one who has been blinded by ambition, apathy, and folly.

My first stop—at the Romanian National Tourist Office—almost proved my last. To my horror, I was informed that the past twenty years had seen many changes up in the Ceahlau Mountains. Hotels and chalets, hiking trails and ski slopes, camping sites and asphalt roads now overran the once wild forests. The Bistrita River had been dammed and the resulting lake become very popular with boaters, water skiers, and fishermen. The young agent in the office recited her litany with pride and satisfaction, but it was a mighty blow to me. Even as I sat there at her desk, my head swam with visions of disaster: If the Conglomeros were still alive, wouldn't it have moved on to more secluded ground? What were the probabilities that it would have remained at the risk of discovery by any passing boy-scout troop? Either way, it was a daunting prospect: If the creature had stayed, my search would be immeasurably complicated by hordes of pleasure-seekers; if it had left, I could simply abandon any hope of ever finding it. It seemed as if, perhaps, my mission was doomed from the outset. I knew that, regardless of the circumstances, I must go to Romania for my own peace of mind; but now, with what prospects of success? I thanked the young woman, grabbed a handful of brochures, and retreated from the office with a heavy heart.

But that night, dejectedly reading through the brochures, I had a sudden revelation. I knew that the resorts would be overflowing with hikers in summertime; were I to go in the winter, however, the heavy Carpathian snowfalls would seriously impede my search; and if I were to go off-season, I would be far more likely to attract unwanted attention to myself. The problem seemed insurmountable until, glancing over an article on customs regulations, I happened across a section on firearms and ammunition, which, it seemed, sportsmen were allowed to import in limited quantities. It occurred to me that visiting the Carpathians as a hunter would be the perfect pretext for going in the autumn. Some further reading convinced me of the practicality of this plan: The mountain forests were abundant with big game, most notably bear and wild boar. Many of the species were protected, I learned, but the boar was not among them. What could be more natural for a seasoned American hunter than to go to Romania to hunt wild boar, a species not found on his native continent? And what better excuse for tramping stealthily through the woods day after day?

I returned to the office the next day, my plan fully formed. The young woman was pleasantly surprised to see me back so soon and, as we talked, my insouciance over expense helped to make her more amenable still. No, there was no problem with traveling alone in Romania, renting a car, moving about from city to city; no problem in hunting wild boar; yes, it could all be arranged from her office—visas, hunting license, import permits for gun and ammunition, car rental, hotel accommodation, an English-speaking guide from the Hunting and Fishing Association, anything I wanted and was willing to pay for. By the end of the morning, the arrangements had been made: Documents were to be sent to my home for signature and payment, guns must be registered, reservations confirmed, and I was to fly to Bucharest in late September, six weeks away.

My next step was equally convoluted and far more lugubrious. Emil Arghezi was a man my grandfather had known before moving to Florida and who was deeply involved in émigré politics. In Romania, he had fought against the Fascists, and later against the Communists, who expelled him from the country; in America, he was the head of a Romanian émigrés' club that met in the basement of his house in Astoria. According to my grandfather, this club was a center for exiled nationalists, and actually provided some nominal funding to an underground group in the old country. Also according to my grandfather, who had never had much taste for politics, there had even been some loose talk in the early days after the war of a Romanian national "government-in-exile" of which Arghezi was supposed to be some sort of minister. Though we had never met, he immediately agreed to see me when I called and told him who I was.

I went to his modest clapboard house off Ditmars Boulevard and he met me with a bear hug on the front stoop. He was dressed entirely in peasant costume—a white linen tunic cinched around the waist with a wide leather belt, a sheepskin waistcoat, and a tall, cylindrical sheepskin hat—as if in anticipation of a folk festival. Saying not a word, but glancing suspiciously up and down the block, he led me down the steps and into the basement, double-locking the door behind us.

The room was windowless and ill-lit, a brown industrial carpet on the floor. It was furnished with an assortment of shabby sofas, wooden and metal chairs, all pushed against the walls, which bore tourist posters of Romania, a map, a dartboard printed with Ceausescu's likeness, and a large coat of arms that I took to be the emblem of the old monarchy. Arghezi, a swarthy, kindly-looking fellow in his seventies, sat me down on a sofa and pulled up a chair for himself.

"Your grandfather was a good man," he said.

"Yes," I said. He shook his head sadly.

"But not enough caring for his motherland," he said.

"He left Romania a long time ago."

"What is born in the flesh is blood in the brain," Arghezi said, and I could only agree. From beneath a set of bushy gray eyebrows, he piercingly stared me down. There was a moment of uncomfortable silence.

"So what is it you are wanting from us?" he asked, as if all his doubts and questions about me had been answered.

I explained my situation to him, naturally omitting any reference to the Conglomeros. I said that I would be entering Romania legally, but that I might need to leave illegally, and secretly, as a smuggler. He was concerned that I planned to steal artworks from the "national patrimony," but I strove to assure him that my intentions regarding the Romanian nation, as opposed to the Romanian government, were strictly honorable. Harder still was it to insist, without risking the loss of his avuncular goodwill, that the purpose of my mission remain known to myself alone. His friends, he reasoned, placed themselves in some danger by helping me—surely they had a right to know why they risked their lives. Like any diplomat, I conceded the right but withheld the privilege. Sensing the approach of an impasse, I resorted to a disingenuous appeal to my grandfather's memory, and that seemed to sway him. He stared at the map a while further, then heaved a heavy sigh.

"It's very expensive," he said.

We discussed the arrangements. I gave him the details, the approximate dates, the necessary parameters, and a down payment. He gave me a name, a place, a password. His people were not spies, he reiterated—they were simply patriots who did big favors for hard currency. It turned out that I was very fortunate in that one of these patriots happened to live at the very foot of Ceahlau. This man would be expecting me sometime around the specified date; he was to be paid handsomely, but I could rely on him implicitly. All I need do was find him and he would finesse me and my contraband out of Romania, no questions asked. In the event that his services should not be required, I should make no attempt to contact him, but my down payment to Arghezi was forfeit. In any case, I was further encouraged out of fraternal solidarity and respect for our ancestors to make a voluntary contribution to the treasury of the émigrés' club. Though my ancestors had been brutally persecuted by Arghezi's ancestors and would certainly have been dismayed by my liberal donation to his cause, I made no objection to any of his demands and our negotiations were brought to a mutually satisfactory conclusion. I thanked him and left.

Should the reader assume that these arrangements were made in anticipation of my capturing the Conglomeros and removing it from its native habitat, the reader would be correct. But the reader would be quite mistaken in believing thereby that this had already become my firm intention. I must reiterate that I was merely planning for every contingency. While subsequent events may obscure it, the fact is that at the time of my meeting with Arghezi I was far from any decision regarding my eventual conduct toward the creature. In other words, I had as yet no intention of kidnapping the Conglomeros, but I would at least be prepared to do so should it prove necessary for any reason.

Over the next six weeks there was very little for me to do but fret and wait. I spent several days in the map room of the public library, studying the terrain of the Ceahlau Mountains, learning it by heart, trying to pinpoint the exact location of my grandfather's sighting. The best I could manage was an approximation within an area of some fifty square miles, which offered prospects both encouraging and disheartening. On the one hand, if my grandfather had not been so dully fastidious, even that negligible degree of precision would have been beyond me; on the other, fifty square miles was a large area to cover in the limited time I would have at my disposal, even supposing there was anything to find within them. Given my assiduous efforts to leave nothing to chance, having in the end to rely on dumb luck was an unpleasant concession to be forced to make. My mood suffered violent swings over the weeks, at one moment reaching the highest peaks of elation and optimism, at the next plummeting to the darkest depths of despair. Aware, however, that this kind of volatility could in no way contribute to the fruition of my hopes, I redoubled my efforts to master my emotions in anticipation of the task at hand. I exercised my mind with games of concentration and self-control. I took long walks late on hot, steaming nights through the most dangerous parts of town, examining my fear like a dissected frog until I understood its every sinew. Such preparation requires more than six weeks, I know, but I did make some progress that was to stand me in good stead.

Similarly, I exercised my body, strengthening and hardening it, and purging myself of the effects of years of self-indulgence. I bought myself two large-caliber rifles and centerfire cartridges, with which I practiced until my marksmanship was adequate at best. I also studied the rudiments of hunting so that, if need be, I could talk it up like an expert. I applied for an international driver's license and studied Romanian in my spare time. Yet necessary as all these things were, my main goal was distraction. By keeping myself busy with a thousand minor preparations, I hoped to suppress the agitation and torment that kept me in a perpetual state of heated fervor; and indeed, the weeks did seem to pass more quickly. It was only at night that the terrible risks and immeasurable rewards of my impending journey welled up to haunt me and to trouble my dreams. But with the help of a venerable escort agency, even these regained a measure of serenity through my nightly ministrations. And so the weeks passed, the oppressive humidity of summer gave way to the cool and gentle breezes of fall, and the day of my departure finally arrived. My bags packed, my wallet overflowing with crisp new bills, and my guns and ammunition safely locked in wooden cases, I flew to England for a brief (last?) visit with my mother, then on to Bucharest. My heart raced as we touched down at Otopeni.

My weapons were naturally of some concern to the customs officials, who milled about them with fervid curiosity. My guns and I were taken to a room secured by armed guards. I was asked several times to take the weapons apart, and they were checked for altered pins, secret compartments, concealed contraband, and subversive literature. I think, however, that the guards were merely impressed with the quality of my arms, for they each took turns weighing, bolting, and shouldering them. In general, they were very friendly and asked me many questions, which I answered as best I could. After they counted my cartridges, everything was put away and the boxes were locked and sealed, the seal to be unbroken by any save my appointed guide. My permits were stamped and I was let loose. I took this unexpected goodwill as a good omen.

I took a cab into town, enjoying a view of lakes and parks along the wide, empty arterial boulevards leading into the heart of the city and to the Inter-Continental, where I checked in, leaving my bags in the room and the gun case in the safe. Then I walked down the road to the National Tourist Office, where my black Volga was waiting for me. By the time the necessary forms had been filled out and I was able to return to the hotel, it was quite dark, though the evening was wonderfully balmy, almost Mediterranean. I ordered some meatballs and a bottle of wine, and sat out on the balcony to take my supper. The city was spread out before my feet and my fantastic voyage was finally beginning, but my heart was cold and empty, as I had conditioned it to be when I was most frightened and anxious. I did not sleep well that night, and was on the road to Piatra Neamt by seven.

I drove all morning, up onto the fertile plains of Moldavia. On either side of the road, bales of new-mown hay and shocks of wheat littered the stubbly fields. Soon, a dark ridge of mountains rose to my left, and the road joined the course of the sparkling Siret to the right. There was very little traffic and virtually no private cars, and I drove with one arm out the window, the wind rushing through my hair, the sun beaming down. The road rose almost imperceptibly with the passing miles, the valley became more populous and lush, the fields gradually yielding to orchards whose leaves were only just beginning to turn. The air was noticeably cooler at noon than in the morning, and I stopped for tea and a roll in the central square of Bacau, under a canopy of lindens.

Just north of Bacau, I left the main highway and headed up the Bistrita Valley on the last leg to Piatra Neamt. Now the road began to climb much faster, soon a mere corridor through a thick evergreen forest. Every so often I passed a lumber mill or an odoriferous fertilizer factory, and huge log-laden trailers roared past out of the mountains. The air grew crisper, the sunlight sharper, the villages more Ger-

manic. The mountains loomed ever closer and more ominous, the river became shallower and more animated, the
road climbed and climbed, I turned a corner and there were
the hills and steeples of Piatra Neamt, nestled in the last
valley before the mountains proper. I drove through the industrial suburbs and on into the historic center of town,
squeezed in amongst the rounded hillsides.

I made straight for my hotel, located above the river and
railroad sidings. I parked outside and left my baggage in the
car as I wandered into the marble-floored lobby. It was de-
serted, except for a young man in a wide-lapel leather jacket
and green stovepipe trousers, leaning against the reception
desk and engrossed in conversation with the receptionist.
My footsteps echoed across the floor, and they both looked
up like startled deer. The young man jumped to attention
and strode across to me, flattening a cowlick and straight-
ening his jacket. Still a good twenty feet away, he stuck out
his hand and broke into a broad, toothy smile.

"Mr. X.?" he asked "Mr. Aaron X., of New York, New
York?"

"That's me."

"I am very pleased to see you, sir. I am Ion Gusti. I am
appointed by the General Association of Sportive Hunting
and Fishing to be your guide and interpreter in all matters,
and of making you as well the happiest and comfortable stay
in our country." His accent was barely noticeable, and I
could tell it was simply youthful exuberance that made him
stumble over his words. Ion seemed like a very nice boy. We
shook hands for several minutes.

"Ah, but your bags," he said, finally coming to. "I'll get
them."

"That's all right, Ion," I said, taking him by the arm, "the
bellboy will get it."

"Ah, but you see, there isn't any." Ion shook his head sadly.

We brought my luggage up to my room, and I set the gun case on the bed.

"Could you open this, please, Ion?" I asked.

"Yes, sure." He beamed at me. He pulled a nail clipper from his pocket and neatly snipped the wires on the seal. He bounced the red wax disk in his hand while I opened the case.

"I keep this?" he asked.

"I don't know, do you? What are the regulations?"

He pondered the seal. "Yes, sure, I keep. It makes a good souvenir. Why not? Oh!"

He had seen the guns, and leaned over them amorously. "What big guns!" he exclaimed rapturously. "Are all American guns so big?"

"No," I said. "But you need a big gun for boar."

"Yes, sure. May I touch it?"

"Yes, sure."

He picked up a gun and weighed it in both hands, stroking the smooth cherrywood of the stock. He pulled back the bolt and peered down the barrel, then he lifted the gun to his shoulder and pointed it out the window. Only he held the weapon the way a child would, with his left hand far down the barrel, near the muzzle, and the stock touching his cheek. He pointed the gun at a wheeling bird, said "boom!" and giggled.

"You'll do more harm to yourself than to the boar if you shoot it that way," I laughed. Ion turned to me with an apologetic grin. "Oh well, you know, guns . . . ," he murmured as he returned the rifle to its cradle.

"Don't you hunt?" I asked, incredulous.

He stuck out his chest like an athlete, slapped his right hand over his heart, and smiled proudly at me. "No, I fish!" he said.

"But I'm a hunter!" I cried.

"Yes, sure, I know. And I am a fisherman. It takes all kinds. To each his own, as you say in America!"

"No, you don't understand. You're supposed to be my guide."

"Yes, sure I am your guide," he said in a tone of injured pride. "I am appointed your guide by the General Association of Sportive Hunting and Fishing. Don't you like me, Mr. X.?"

"Yes, sure I like you, but . . . oh, never mind."

It had suddenly dawned on me that Ion's youth and inexperience in hunting would work very much to my advantage in a number of ways. It was especially vital that I avoid having to shoot a boar, since, having reached my limit of one kill, I should have lost my one plausible pretext for scouring the wild hinterlands. Meanwhile, I was already familiar with the local topography from my studies, and any sort of competent guide would in any case have been superfluous, a hindrance even. But with Ion's amiable ineptitude, and his inability to discern mine, we would be even less likely to stumble upon any real game; most important, however, he would be oblivious to my deception when I led us along tracks that had nothing to do with hunting wildlife, should such an opportunity happen to present itself. With a few conciliatory words and a wink, I sent him back downstairs to the receptionist, unpacked my bags, and lay down for a nap. As usual, my dreams were troubled, and I awoke unrefreshed at dusk.

I wandered onto the balcony, and the crisp mountain air soon dispelled any vestiges of a lingering headache. The sun was already behind the mountains, whose black silhouettes hung over the town like a promise unfulfilled. I thought of Victor Brauner's "The Metamythic Muse," and of how once, perhaps, it had called out to him on a night such as this. Somewhere out there, I mused, somewhere out there, bending over a darkling brook, or grazing in a forest clearing, or gazing at Venus newborn beneath the rising moon, or lying to in a thicket, listening to the gathering of the night winds and shivering at their portent of winter, somewhere out there the Conglomeros roamed, waiting for me. And perhaps, too, the winds had brought it news of my arrival, and like me it stood pensive, and turned its gaze to the lights of the city on the eastern horizon, and wondered wordlessly what they would bring. I shuddered and returned to the room, drawing the curtains.

I dressed for supper and met Ion in the lobby, where a few desultory tourists lounged about, slumped in the armchairs or staring at the picturesque landscapes and portraits of the dictator and his wife adorning the walls. Ion was again engaged in intimate conversation with the receptionist; he had not changed his clothing and seemed not to have left the hotel all afternoon. He startled and blushed very sweetly when I tapped him on the shoulder, but quickly regained his composure and clapped me on the back.

"Look, Mr. X.," he said with a broad sweep of his arm toward the receptionist, who turned red and smiled, "I want you to meet my fiancée, Ana Hogas. We're married soon."

"Well, congratulations," I said, and to the receptionist, *"Buna seara."*

She giggled and lowered her eyes. Ion gazed at her lovingly for a moment. "She is the sweetest thing," he said, and at that moment I could not disagree. "Come on, now," he went on, pushing me toward the door, "we go eat."

"La revedere," I called over my shoulder.

"Hallo," Ana Hogas called back, and we were on the street.

We ambled up into the central square of the town, which was not far at all and a very pleasant walk on this autumn evening. The three hills of Piatra Neamt, bearing down upon the narrow streets, almost gave one the impression of being indoors, as if the town were under a glass dome. Piata Stefan cel Mare was a lovely grassy square lined with ancient churches, museums, and statues, and much animated with local color. Young men stood around in their shirtsleeves, arguing or singing, and weaved through the crowds on rickety bicycles. Old men sat on the benches, drinking and spitting, young ladies paraded in vinyl boots and midiskirts, and the intellectuals congregated in the sidewalk cafés sipping coffee and cognac. I was amazed by the tenacity of the Latin spirit, flourishing in repressive circumstances so far and isolated from its center. Ion and I took a table outdoors to admire the scene, and our conversation was continually interrupted by greetings. We ordered some pork chops and brandy.

"Have you lived here all your life?" I asked.

"No, no," Ion tsked. "I went to university in Iasi for five years."

"What did you study?"

"I studied two majors," he said with a hint of vainglory. "American literature and sylviculture. Sylviculture is a fascinating study of natural phenomenons, but without American literature I wouldn't be sitting here with you drinking brandy. I wrote a thesis on John Updike. Don't you think John Updike captures the wealth of the American Scene in all its particulars?"

"You read John Updike here?"

"Not much. A little. Don't you believe that John Updike relates in vivid prose . . ."

"He's a highly respected author," I said. "Aren't you a little young to be thinking of marriage?"

"What young?" he asked, genuinely surprised. "I am twenty-three, Ana is nineteen, I know her since she was six. Not young, I think, but we must wait. We live still with our families, we are waiting for an apartment. Even here," he made a vague gesture toward the square, as if it were Shangri-la, "it is difficult, but great progress is being made in all social spheres, thanks to our great leader. And then, Ana is a Magyar by origins, and that makes it difficult for us. Ah, but love is a beautiful thing, you know, Mr. X., and all the problems mean nothing to Ana and I. Are you not married?"

"Widower."

"Oh, that is dreadful, and you are so young too."

"Yes, my wife was only your age when she died. She killed herself with drugs."

"Oh, oh, that is terrible. I hear you are having these terrible problems in the West with cocaine and amphetamines. You have this writer, Henry Miller, who . . ."

The conversation ran on into the evening, floating among topical issues of the day, inevitably drifting back to America and its arts, its politics, its living conditions. Ion was not at all shocked to hear of the homeless on our sidewalks or the criminality of our elected officials, but he was surprised to learn that I did not possess a handgun and that I was not, to my knowledge, acquainted with anyone who did. The talk of guns led us round to the topic of hunting, and Ion let me know that, as my appointed guide, he had done his homework.

"Tomorrow we drive up into the Stinisoara Mountains, we climb Netedu Peak to . . ."

"The Stinisoara Mountains?"

"Yes, sure, why not? It's good mountains for hunting."

"It's nothing, only I thought . . . Ceahlau . . ."

"Yes, sure, Ceahlau, Stinisoarei, Tarcalui, what difference? We have two weeks time, we can do them all. More haste less speed, that's right?"

I didn't care to press the point, though Ion was hardly the suspicious type, and the conversation drifted onward. The crowd milled and lingered, basking in the last warm evenings of the year. Though the city is a gateway to the mountains, and we were sitting in front of the only *de luxe* hotel in town, there were very few foreigners to be seen, and those seemed mostly to be Russians and other Slavs. I was very gratified to note that my calculations in that regard had been correct, and Ion confirmed my hopes that I had arrived in the slump between the summer and winter seasons. Eventually, around eleven, I walked him to his parents' apartment down the block, next door to the Museum of Natural Sciences ("thence is my passion for sylviculture," he grandly proclaimed) and we parted for the evening, good friends already. It was only as I made my way back to the hotel, winding around the strolling lovers and drunken comrades propping each other up, that I realized with a twinge of conscience that I might find myself before long in the position of having to betray Ion, perhaps destroying his career in sylviculture, his prospects for a subsidized apartment, and his matrimonial aspirations. And now, in retrospect, as I recall those sad, prophetic musings, I can see that even then the evil seed that was to be my eventual undoing had taken firm root in my all-too-purposeful thoughts. When I reached the hotel, I was glad to find that Ana was off duty, for the cheap brandy had made me quite morose and I dreaded having to meet her cheerful, optimistic smile. I set my clock for six A.M. and fell asleep reminding myself of all the potentially great and noble motives for my mission.

The sun had not quite risen and a light mist hung about the treetops when Ion and I set out the next morning. All of the equipment was securely locked in the trunk as we headed west out of town, through tiny sleeping roadside hamlets, and up into the heart of the mountains. The river was lost in a steaming swamp to our left, then suddenly emerged as a rushing torrent to our right. We crossed it a number of times as the road rose and wound up the valley, ever higher, ever more narrow and oppressive. It took us an hour to reach the dam at Bicaz, and another half hour following the shore of the dark lake until we pulled off into a dirt road on the outskirts of an apparently abandoned village.

We unpacked the equipment—guns, cartridge belts, two twelve-inch hunting blades, various provisions that Ion had prepared, and emergency equipment that included flashlights, flares, and sleeping mats rolled into cylinders and bound with leather thongs. Everything but the rifles and belts was packed into two small green knapsacks, and we set out into the wood, weapons slung across our shoulders. My fingers trembling, I had some difficulty adjusting the fit of my cartridge belt.

We followed the bed of a stream up the mountain. I explained to Ion that we would be able to detect tracks more easily in the mud on the banks, and follow them thence into the depth of the forest. But in fact, whenever we came across any hoofprints, I either deleted them under my heavy boots or ascribed them to deer, which have cloven hooves similar to those of swine, though I myself could not tell the difference. To be doubly certain that we would encounter as little wildlife as possible, I had liberally doused my clothes and person with a rather vulgar French cologne, and as I had suspected, Ion had neither the experience nor the presence of mind to question the wisdom of wearing scent on a hunt. He did, however, object to my whistling, so I came down with a nagging cough. As I have said, the last thing I wanted was to be compelled to kill some harmless mountain creature. Of course, if by any chance my intended prey were within earshot, it too would be warned of our approach. My grandfather's description had portrayed it as a timid creature, shy of human contact; on the other hand, Victor Brauner had had the opposite experience. Perhaps the Conglomeros would be attracted by any sign of our presence, the way dolphins are said to be drawn to the sounds of human activity. In any case, the risk had to be taken.

We climbed all morning, abandoning the stream when it appeared to be rising above the tree line. At one point, we stumbled onto a small alpine pasture, which afforded a magnificent vista onto the lake and the valley. On the other side glittered the stony peaks of Ceahlau. I stared at it for a long time.

"That is Ceahlau," Ion said.

"Uh."

We took our lunch in the pasture—black bread, soft cheese, powdery red apples, and some warm and very salty mineral water. The sun had already passed its zenith when we finished, and I suggested a short nap before heading down the mountainside. Ion was flushed and exhausted from our morning exertions, and he readily agreed. Later, when we reached the car, he seemed completely worn out, and I knew that with a few days of such exercise he would be putty in my hands. We drove back to Piatra Neamt in silence, and Ion went straight home to bed.

I showered and changed in a very pensive mood. The day's hike had highlighted my greatest misgiving—that not only did I not know what I was looking for (let alone *why* I was looking for it), but that I also did not know how to go about looking for it. Footprints, a nest, a cave, a hole in the ground, bent saplings, a hut—which if any of these was a clear indication of the vicinity of a Conglomeros? And should such a sign exist, how could I hope or expect, in an area of over three hundred square kilometers, to find it? The experience of the day had shown how little ground could be covered on foot, yet on foot was the only practicable means of exploration. Increasing my hours on the prowl might prove of some extra help, but would barely suffice in truth. Covering every square inch of ground might take months, years—and my visa lasted but two weeks. With an onerous burden of weariness and anticipation, I was forced to concede that I had my whole life ahead of me, that I could return year after year to Romania in quest of my elusive quarry, and that I would, if need be. This was only the beginning—if it existed at all, the Conglomeros would be mine.

I sauntered up to the central square, found a table at the same restaurant as the night before, and ordered a beer and a dish of noodles smothered in stew. I sat and watched the young people on display, some of whom, evidently friends of Ion's who recognized me, greeted me and somewhat skittishly agreed to join me for beers. They all possessed a smattering of English, and where that failed we made do with a smorgasbord of other languages. Mostly, they just wanted to know about stereos, VCRs, dishwashers, and the like, but they were affable and talkative and I very much enjoyed being the focus of their curiosity. As the evening wore on and the beer gave way to brandy—and despite the very obvious supervision of sober, glowering security agents in close proximity—the crowd around my table swelled to seven or eight young men and women, openly smiling and laughing at my narrative of life in America. Passersby stopped to stare unashamedly, and a constant flux of changing faces kept the conversation animated and convivial. It was really a very pleasant evening, and as I finally rose to leave I promised to return the next evening to continue our chat.

By one o'clock the next afternoon, Ion and I were already high in the woods of Stinisoara, this time on the eastern slope, even further from Ceahlau than before. We had crossed over a ragged, stony ridge and swept across the slope in a wide arc. Ion was looking peaked and haggard, and he lagged some distance behind me. The day was actually hot, though some fleecy clouds scudded across the horizon. The only sound to be heard was a roaring stream ahead. My face was covered in a slick film of perspiration and my camouflage suit was distinctly stuffy. Whatever birds there were in these woods fell silent at our approach, though the occasional lonely echo of a crow could be heard ringing in the glens. And then I noticed the trail. It seemed to be a deer trail, marked by brown, trodden grass and a certain concavity in the surrounding brush; but of course, it might have been made by any number of species, including bear or . . . A few light tracks under the pine needles were inconclusive. I followed the trail, leading toward the sound of the water, which grew steadily pervasive.

Not far ahead, I could make out a patch of sunlight where the forest canopy was broken along the path of the stream. As the trail neared, it widened out and the brush grew thicker. I found myself on a mossy bank above a curve in the stream, which was deep and fast and clean. In my heated state, it was irresistibly tempting, and I sat down on the damp moss to remove my boots. But as I laid my gun to one side, my eyes fell upon the unmistakable prints of bare human feet. It was difficult to tell how many feet had made these prints—perhaps four, perhaps six—but they were definitely small and delicate looking. And they led around the curve in the stream, whence I now detected the sound of splashing. My heart thumping, I lay on my stomach and inched my way like a soldier under fire to the edge of the knoll. And there they were—two young women skinny-dipping in a shallow pool, giggling as they tressed one another's hair, their wretched breasts bobbing on the surface of the water. I swore disgruntledly under my breath and inched back to my gun and knapsack. Only then did I notice the blouses, bras, and other clothing hanging on some low branches, and I vowed to be more attentive to detail thenceforward. As I stood to leave, Ion stepped out onto the bank, puffing and sweated. I motioned to him to turn back, and we called it a day.

The following days passed quickly but just as fruitlessly. During the light hours, and frequently past sunset, Ion and I roamed the mountains around Ceahlau—the Stinisoarei to the east, the Bistritei to the northwest, the Tarcalui to the southeast, the Hasmas to the southwest. If the Conglomeros were anywhere in the region, it would have to be on Ceahlau. And even though this was as I had expected, and even though I had now dismissed all other possibilities, and even though I might consider myself measurably closer to my goal, I became more and more despondent with each passing day. I could repress neither the dismal visions of failure nor the paranoia that stifled my every optimistic impulse, and I even began to wonder whether I hadn't fabricated the entire phantasm in the ugly recesses of my jaded imagination. On the hunt I was sullen and morose, stalking ever further ahead of Ion and taking an occasional potshot at the woodcock; at night, I drank more heavily with my companions, and began sniping maliciously at all that was good, bad, or indifferent in our respective societies. Gradually, the number and enthusiasm of my youthful admirers dropped off, until within a week only the most mercenary few continued to dare my brazen tongue. And, to make matters worse, I was coming to suspect that I was being watched.

I had seen him on my very first night in Piatra Neamt, but in the early flush of elation had paid him no mind—a little old man sitting alone at a table in the corner of the sidewalk terrace, drinking tea. Like me, he was on the terrace every evening; unlike me, he was always alone. Sometimes he was reading a book, sometimes a newspaper, sometimes he just stared out at the square; but whatever he was doing, I gradually became aware that he always had one eye for our group, and, it seemed, for me in particular. And when I say one eye, I mean it literally: He wore a black eyepatch over his left eye, which did nothing to dispel the aura of mystery that hung about him like a pall.

There was something vaguely troubling about him, vaguely familiar. At first, I thought I had seen him somewhere before, but then I realized that he was a foreigner, a westerner like me, and that what I had recognized in him was the cut and material of his clothing, so different from that of the locals. Of course, I was aware of the rumors that placed many foreigners in the ranks of the dreaded *Securitate,* but those were said to be mostly Arabs. This meant that, unless he were using his Western apparel as a deceptive cloak, he was at least no government agent, which I had every reason to fear. What, then, could he be, or want here, or want with me, if anything? I thought merely that he was lonely, and that the good cheer and laughter of our conversation gave him some vicarious pleasure, but night after night and despite ample opportunity he failed to make any move to approach my table. His solitary, supercilious observation began to seem intrusive, and finally irksome, and I was eventually forced to take some note of him, to return his stares, which he frankly bore without shifting his gaze from my person. I found it all decidedly unsettling.

Eight days had gone by since my arrival in Piatra Neamt, eight days of grueling but futile search, eight days of increasing despair and depression. As if in reflection of my state of mind, the weather grew ever more unpleasant; though it had yet to rain, a brooding cloud cover now continuously enshrouded the sky, the temperature dropped, and a cold wind blew in daily from the north. The crowd evaporated from the square with the warm weather, and I began to take my meals inside, looking out across the windswept lawn and past the medieval turrets and towers to the black slopes above. I was occasionally but with growing infrequency joined by Ion, who was visibly pained and bewildered and saddened by my degeneration; in obvious deference to the stronger Ana—who had recently taken to throwing me malevolent looks as I skulked across the lobby—he was at odds to find excuses to avoid me.

And still, my old man sat and read and watched. It was a Sunday night, dark and empty; Ion was at the cinema with

Ana; my friends were at home with their families; my wife was nearly three years dead; I was alone in a foreign country, looking for a monster that most probably did not exist; and on my fourth or fifth brandy. As I stared out into the night, I became aware of a reflection on the window pane, the reflection of the old man behind me. I drained my brandy, stood up, and walked across the room. "Excuse me, *poftiti,*" I said, standing directly before him. "Do you speak English?"

The old man looked up at me, discomfitted. He pulled at his ear nervously. I repeated my question.

"Minute, just a minute," and motioned for me to sit down. He pulled at his ear again, and I realized that it was not a nervous gesture, but that he was adjusting a hearing aid secreted behind his left ear. When he seemed satisfied, he offered me a sheepish grin, and spread his hands, palms upward, in token of apology.

"I am very sorry, sir," he said in a light accent that might have been German. "They confiscated my batteries at the border. Now I must economize. I turn them off when I am not talking."

"They confiscated your batteries?"

"The little round batteries, they look like listening devices or radio receivers or some such, I don't know." He rolled his right eye in a most disarming manner, as if to suggest infinite patience. "Now," he said, leaning forward and clasping his hands like a therapist, "how may I be of service to you, sir?"

I stuttered out the beginning of some improvised excuse, but he cut me short with a little wave of his hand.

"I seemed to be watching you, is that it? Yes, I'm sorry, it is true. I'm an old man, traveling alone, you see, and I notice a compatriot, well I . . . ."

"I am an American."

"So am I, sir, so am I. I'm an American longer than you, if

I may say, since 1947. But I am not so . . . so social as a born American. You, you just sit down, they come to you, you make friends. Me they leave alone, an old man . . . An old man, by the way," he smiled, offering me a tiny, wrinkled hand, "whose name is Richard Hand."

"Aaron X."

"And what brings you to Romania, Mr. X., may I ask?" he inquired with a mischievous glint in his eye.

"I'm hunting the famous Carpathian wild boar," I said.

He threw up his hands in mock dismay. "Ah, a hunter! And have you had any success on your hunt, may I ask?"

"None so far, I'm afraid. But I have great hopes for a mountain range called Ceahlau."

"Ceahlau, you say?" He seemed taken aback. "I know it well."

"Really?"

"I have never been, you understand." He waggled his index finger like a metronome. "No, I know of it from books. It is very famous for its folklore." He paused a beat, then added, "Its mythology."

"I didn't know that."

"Yes, yes indeed. It is sometimes known as the Moldavian Olympus, so legendary is it. Ceahlau is believed to be the mountain which Strabo in his *Geography* called Kogaionon, before the Roman conquest. Kogaionon was sacred to the Getae, or the Daci as the Romans called them, as the sanctuary of their great god Zamolxis. The Dacians had a great king, Decebalus, who had a beautiful daughter, Dochia. When the Romans attacked Dacia, Decebalus sent his daughter to the sanctuary for protection. But Dacia fell to Trajan, Decebalus was killed, and Dochia in her misery pleaded with Zamolxis for mercy. The god heard her plea, took pity on her, and granted her wish—he turned her to stone. And to this very day, the stone Dochia stands atop Ceahlau, staring out for eternity across her beloved Dacia."

He was silent for a moment, shaking his little withered head. He took a sip of his tea. "But that was a long time ago, and much has befallen the poor Dacians since then," he said.

"There are other legends associated with Ceahlau?"

He looked at me, and the stare of his one eye pierced me to the core. "And what legends might those be, sir?"

I was filled with confusion, and lowered my eyes. "I . . . I don't know. I was asking you," I stammered.

"Perhaps," he said nonchalantly, rolling the *r* into a little ball. "I do not know of any others."

"You seem to know a great deal about it."

He dismissed my compliment with a wave of his hand. "Ah, it is my job to know it. I am a historian. Or I was once a historian . . . I am a teacher."

"You are retired?"

"No, no, not so. I still teach. But I no longer teach history," he said ruefully.

"May I ask why you gave it up?"

"Ach," he said, again with a gesture of dismissal. "It is a long and silly story." He paused, cocking his head like a sparrow. "Though I think, instructive in its own way. I will tell you, if you like." He looked at me eagerly, and it was easy to see that this lonely old man was anxious to talk, and pleased to have someone to talk to, for once.

"I should be very interested," I said.

"I tell you then." He shifted in his chair, settling in for the narration. "I was a young man, much younger than you, after the Great War. I was too young to fight in the war, and I was an idealist, you see, and very happy. I am an Alsatian by birth, you see, so I was born in Germany, but not German, French. And after the war, Alsace was returned to France, and we were all very happy. I was a student at the university in Strasbourg, it was a very . . . a very vital time, many issues, much argument, much passion. I studied the history of Europe, the history of war, the history of Mankind, and I was one of those who was going to make the world better. I was a very intense young man, I studied very hard, perhaps too hard, for I had a rather delicate constitution, high-strung. In my fever for learning and the tense competition for scholarships, my mind snapped, and this was to ruin my life, so to speak. I remember like it was yesterday."

He leaned forward and dropped his voice to a whisper.

"It was very late at night, I studied by candlelight for an examination. I was reading Froissart for a course on the rise of the bourgeoisie in medieval Europe. I was reading about the battle of Roosebeke, 1382, between the French and the Flemings. The armies were camped for the night on either side of a hill, where the battle was to be fought the next day. They were sleeping, no noise but the horses stamping, soldiers mumbling in their sleep, the crackle of the camp fires, the wind whistling on the heights. Suddenly, the Flemings were awakened by a great noise on the hill, shouting, laughing, sparks flying into the night sky. They thought it was the French preparing a surprise attack, but scouts were sent and reported no movements, and the army was not roused. The next day, the Flemings were utterly crushed in battle, their leader slain. And many believed that the noise heard on the hill had been the sound of devils and demons dancing and whirling on the battleground, in celebration of the many souls they were to reap the next day.

"Now, this story had a deep effect on my heated brain. It was like a fever, a fire that consumed me, and I became obsessed with it. I said to myself that I was studying history, but I was only following an obsession. I was convinced that the story was true, and I became determined to prove it true." (He paused to clear his throat, then went on.) "I traveled to Roosebeke, I camped on the Golden Mount, as it is called, I read every source, I wrote a long dissertation. But even this was not enough to satisfy me; I can't explain it, it was like a terrible sickness. I became a correspondent for a

Paris newspaper, I traveled the whole globe in search of wars and dancing demons. I was with Frunze in Russia, Abd-el-Krim in Morocco, Amanollah in Afghanistan, Sandino in Nicaragua—anywhere there was a war, there was I, in the front line. It was in the battle for Fez against Pétain, a fellow Frenchman, that I lost this eye. But fight I never did—I listened. The night before battle, I crawled like a snake on my belly to listen for devils. Wherever there was a pitched battle, I listened. But I tell you what—I never heard anything, not one devil. And you know why? Bombardment. In modern warfare, you always bombard your enemy before attacking, day and night, softening the enemy's lines. So I listen for the devils, all I hear are bombs, day and night, the devils are drowned out. Maybe they dance, the devils—who knows, you can't hear them, just bombs. They can't compete with the modern world. So I lose my eye, I lose my hearing, and I lose hope. I became a bitter man, and I abandoned my studies, my history. I'm better now, I don't care, only I wasted so much of my young life, that's why. I went back to university, I studied art, and I began to teach, first in France, later in America. It's not bad, though my health is no good. Many people waste their youths in obsession, and I did it too, in my own way. And now I can say, I tell the young people like you, don't be obsessed, don't lose your youth. It's not so bad." His eye shone, and he sipped at his tea. I shook my head in wonderment.

"You are quite a storyteller, Mr. Hand" was all I found to say.

"It's all true, yes."

We sat there in silence for a while, bobbing on an atmosphere of vague sadness and regret. I watched him sipping his tea, staring into his cup, a sad grizzled old gentleman with a past. He seemed so immeasurably small and gentle and wise, I was almost tempted to ask his advice. It is perhaps the greatest misfortune of my life that I remembered in time the necessity for absolute discretion, and instead, embarrassed, I changed the subject.

"So now you teach art?" I asked tactfully.

"Well," he hesitated, "not art, no. Art history, to be exact. That is why I am here, I study the ancient Moldavian churches, the monastery here. Beautiful religious artworks are all around, and perhaps soon to disappear."

"I see," I said; then, to show interest: "Do you specialize in any particular period or subject?"

He warmed to my question, smacking his lips. "Why yes, I do. What I teach, what I study, is realism."

"Soviet realism?"

The expression on his face suddenly changed, the furrows on his brow deepened, and again he gave me a piercing look of such sagacity and cunning that I shuddered involuntarily. "I mean surrealism," he said, and stood up. His countenance had instantly recovered its benevolence.

"It is late, sir," he said, smiling and shaking my hand, "and I must say goodnight. I have very much enjoyed the pleasure of your company, and I hope we shall meet again. Happy hunting, sir! Goodnight! Goodnight!"

He shuffled across the room and out the door. It was only then that I realized how very small this strange little man really was. I stared after him, bemused and not a little shaken. What it all meant—the veiled allusions, the meaningful looks and questions—was beyond me to fathom. While it seemed paranoid to imagine in him anything but a lonely old man, anything even resembling a spy, or that he had guessed the nature of my mission, there was yet something undeniably mysterious about him, something that made me suspicious and uneasy. For instance, why had customs confiscated his hearing-aid batteries while I had been permitted to enter with two dangerous weapons? Why, if he specialized in surrealism, was he studying ancient monasteries in Romania? Perhaps I was just imagining these things. As I sat there pondering, I realized how lonely I myself was feeling, and I was inclined to attribute my fear of Richard Hand to the work of my own depression. I swallowed my drink, threw a handful of change on the table and left the empty restaurant, my shoulders hunched against the rising wind.

Of course, it was not until I lay in bed, examining the seed of paranoia that was growing in my gut like a newly fertilized zygote, that I realized where I had seen Richard Hand before. In all my assiduous and detail-oriented preparation, I had failed to take into account perhaps the most egregious and dangerous obstacle to my search—the existence of a second person who knew of the Conglomeros and who, like me, might undertake or had undertaken the task of hunting it down! It is understandable that I had not fully grasped the situation at my first meeting with Richard Hand in the museum; but that I had come this far without suspecting was an unforgivable arrogance. Surely Hand had suspected me from the very first moment, and had since been closely following my every move and every progress; indeed, it could well be that, possessing no clue himself to the creature's whereabouts, he was simply shadowing me until such time as my adventure should culminate in success, only to snatch my prize from under my very nose. On the other hand, it was equally possible that we had stumbled independently but simultaneously upon the requisite information, and that we now found ourselves engaged in a frenzied race to the finish. But in either case there could be no doubting that he was my rival, though the threat he posed was impossible to calculate.

What did I know about him, other than that he was tenacious, single-minded, and iron-willed? He was surely not all he claimed to be and much more than he let on. Perhaps he had known Victor Brauner, or my grandfather, or, god forbid, even the Conglomeros itself! And what did he know about me? Certainly more than I did of him. These were my disadvantages. I, however, was young, strong, and well armed. I had already scoured the countryside and narrowed my field, an exercise the old man could not possibly have considered attempting. Most weighty of my advantages, however, was the vitality that righteousness lends to fortitude. Whatever Richard Hand's strengths, motives, or intentions, I would pursue my goal and I would achieve it. Should I or would I succumb to fear? As I stared at the ceiling, dappled with the harsh glare of the lamps in the railyard below, I steeled my determination with a triumphant "Never!"

By the next morning both fear and depression had dissipated, for this was the day we were to broach Ceahlau for the first time, Richard Hand or no Richard Hand. I had in mind a very particular area of the massif that I wanted to explore: the southwest slopes, where, by my calculations and guesswork, my grandfather had had his encounter with the Conglomeros. I knew, of course, that there were any number of reasons that I might not find it there, but this was not, after all, the most rational of quests to begin with; by the same token, the creature might just as credibly be where I expected it to be, and the southwest slopes, as in my grandfather's day, were still the wildest part of the range—were, in fact, a kind of corridor into the uninhabited reaches of Transylvania. If the Conglomeros was anywhere—and I believed that I had proved, at least, that it was nowhere else—it would be here, if my rival had not gotten to it first.

Ion and I drove farther into the mountains than we had ever driven before, up where the peaks of eternal snow glowed pink in the dawn sunlight, high up in the Bicaz Valley. The sky had cleared overnight, but the air remained brisk. Eventually, we pulled off the road onto an old logging track that soon faded into brush. It was evident that the track had fallen into disuse many, many years earlier, long before Ion or I was born, and it took me several moments after the engine had been cut to notice the silence. No sound of traffic intruded from the road; no distant airplane, motorcycle, jackhammer, chainsaw, radio, or picnic party polluted the air with their voices. We seemed on the very periphery of civilization here—nature alone was speaking, or seemed ever to have spoken, in this quiet little place. The rustling of the leaves overhead, the billing of wood pigeons, the *clac-clac-gwob* of the river: These alone were heard. A flock of starlings swung past above, and a branch moaned as it rocked in the breeze, heavily scented with pine. I reached into the trunk for my rifle.

I strapped on my belt, hoisted my knapsack onto my shoulders, picked up my gun, and off we set. We were soon deep into the forest, and I examined my map and compass: If I had correctly interpreted the location of my grandfather's sighting, we were about eight miles from where it had occurred. I was confident of having a better grasp of the lay of the land than Ion, who had not had my motivation in studying its topography. I was faced, therefore, with the task of guiding us to the destined area while giving the impression of haphazard. The slope had begun to steepen sharply when we heard flowing water to the left.

"Hark," I said. "A stream."

"Yes, it is the . . . the Parau Neagra," said Ion, stopping to consult his map. "It flows down from Piatra Neagra, the Black Rock. That is directly above us."

"Good. Shall we follow the stream up, then?" I asked.

"Well," Ion hesitated. "If we do we'll soon be out of the trees. The peak is just bare rock. No boars, no nothing."

"That's all right," I said, already making for the stream. "It will give us a good chance to look around, maybe see some chamois." In those woods, rich with lynx and pheasant, I whistled as I strolled along. Behind me, already puffing with exertion, Ion mumbled, "Chamois, yes sure," and spit.

We continued climbing by the banks of the gurgling

brook, occasionally walking ankle deep along its stony bed. Now and then a woodcock hoarsely cried out, but otherwise the song of the stream drew a merry, impermeable curtain of sound around us. Though our packs were heavy and our way precipitous, the uphill hike was made pleasant by the serenity of our surroundings, which remained lush despite the lateness of the season. With the wind and the swaying trees and the sunlight, it was an unharnessed sort of morning, and I felt as if I might be in Siberia, a thousand miles from the nearest road. Still, I kept a wary eye out for any signs of our having been preceded to this place, or followed and tracked at this very moment. With no such sign forthcoming, we came after several hours' climb across an old logging trail that cut through the woods to our north, precisely as marked on the map. Through the gap in the trees were plainly visible the two landmarks I had been waiting for.

"Look," said Ion, pointing in that direction. "You see this smaller peak, this cliff ahead? That is Dochia. And behind it, that giant rock like a pyramid, it is Toaca Peak, the highest on Ceahlau. Beyond, the land is much more wild, dangerous."

"Beyond" was my destination. Like a sentinel, Dochia marked the entrance to a small pass between the enormous rocky domes of Piatra Neagra and Toaca. The pass led into the coveted slopes, and further, into the savage Harghita mountains. It was only a few miles below this pass, on the other side—the wild side—that my grandfather had seen the Conglomeros. Indeed, both he and Victor Brauner might have followed this very path to their meetings with the creature. Was this what Victor had meant by "Prenuptial Exercise"? I suppressed a chill and looked about.

"Come on," I said. "Let's follow this path."

Another hour's climb through the forest brought us to the

treeline and to the foot of Dochia, a granite chimney some hundred meters high. Dochia looked out over the valley to the east, whence had ridden the invaders, and ignored the wilderness at her back, which to me seemed like a good omen. The path continued up her side, worn smooth by the wind, and perhaps once by shepherds, smugglers, legionaries. At the top, gazing down upon us with their chests thrust regally out, was a family of chamois. I let out a hoarse cry as I stumbled on a smooth stone, and when I got to my feet, uninjured, the chamois had gone. We continued our climb and shortly reached not only the top of the chimney, but the level entrance to the pass, which snaked away above us and was lost in the rocks. Though the actual summit of the pass was not visible, it very obviously lay hidden in the deep and mysterious cleavage between the two towering peaks. With the wind blowing hard about us, we forged ahead into the rocks. We pressed ever upward, Ion giving an occasional nervous glance behind him, toward civilization. I kept my gaze focused obstinately before me, ignoring all else.

We soon reached the top. A small turn about a large boulder, and suddenly there was the other side, the mighty Carpathians, spread out at our feet like an army of prostrate slaves, their great backs bowed in submission, dimpling the horizon as far as the eye could see. There was Transylvania, and at our feet the home of the Conglomeros, freely roaming somewhere below, perhaps within earshot, or eyeshot, or gunshot. I swooned, just a little bit, inside.

Shortly thereafter, having recovered, I began the descent, Ion directly behind me. Now that I had it before me, this country, I was suffused with an ineffable sense of confidence; where it came from I cannot say, yet it was reaffirming and inspiring to the highest degree. What we cannot confirm we accept on faith—faulty logic indeed, thank god, but faith such as mine, as I felt it then swelling in my heart, could not be unfounded. Now, on the brink of my own journey into the heart of darkness, uncertainty was the least of my handicaps.

We stopped for a brief lunch, though I had lost all appetite. By my reckoning, we would have to begin the return journey by four o'clock at the latest if we were not to be caught in the forest at sundown. The spot I had in mind to begin my search was a gentle slope of spruce and pasture that could be made out to the north, less than an hour's walk from where we sat, and I was understandably anxious to make some headway. We scrambled off, cutting a northwesterly line diagonally across the gravelly slope until we reached the trees. We then changed our course and headed southwest with the sun directly overhead. At last, we arrived at the edge of what I had more or less gratuitously designated as Conglomeros habitat. I sniffed the air skeptically.

"I think we might start looking here," I said.

"And why?"

"Oh, you know—hunch."

"Hunch?"

"Know what you're looking for, do you?"

"Yes, sure."

And off we made, tiptoeing like nymphs through the trees, rifles hanging like ripe shining fruit from our limbs, ears cocked. The quiet here was stupendous: no water, very little breeze, few birds, only the plumping of new-fallen leaves beneath our boots to break the silence. I began to imagine that we were trespassers in some enchanted grove—the one depicted in "The Meeting at 2 bis rue Perrel"?—and that we would soon be turned into stags by an angered Diana, and later shot at by our fellow hunters. I tried to clear my head of these distracting visions and to concentrate on the task at hand, but the power of such silence is not to be underestimated.

We scoured the valley for hours, my eyes sweeping the ground in vain for footprints. Ion walked about twenty paces behind me, going over the same path in case I had missed anything. Deeper and deeper into the wilds we foraged, while the sun slid inexorably toward the horizon. Though on several occasions Ion pointed out the lengthening of the shadows, I could not abandon the search, nor shake the intuitive feeling that I was on the verge of a breakthrough. Still, not a trace was forthcoming, not a hair, and finally I could no longer ignore the lateness of the hour. I sat down on a rock by the side of the stream and stared moodily into its waters. Ion kneeled to drink. All around us, the afternoon was falling like a rent parachute, quietly collapsing.

"Look," Ion said. "We are not the first ones here. There have been others, perhaps hunters like us. A picnic, maybe."

I looked at the muddy bank where Ion had pointed, but could discern no sign of anyone having picnicked there recently. Still, I mused, it was a very bad sign indeed if there were people—and a certain little person in particular—wandering about these parts, frightening the wildlife, driving it further and further afield. I spat, disgusted.

"No, I am mistaken, there were no hunters," Ion said, continuing to search the banks.

"That's good," I sighed.

"No hunters—bathers," said Ion, peering intently at the mud. "You know, Mr. X., it's like Sherlock Holmes, this hunt."

". . ."

"Like what you can be reading in the mud, clues," he babbled on. "Look here, for example. With my own eyes I see what has been happening in this place. There were others here, I see their feet. And they were swimming, I see they were wearing no shoes. And, you know, I think they were children, for their feet are small. Yes sure, children, and they were dancing children, playing. So, I am Sherlock Holmes: I know there were three children dancing on the mud in this place, just a few days past. Pretty good, yes, Mr. X.?"

"Yes, yes, good," I muttered. Sunk in my dark thoughts, I had barely listened to his monologue. Ion could hardly be expected to understand the depth of my disappointment in the day's hunt, and his good-natured rambling was clearly but a ploy to raise my foundering spirits. But then, though I had not really heeded them, his words echoed in my ears. "Three children dancing . . ." I leapt from my perch and rushed breathlessly to his side. And there they were, clear and shining beacons to the intellect, perfectly formed little emblazonings printed in the rich mud, waiting for me to read and interpret as if placed there expressly for the purpose—which perhaps they had—the indentation of each dainty toe, the rise of each shapely arch, the voluptuous swell of each heel. So true and whole was each print, one might almost project the delicate curve of an ankle, the taut calf, rising from each one. Quite clearly, there had been six feet prancing in this mud, three pairs, three people—three very young people—or one Conglomeros. The patterns of the prints were random, but not quite: They seemed to snake after each other, as if the revelers had been dancing a mambo, their hands upon each other's lissome hips; either that, or they were all somehow attached to one another, Siamese triplets joined at the head or chest. Either that, or *they* were an *it*, one monster bathing its supple, downy body in a mountain stream, gazing up at the sky as it popped bilberries under its tongue, dangling a plump toe in the limpid brook as it warmed its limbs beneath the life-giving sun. And sniffing the air, knowing that something is coming, loping off to its lair to await the unknown's inevitable arrival. A Conglomeros waiting for me, I just knew it, a Conglomeros that was and would be mine for the finding, mine alone!

I poked desultorily at the mud. "Yes, bathers," I said, concealing every trace of my emotion. "I'm certain they must have scared off the game. Goodness, is that the time? We'd better start back, don't you think?" I spoke not a word on the hike back to the car, nor during the drive home, but Ion said I looked feverish—pale and shaking, was what he said.

I arrived at the hotel by eight, bathed and changed, then met Ion for supper at our restaurant. All I ordered was half a roast chicken, yet even that, despite all the exertions of the day, I could not force down. I looked about for Richard Hand, but he was absent that evening, which did nothing to alleviate the tension I was feeling. And if he were at that very moment following the trail I had discovered earlier? If that were the case, there was of course nothing I could do about it but brood. Ion remarked upon my abstraction, which I put down to fatigue. In fact, I said, I thought I might forgo the next day's hunt and do some sightseeing about the area instead. He was most appreciative for the day off. Before leaving him for the night, I gave him a large gratuity, explaining that I wanted to do so now, in case I forgot later. I also promised to send him John Updike's latest.

I lay down on my bed at ten, and felt feverish indeed. I tossed and turned the entire night, troubled by dreams of violent, erotic imagery, and was up by five. Into my knapsack I packed provisions bought in anticipation of this day— canned fruit, granola, fortified oatmeal biscuits, and the like. I was on the road well before dawn, and pulled onto the same old trail where we had parked the previous day. This time, however, I drove the car further into the woods, and camouflaged it well with brush and downed branches. The first rays of the sun had just crept over the ridge when I set out into the woods and, unencumbered by weaponry and having a definite goal in mind, I made good time to the banks of the stream. Apart from a light film of frost, the prints were just as we had left them, and no new ones seemed to have been added overnight.

I examined them minutely. No expert in such matters, I was able nevertheless to determine certain crucial clues from the evidence. The Conglomeros—or whoever it was that had left these tracks—had come from the direction of the woods, where the prints dissolved in the carpet of fallen leaves. It had walked directly to the bank of the stream, where the depth of the prints, particularly at the balls of the feet, indicated that it had tarried some considerable time without moving—perhaps for a drink or a wash, or to stare at its reflection in the waters. Then it seemed to have turned about itself several times, as if it had been disturbed by some sound and had spun around to locate the source of the disturbance. These were the prints that had reminded Ion of a dance step. Then it seemed to have waded into the stream, and its trail vanished. Though I searched the opposite bank for a hundred yards in either direction, I could find no place where it had emerged from the stream bed. I deduced, somewhat panic-stricken by this dead end, that the creature had moved off along the course of the stream itself. But in which direction? It was, of course, impossible to tell. On the other hand, as my map told me, there was a large commune just six kilometers downstream. Any man or beast familiar with the area would be aware of that and, if desirous to avoid human contact, would head in the opposite direction, where the headwaters were born in a densely wooded and sheltered hangar. As that seemed by far the most likely direction for a Conglomeros to take, I hiked my trousers above my knees and waded upstream, in a southwesterly direction.

The riverbed was mostly small pebbles and flat stones, which should have made the going easy; but the current was quite forceful and the water extremely cold, so it took me over an hour to walk less than a mile. My brow was bathed in sweat and my feet numb when I flung myself on a cushion of moss for a rest. It occurred to me that if I had missed the telltale sign at the point where the Conglomeros had left the stream, I might scour the woods for weeks without another scent of it. The condition of my feet suggested that the beast could not possibly have walked all this way through the water without boots, and yet nowhere had I seen the slightest evidence—a fresh print, an oddly broken branch, whatever—that my prey had deviated from the path I was following. Reasoning in this manner, I fell into a deep sleep, troubled once again by the same erotic visions.

I awoke, startled, as a leaf dropped onto my forehead. I looked about, disoriented, and then at my watch. I was horrified to find that it was already two o'clock, and that I had slept for over three hours. What precious time I had wasted while the trail was fresh! Though I had not formulated any specific plans, I had hidden the car on the contingency that I would not be needing it anymore. But with the best of the day behind me, and vainly lost, I would be sore pressed to spend a wretched night in the wilderness if I did not retrace my steps soon, and abandon this, my only promising lead to date. But I had no choice: The woods were far too dangerous to be stumbling about in after dark, and even if I left immediately I would be lucky to get back to the car unscathed. I did, eventually, but what agonies of self-recrimination and anticipation I suffered that night!

For the next few days, I retraced my steps relentlessly along that accursed streambed, combing every inch of brookside brush and moss for the signpost I must have missed the first time around. Every day, I put off the bemused but grateful Ion with some farfetched excuse or other; every day, in the desperate and slightly ridiculous hope that I would no longer be wanting it, I dutifully camouflaged the car in the abandoned logging trail; and every evening, I wearily uncovered it again for the miserable drive back to Piatra Neamt. But though my morale flagged pitifully from day to day, and though I felt ever more inclined to abandon my quest at the end of each fruitless foray, and though I sank daily deeper into a morass of self-loathing and doubt—and this is a lesson I would gladly impart to any who would receive it—I persevered.

Thus, when it seemed as if I had exhausted my last resource, and late one afternoon had reached the farthest limit of what I had designated as Conglomeros territory, I stumbled on, onward, ever uphill, until the stream had all but disappeared beneath my feet. Impelled, in a strange way, by the very sense of futility that should have sent me homeward in defeat, I left the streambed and climbed to the ridge overhanging the hangar. By now I was in deepest wilderness, very near the top of the valley, and it was a frighteningly serene view that presented itself to me, there above the trees on a steep green slope of natural pasture. The moaning of the wind was my only companion.

I dragged myself along the crest of the ridge until it began to swing around to the north in a great arched bow. This ridge was the dividing line between the two river valleys and, for me, it was the end of the line—having reached the outer perimeter of my quarry's habitat, I had failed to locate the beast, and though I knew objectively that my search had only just begun, and though I tried to console myself with such platitudes as that it had been hopeless from the outset, mournful thoughts nevertheless crowded out any prayer of consolation. Had the snaking footprints formed patterns only in my imagination? Was this what it had come to, a silly delusion printed in sweat on mud? As I stood on the ridge, looking out over the Schitu valley, I was forced to wonder whether the very mystery I had hoped it to hold was nothing but a fantasy, the setting sun of a setting sun. Oh yes, I had been discouraged before, but never so low as this. The world turned, perhaps, but the myth, my lovely metamythic archetype, did not: It was as still and as stony and as coldly eternal as Dochia there, as a dead moon, as a dead tooth snapped off in the dead of night, no more alive than an Assyrian idol, than old Zamolxis himself. As I stood there on the ridge, beset by these and similar thoughts, my brow set ablaze by the sun dipping toward the horizon, a light flashed in the corner of my eye. At first, I thought it was just the effect of staring at the sun, but then I saw it again: the bright spark of light off some reflective surface—and it seemed to emanate from the depths of a small, isolated copse of larches, a few hundred yards below.

I descended cautiously toward the copse, and the flash blinked a few more times as I did so. Soon I stood at the very edge of the trees, which formed a ring so dense that I could make out nothing but wood and needles and a deepening twilight within. Whatever I had seen was now shrouded in its depths, for the sun had sunk below the mountain tops. I pushed myself through the first ring of trees, but still saw nothing. I proceeded inward toward the center of the copse, and though I am not a pincushion, the trees sorely pricked me as I slid between them. Finally, I broke through the barrier of branches and stepped boldly into the center, clear of trees but in no way empty, to my great wonder and astonishment.

The little clearing was almost perfectly circular, some twenty feet in diameter and completely screened by the palisade of larches from the outside world. It was like a tiny, verdant chapel, carpeted with firm layers of green and yellow mosses and fallen needles, which seemed ever so softly to glow in the dying light, reflecting the candescent dome of sky above. The branches of the trees were interwoven like a screen of wattling, unbroken save by a low, arched entranceway at a point roughly opposite that where I had entered. Thick drifts of needles were piled at the trees' feet, and the cloistered, emerald seclusion of the clearing gave the general impression of a large nest in its structure and womblike atmosphere of security.

On the other hand, if nest it were, the tenant was surely

some monstrous, insatiable magpie. The accumulated artifacts and detritus of many centuries made up its odd décor, strung across the opening above, hung from the drooping branches, spread out upon the floor and heaped pell-mell in the corners. As I looked about in awestruck confoundment, I was able to identify objects from many cultures and many professions, thrown together in distorted and disordered decorative pastiches in complete disregard for their original functions.

Several filthy yashmaks, for instance, were suspended like tapestries around the edges of the clearing, evidently as windbreaks. More lay in heaps on the ground, while some were draped over several votive crosses exquisitely carved in the Byzantine fashion, certainly many centuries old and probably of immense value. The crosses themselves were hung with fiddleheads, feathers, and clumps of raw wool, strung together on bits of wire and looped from cross to cross. Anything that could be hung, strung, or suspended dangled from branches, pieces of driftwood, or metal stakes jammed into the ground. I stumbled through, around, over and under this bizarre collection as one might through the senile memory of a grandparent.

I saw a magnificent, tarnished brass reliquary—empty— sitting near the center, capped with an ancient leather imperial shako, its blue dye faded into translucence. From the reliquary's slots and arabesques protruded the ivory hilt of a dagger and a rusting bayonet, at the tip of which swung a pair of goatskin gaiters with wool linings. A scrap of Brussels lace fluttered from the hilt. A heavy, cast iron weathercock in the shape of a ram was struck into the earth, a cracked briarwood pipe jammed onto one of its horns and a fairly new rubber douche sprouting from the pipe's bowl; a bamboo cricket cage hung from its tail. Many well-rounded pieces of colored glass were strewn haphazardly about the ground amidst a scattering of ivory piano keys, old bronze coins, and writing implements of every kind and age. The six of clubs from a pornographic deck of cards was pinned to an icon—a Virgin and Child on wood—by an extremely ancient silver brooch, possibly Roman, depicting the half-portrait of a braided woman in a tiara. I pocketed the brooch and the playing card fluttered to the ground, landing atop a train schedule bound in green oilcloth and containing the timetable for trains leaving from Iasi in 1926. There were other books lying around or propped against bottles: I found an Eastern Orthodox Bible, a Latin grammar, a farmer's almanac in Hungarian, an Austrian etiquette from the nineteenth century, and a book in English entitled *Secret Memoirs from the Court of St. Petersburg*, published in 1781. Hanging from lengths of ribbon, string, and broken fan belts tied to boughs was an assortment of nuts, bolts, stirrups, wooden and metal cutlery, a pince-nez, a tiny Canadian flag and a YHA insignium, an unopened can of smelts, a typewriter platen, a moldering silk fan, an old celluloid collar, a haydoll, a tuning fork, a phylactery, unfurled condoms, a clay ocarina, a few brass earrings, and a blond wig.

These are but a few of the objects that I saw there, many of which I was unable to ascribe to any specific use or origin. Some of these things, as I have mentioned, were antique and of incalculable value; others were old and worthless, while many were new and worthless. The manmade objects were interspersed and superimposed upon the natural objects with a complete and utter lack of inhibition, so that all the artifacts, regardless of origin, seemed in some eerie way to have become natural products and refuse, like articles in a garbage dump or a museum. And in a very real sense, the atmosphere in the clearing was a combination of the two—it was like some museum in the distant future, whose collection was composed of antiquities exhumed from ancient civilizations of which the curators knew absolutely nothing except that they were extinct. And though, in this case, the collection was relatively modern, it was stripped by the very nature of its setting of all meaning, of any reference to the cultures that had spawned it. In fact, if anything, it was the feathers, the fiddleheads, the pebbles, and the unpolished gemstones that defined the unknown collector's under-standing of the manmade objects—they had become the produce of nature, as much as if they had sprung from the earth, or been formed in the waters of the rivers, or shorn from the backs of wild animals. I must say, I found in all this something fundamentally offensive to my iconic Western sensibilities, but then again it would be fair in that regard to recall my state of extreme agitation at the time.

I think the reader can appreciate my wonderment in stumbling across this incongruous cache in the middle of the wilderness. If so, then the reader may also appreciate my terror when, as I stood marveling at my find, a low moan echoed through the space, a moan such as I had never heard before. I spun about, the hair rising on my head, but the clearing was empty. Had it been the wind rising off the heights? No, for I heard it again—a moan of pain, clearly, neither quite human nor quite animal. And imagine, then, my horror as I watched a pile of filthy yashmaks begin to shift and quiver like some revolting, diabolical stew, and rising from its depths—a hand, a human hand, a tiny hand, the trembling hand of a baby! The fingers were splayed and groping, the tiny arm swaying, as if feeling for a phantom mother. And again, for the third time—that moan!

My first and almost overpowering instinct was to run, to flee this hideous apparition as fast as my legs would carry me; but instead, mastering my terror and shivering with fear, I inched toward the vile bundle quivering on the ground. As I neared, I extended my arm toward the hand, and it seemed to sense the presence of a companion, for it started to reach and grope in my direction. Finally, infinitely slowly, our index fingers grazed one another, and the hand leapt at the contact. It shot forward and grasped my finger with a strength and tenacity not at all commensurate with its size, but just as a baby grasps at a proffered finger. I jumped backward with a yelp of fright, but the hand did not loosen its grip. Instead, the entire arm was exposed as I pulled it from the bundle, and also what was attached to the arm—not the body of a baby, but a great domed head, a head as big as a watermelon—the head of a Conglomeros! The arm I held sprouted like a tentacle where an ear should have been. The creature blinked its eyes slowly, licked its lips, and stared languidly at me. Then it closed its eyes, moaned again, released my finger, and seemed to fall away into a dead faint.

I stood spellbound for several minutes, unable to move yet unable to tear my gaze from the fabulous creature before me. Its nostrils quivered, and its breath came in rasping pants through half-opened lips. It was immediately clear that there was something wrong with it—this was not the vibrant Conglomeros of Brauner's paintings: Its lips were parched and cracked, mucus flowed from its nose, its tongue was swollen, its skin dry and peeling, its eyes caked with crust. Furthermore, it appeared to be unconscious and was having some trouble breathing. Though no veterinarian, I understood that the creature required urgent attention. I overcame my fear and revulsion, and knelt by the side of the bundle, ripping away the rancid rags in which the beast had swathed itself. As I was engaged in this nauseating task, I could not help but wonder: Had I finally found it, only to watch it die?

A gasp exploded from my lips as the last piece of cloth fell away. There, in all its mythical reality, was the entire Conglomeros, a sculpture in flesh, its three bodies hugging each other, arms and legs entwined like those of sleeping lovers, and so young, so tender, as to make one weep. A noxious stench rose from the bed, and I saw that the bodies, too, were covered in dirt and feces, and seemed unnaturally emaciated. I touched my hand to the beast's forehead—it was burning with fever. Of course, I had no idea what its natural temperature might be, but all the evidence indicated that the creature was seriously ill.

I let my knapsack fall to the ground, and retrieved my canteen and a handkerchief. Gently lifting the creature's head and cradling it in my lap, I soaked the handkerchief in water and swabbed the burning forehead. At the touch, the Conglomeros opened its eyes, so slowly and serenely I could count the seconds like drops of honey dripping. We stared at one another. The monster's eyes displayed neither fear nor surprise nor rage, yet they were wide and round enough to show the whites above and below the diaphanous, lime-green irises, deeper than a night of despair. I felt I could sink my arm up to the shoulder into one of those eyes and touch nothing but a warm undertow, an undertow whose pull was strong even from where I sat, motionless, petrified. I dabbed at its forehead again, and the eyes closed, and the creature sighed like a babe in arms. And when I dripped some water onto its lips, the shadow of a smile floated across its features like marsh flame. It was, indeed, as Brauner had painted it—an "Archetypal Identification."

The Conglomeros then sank into a deep oblivion, and though I feared greatly for its life, all I could do was sit and admire the miracle of its form. A little later, I removed all of the soiled yashmaks, gave the Conglomeros an improvised spongebath, and wrapped it up again in the cleaner shawls that hung on the crosses. Though it was risky—even now the alarm might already have been raised at my disappearance—I lit a fire which I kept burning through the night. I sat up until dawn, occasionally cooling the brow of the fevered beast, wetting its lips, and offering little comforting sounds to its troubled sleep. And as the sun rose the Conglomeros awoke, and the fever had been broken.

We sat and stared at each other for a long while, and I knew now that I had nothing to fear from the creature. It smiled at me continuously, closed-lip smiles broad enough to engulf my entire head, smiles of such gentle mystery as is more commonly experienced in medieval icons of the Virgin. It seemed already to have formed some improbable attachment to me—with its tentacular arms it repeatedly took my hands and pressed them to its glowing cheeks, which felt like warm peaches beneath my palms and amazingly delicate despite the creature's size. This silent communion lasted through the morning, but time seemed to stand still as I contemplated the Conglomeros in awe and wonder, and it contemplated me in apparently equal fascination.

Eventually, though, I became aware of a gnawing hunger, and I emptied the contents of the knapsack onto the ground. I opened a can of peaches and ate a few halves, then spoon-fed the Conglomeros, its head in my lap, while never for an instant did it remove its benign gaze from my countenance. It brought up the peaches in a great steaming jet a few minutes later, but after a while we tried some pears, which it managed to keep down, though with evident difficulty. It consumed some biscuits with relish, but, after a sip and a grimace, balked definitively at the evaporated milk. Through the afternoon, while the monster remained motionless in its swaddling cloths, we made a sampling of all the fare in my knapsack, and my suspicion that the Conglomeros was vegan, if not quite herbivorous, was confirmed. Spinach, peas, and the rest of the biscuits disappeared down its throat, while it simply stared at the boiled eggs and Spam in horror and confusion. I, like a child with a new puppy, was simply and frankly delighted by its every movement, its every reaction, its every glance. What had been the cause of its mysterious illness, or whether indeed it was at all cured, remained an enigma. The creature did not respond to my questioning, though it plainly understood

the fact that it was being questioned. Had Brauner communicated in language or gestures? I tried Romanian, English, French, Italian, and even some Latin—all met with the
same blank curiosity and silence. In fact, with the exception
of a rare, grunted expletive of disgust at the food I offered it,
I did not hear it speak a single word that day. The tiny arms
projecting from its head, however, were most expressive:
When placid, they linked fingers beneath the chin, like the
ribbon of a bonnet; when impatient, the fingers drummed
upon the forehead; when curious, they waved about like the
antennae of an insect, and when upset they clenched and
unclenched like the fists of a pugilist. It was a very edifying
if somewhat disconcerting experience, for in every particular the Conglomeros's face was emotive just like a human's—indeed, almost overly so, for like a simpleton it
seemed to have little or no control over those emotions.
Like its every feature, its affective states seemed larger than
life. The Conglomeros, it seemed to me, was baby, wild
beast, and some sort of sylvan silenus all in one, very much
the "Image of Uncreated Reality" that Brauner had claimed
it to be.

When next I looked up from our play, I was surprised to
find that the sun had already disappeared below the rim of
trees encircling our enclosure. Engrossed as I was in my
study of the monster, and as anxious, too, to prolong these
quiet moments, I knew that I must begin considering the
practical exigencies of my situation. There was an important decision to be made and, given my distraction and a
perhaps natural reluctance to confront certain harsh reali-
ties, I had not prepared myself to make it. The nascent sense
of panic that now gripped me with the full realization of my
predicament most certainly contributed in part to the course
of action I was to take; but I might just as truthfully admit
that this course of action had been determined from the first
moment I had set eyes on the mysterious and compelling

monster. Whatever the factors that determined my eventual decision, I now made an assiduous effort to examine the situation with a cold and objective eye, and my reasoning went as follows.

I would undoubtedly have been missed by now, thirty-six hours since I had last been seen at my hotel. Search parties would have been sent out, but not the humanitarian kind organized for wayward mountaineers: They would be armed posses of soldiers seeking a fugitive spy. I had given Ion deceptive information on my plans and whereabouts, but that wouldn't afford me any significant amount of lee-way. There was also the risk of Richard Hand's betraying me to the police. In any case, when the car was found, as it must be, it was only a matter of time before I would be traced to this refuge.

As I understood it, I had two options. Come the dawn, I could return alone to my car and to Piatra Neamt, claiming merely to have been lost overnight in the forest. This option had the advantage of forestalling any fortuitous discovery of the Conglomeros by the search parties, but it was also full of risks. If the car, carefully camouflaged as it was, were discovered, it would be clear that I had hidden it for reasons that were at the very least suspicious and, to minds already accustomed to habitual suspicion, probably damning. I would be interrogated and, if not indicted, certainly deported, precluding any opportunity for return in the future. On the other hand, a mechanism for my surreptitious flight had already been set in motion, and I had only to take advantage of it. This, too, entailed great, potentially lethal risks, though of course the rewards of its successful conclusion were enormous. Those rewards, however, were contingent on one crucial variable: my taking the Conglomeros with me.

In light of all that has happened, how can I now hope to justify that decision? A choice had to be made, and I had been prudent enough to foresee this moment and forearm myself with alternative solutions. Had I not, I would now be compelled to leave alone; instead, I had the choice: I could leave with the Conglomeros or without it, according to my whim. I chose the more attractive alternative. A mistake, perhaps, but who has not made them? Self-delusion, undoubtedly, but show me the sacrifice devoid of self-interest. The apathy to ignore scruples and the ambition to overcome them inform my every action—tell me, how could I have acted otherwise?

Dutifully, I presented myself with altruistic motives: The creature was ill, perhaps dangerously so, and required (my) care; it lived in constant danger of discovery by people who would be less compassionate than I; its natural habitat was being eroded by development and might soon disappear altogether; and most important, it was being stalked by an evil man who could appear at any moment to spirit it away to some cage in a zoo, or some laboratory, or some circus sideshow. Every thinking man has his reasons, and these still seem good to me. The problem remains that no crime is a mistake and every mistake a crime in a moral universe, and that we human beings cannot help but be criminals and fools. I am in no position to preach but I am in a position to know, for I made a criminal mistake. I decided to abduct the Conglomeros.

To the casual observer, "abduct" may seem an inappropriate expression, with its implications of forcible action and unwholesome design. Obviously, the abduction in this case depended on the subject's willingness to be abducted. There was no way I could force the creature to accompany me—even should I mange to subdue it, I could not possibly hope to carry it down the mountainside, since in its present condition there was no certainty that it could complete the journey without some sort of relapse. I understood that a gentle,

insidious persuasion was called for, one in which the ab-
ductee would have every experience of voluntary action.
This, then, was the task at hand, and no sooner was it con-
ceived than I undertook it.

With great patience and tenderness, so as not to frighten
the gentle beast, I began peeling back the layers of cloth in
which it was wrapped. It watched me curiously, with no
trace of fear or suspicion. When the creature lay exposed in
all its nakedness, I rose and walked to the other side of the
clearing. I gestured for it to rise and follow, I pantomimed
the act of rising, I asked, begged, and commanded it to rise
and walk; but though it shifted so as to be able to observe my
actions, all three bodies moving in perfect unison and coor-
dination, it did not seem to understand what I required.
"Stand up! Stand up!" I shouted, but it remained supine. Finally, I approached it and grabbed it gently by an arm, tug-
ging upward. Still, the creature did not move, and it was
surprisingly heavy. I squatted by its side and tried to coax it
with sweet whisperings. As I reached again for its arms, it
suddenly leaped to its feet, so fluidly and with such speed
that I was bowled over and found myself on my back, staring
up at the monster that towered, smiling, above me.

At that moment I understood for the first time the cryptic
title of Victor Brauner's 1949 canvas, "The Hunter of the Unconscious." Nothing—no painting, no sculpture, no description, no fantasy—could have prepared me for the physical
presence of that beast. From childhood, we are familiar with
the image of a centaur, and quite take in our stride its unlikely figure. But actually to stand next to one, close enough
to feel the heart of its body, to smell its earthy scent, to caress
the line where skin gives way to pelt—to imagine that is to
know how I felt with the Conglomeros's many-limbed body
above me. Its grace was purely animal, despite its incongruous bulk no less natural than a cheetah's, than a giraffe's,

while yet disconcertingly apprehensible as human. Technically, the creature was precisely as portrayed in the statue. Yet now, standing there, how far in truth! How could Victor have described the sway of its long necks, or the simultaneous rise and fall of its chests, the crystalline fragility of its rib cages, the slimness of its arms and legs and fingers, the softness of its down, the firmness of its breasts, or the slender pubescence of its sexes? Certainly, I could see how Victor might have interpreted his awe before its raw animality as sexual desire. Indeed, I have never yet beheld anything so beautiful as its eyes, its bodies, its grace—nor do I ever expect to. Neither the most perfect thoroughbred horse nor the whitest swan nor sleeping Endymion nor immortal Psyche are anything in comparison.

The monster extended an arm and helped me to my feet. We examined each other frankly, both marveling. We were of about the same height—slightly under six feet—though the Conglomeros was of course much larger than me—at my estimate, somewhere between three hundred and three hundred and fifty pounds—and, despite its comeliness, somewhat intimidating thereby. Furthermore, it seemed to have entirely recovered from its illness, and such powers of recuperation were in themselves astonishing, though I had perhaps misjudged the severity of its symptoms. Whatever the circumstances of its recovery, it now seemed as fit and as sound as it could be. I paced back and forth across the clearing—it followed me. I jumped up and down—it jumped. I ran in place—it ran in place, six legs pumping, eight arms swinging, without the slightest trace of awkwardness: indeed, with the same agility as any wild beast. I was reassured, at least, that it was physically fit to make the arduous journey ahead. But would it? And how could I find out? The sun was already beginning to set, and I must leave soon—alone or not.

I sat down to ponder the dilemma, and the Conglomeros

sat down beside me, now and then mimicking my gestures. How to convince it that it must follow me? I tried the direct approach: I pointed toward the exit to the clearing. "Out? Out?" I asked, as if it were a dog, and, just like a dog, it stared at my finger instead of in the direction in which it pointed. I said, "Look, you really must come with me. We're both in trouble. Even if I leave without you, they'll trace me here and find you. You don't want that, do you?" It shook its head vigorously, but I realized that it was only copying me. "So you'll come, then?" It mimicked my nod. I was getting nowhere, and the time of departure was upon us. I began to pack my knapsack, and the Conglomeros looked on—sadly, as I thought. It scratched its thighs. Where would I go? I decided to take my chance with the authorities—at least there would be some hope of return, even if it was slim. I could waste no more time, and though I knew it to be a lie, consoled myself with the thought that I had, in fact, found what I had come to find. And as for Richard Hand—there was every chance that he would encounter precisely the same problems as I, or worse, which offered me some modicum of comfort.

I looked at the Conglomeros and it looked at me, its hands folded in its laps. I was shocked to find tears springing to my eyes, and my sight blurred. Would I ever see this lovely creature again? I leaned over and stroked its bald, downy head, and gently kissed its brow. The two tiny arms wrapped themselves around my neck, and the Conglomeros kissed me full on the lips—I could smell its moist, herbaceous breath, redolent of newly mown grass. It didn't seem to want to let me go, but go I must. I disentangled myself from its arms, and moved to the low, branched archway at the far side of the clearing. I turned around, hoping that the creature might follow me, but it just sat forlornly watching me leave and distractedly rubbing its thighs. A moment later I was back in the outside world, somehow repellent in its cold expanse after the warmth and seclusion of the clearing. The last dying light of day glowed against the distant back of Dochia, and it was thither that I turned my heavy steps.

I was but a half-mile down the slope, lost in thought, when the Conglomeros tapped me on the shoulder. It laughed and gurgled like a baby, but it was obvious from the bright spark of panic in its eyes that it was aware of having made a great and irreversible decision, just as it knew that it had been fated to make it. I smiled, spoke a few words of solace, and we retraced our steps, past the copse, over the ridge, and down the other side into the darkling valley.

We scrambled down the rocky slopes as fast as possible, making the most of the remaining light. I slipped and fell often, cutting my hands rather badly, but the Conglomeros was as surefooted and silent in our flight as a mountain goat. It was already dark by the time we reached the woods and I felt hidden enough to switch on a small flashlight I had brought along. Soon thereafter I heard the rushing waters of the Bistrita off to our right, and we followed the stream the rest of the way down. In the dark, the Conglomeros's eyes flashed like a cat's, like the breasts of the sorceress in "The Philosopher's Stone." Once it understood that we were to follow the stream it took the lead, and I almost lost it from sight as it bounded ahead of me, running low and skipping nimbly through the undergrowth. But every so often, after I had stopped to catch my breath and it had disappeared in the darkness, it would wait and startle me as it stepped out of the shadows. We ran this way for several hours, and the stream grew louder and louder as it was fed from the gurgling tributaries we forded. By the time we emerged from the forest and found ourselves on the edge of a meadow, the stream had been swollen into a full-fledged creek. With words and gestures, I persuaded the Conglomeros to remain behind in the safety of the trees while I crept on into the village of Telec.

The village was tiny, no more than a dozen wooden bungalows lined up on the left side of the road and hard by the shoulder. Lights blazed from all the windows, and I realized that it was still too early to contact my guide. I backtracked to a small bridge, and hid myself beneath it on the bank, whence I could watch the activities and lights of Telec. I sat there for several hours, saw one old couple visiting from house to house, the scuffing of their boots on the gravel clear and sharp in the night air. At last they arrived at their own home, looked up at the clouds and whispered about the weather to each other, then retired indoors. Fifteen minutes later, their lights went out. A half-hour later there was not one window left alight in the entire village. Though I was concerned that the Conglomeros might wander off into the woods, being not quite a brute yet still a beast, I allowed another hour to be safe, then tiptoed down the road and into the village, looking for the landmark that Emil had described for me. I found it in front of the fourth house: a small granite milestone with the number 1 carved on it. I crept round to the back of the house and tapped three times on the window, paused, tapped twice, paused again, tapped once. A moment later the window was opened, and in the darkness I discerned a swarthy, black-bearded face.

"Vreti sa plecati acum?" a voice hissed at me.

"Da, vreau sa vizitam la mare," I hissed back.

"Am uitat da costum de baie?"

"N-avea grija, ne-au invitat sa stam."

"Da doo run run run."

"Da doo run run."

"Come to the front."

I crept back to the front door, which opened silently at my approach. The house was pitch black inside. A large hand grabbed my shoulder and pulled me to the side. I felt the man's beard against my cheek, and smelled wine and garlic on his breath as he whispered in my ear.

"We must go soon," he said. "You have money?"

I pulled a wad of dollars from a pocket of my hunting jacket, and handed them over. A match flared in the darkness, shedding only enough light to illuminate the money. He flicked through the bills, all hundreds, but didn't bother to count them. The match went out.

"Is good. We go, come." He pulled me to the door.

"Wait," I balked. "I've got to get my friend from the woods."

"*Ce?*"

"My friend," I hissed.

"Da, you friend. You come here. *Repede.*"

I ran back to the woods on tiptoes, and found the Conglomeros by its enormous glowing eyes. It was sitting under a tree, and didn't seem at all put out by the long hours it had had to wait; no more did it seem inclined to get up, despite my frantic pleading, until I jerked it forcibly to its feet. Even then, I could not have budged it unless it had wanted to be budged, and I remember thinking even then how strange it was that such a simple, gentle creature could be so moody. We crept back toward the village and I made the Conglomeros wait under the bridge while I returned to the house. I was about to knock at the door when I was hailed with a "psst!" from the darkness. It was the bearded fellow, sitting in the blacked-out cab of a minivan parked before the house.

"Where you friend?"

"At the bridge."

"Go get. *Repede.*"

At the bridge, the Conglomeros balked once more. It seemed to sense that this was its last chance to turn back, and it would have been no use explaining that its life was irrevocably altered whether it chose to stay or not. It rolled its eyes in a most pitiful manner, turning its head from side to side as if seeking help from the surrounding night. It moaned and whimpered softly. I pleaded with the beast, stroking its head and hands, but in its growing panic it looked right through me. Finally, in desperation, I planted a firm kiss on its mouth, and it seemed to see me for the first time. I looked deep into its eyes, cooing little reassurances, and though it continued to tremble like a terrified animal, it smiled hesitantly. I patted and pulled at a hand, and finally it rose. I threw my jacket over its shoulders so as to confuse its monstrous silhouette, and we ran back to the minivan. The back doors were open, and I urged the Conglomeros inward. It gave one last look at the dark slopes overhead, and clambered inside. I was about to follow when the driver called softly to me.

"You push," he whispered.

"Push?"

"No good drive in village," he said, and I understood. Our way was downhill, and the minivan rolled easily enough as I panted, jogging, beside it. When we had cleared the houses, the driver said "In!" I threw myself into the back of the minivan and shut the doors. The motor coughed to life. We were in total darkness, and over the engine's whine I heard the Conglomeros's plaintive whimpering. I curled up within the warm hollow of its bodies, kissed it goodnight, and fell asleep.

I slept all night, and when I awoke the daylight was clearly visible through the seams of the doors. I had no idea where we were, or where we were headed. Emil had warned me to ask no questions, but simply to trust: His people had done this many times, and only rarely had something gone wrong. Still, I could not restrain my curiosity. I crawled to the door, opened it a crack, and peered outside. We were driving along a lonely, two-lane country road, with no other traffic in sight. The landscape was flat, allowing no view of the surrounding countryside, and the road was lined as far as the eye could see with tall, brownish reeds. There was a vague hint of salt water in the air, and the cloud-cover hung menacingly low and gray. It must have been sometime after dawn, but the sun was invisible. I closed the door and turned back to my companion.

The Conglomeros was wide awake, and still in the same state of animal panic. Its great green pupils were dilated in terror and it trembled from head to toes. I had noticed that, in fear, its bodies clung to one another, arms tightly wound about its chests, legs wrapped about the waists, similar to three children playing choo-choo train. And so it sat now, huddled in the corner, its head leaning and bumping against the corrugated tin wall. I crawled over the squeezed myself in, encircling its shoulders with my arm, cradling its head in the crook of my neck and whispering in dulcet tones. "There, there," I whispered, and my voice echoed against the metal walls. It took me several minutes of this finally to realize that there was no echo. "It's all right," I said. "Sol-rye," the Conglomeros said, unconsciously mimicking me under its breath, its voice that of a pubescent child, neither quite male or yet quite female and somehow indefinably Latin. "Don't be afraid," I said. "Dobey-fray," the Conglomeros said. I laughed, and it looked up at me, a spark of warmth and affection in the depths of its gaze. I kissed the top of its head, a texture like that of an unripe peach, and hugged the creature tight. We stayed in that position for a long while, until I became aware from the rhythm of our driving and the sounds outside that we were no longer in the countryside. I heard voices, other engines, a variety of clattering and banging noises that told me we were in a town or city. The Conglomeros, too, understood the import of these sounds—its entire body grew tense and rigid, and its breathing came in fast, shallow pants. We came to a stop soon afterward, the engine was cut, and the door of the cab opened and shut. I looked frantically about me, and in the dim light

I found a plaid blanket in the corner that I had not seen in the dark the night before. I grabbed the blanket and threw it over the Conglomeros, covering its many limbs as thoroughly as possible. I forced the creature to the floor, and sat so that it would be hidden behind me. The doors opened, and our driver peered in at us, his eyes groping for a glimpse of my companion. Looking past him, I was able to determine that we were in a garage on a narrow alleyway.

"You wait, not move," he said, and slammed the door. I heard a key turning in the lock. A few minutes later he returned with a loaf of bread, some cheese, a large bottle of water, and an enameled chamber pot with a lid.

"We leave this night," he said. "You not talk." And he was gone.

The day passed slowly. In the renewed darkness, the Conglomeros calmed down somewhat, though the slightest noise would cause it to jump, its eyes wide with fear. We slept fitfully, ate our food (the Conglomeros would not touch the cheese), and filled the chamber pot. I was gradually beginning to understand the creature's biological functions—each body seemed to function independently of the others, equipped with all the required organs for respiration, circulation, digestion, excretion, reproduction, and so on. As I sat there, listening to its soft breathing, I tried to imagine the miracle of its skeleton, more arcane than that of any dinosaur, the terrible complexity of a nervous system that could coordinate such a body, the enigma of a monster that possessed three sets of genitalia but no navel. Despite myself, I began to envision all the tests and examinations that would reveal this marvel to modern science. But I quickly shook my head clear of such nocuous thoughts—the Conglomeros was mine, I had taken it under my protection, I was beholden to it, and I had no intention of allowing it to fall into the greedy, insensitive hands of the scientific and commercial establishments, should I ever succeed in getting it to

America. What it needed was not to be prodded and put on display like some circus freak—it would require love and nurturing and the security of seclusion if it was to thrive in its new life in the new world. I would be its guardian and educator, not its tamer. With these and similar thoughts I soothed and repressed any doubts I might have had about my own altruistic motives. As if it had read my thoughts, the monster took me by the hand and murmured "sol-rye" in my ear.

To pass the time, I tried to teach it some English. We began with body parts, and the creature took very well to its lessons. Within an hour it had memorized all the major limbs and extremities, but it fell short of grasping the concept of names. "Aaron," I said, pointing to myself. "Arrow," it repeated. I planted my index finger in its foremost chest. "Chess," it said. "No, no, this chest, but all of this—Aaron." "Arrow." "And this?" "Arrow." "No, *I* am Aaron. You are . . . ?" "Hans." "No, don't look at my hands. *You* . . ." and so on, throughout the afternoon. Later we took another nap, and despite the cramped conditions, despite the hardness of the floor and the odor of the chamber pot, I found great serenity enfolded in the arms of the beast.

We were wakened by the creaking of the garage doors. There was no way to determine the time of day. A moment later, our driver poked his head in the door.

"Okay?" he whispered.

"Sol-rye."

"We go."

The engine started up and we reversed out of the garage. We hadn't been on the road more than five minutes when we stopped. The moment the engine cut off I could hear the lapping of waves. The doors opened, and our driver said, "Out." We got out, the Conglomeros wrapped in the blanket and wearing a woolen hat of mine to cover its antennal arms. Though the night was pitch black and the sky heavily overcast, it was clear that we were on a wooden dock. The lights of the town we had just left glowed around the curve of the river. Moored to the dock was a barge piled high with reeds, and a small fishing smack rigged like a sloop. It was to the smack that our driver guided us. It was just dark enough, and the blanket just long enough, for him not to notice anything unusual about my companion. We clambered down into the smack, where a pilot was waiting by the jib. The driver disappeared without a word, the pilot cast off our mooring, and the boat slipped out onto the water, mainsail billowing.

"You speak English?"

"No."

"Where are we?" I asked in Romanian.

"Tulcea," he said.

"What is this river?"

"Dunarea."

The Danube! That meant that we were somewhere in the delta, heading east, out toward the Black Sea through the marshes. How long it would take us to reach the open sea, and what we would do once we reached it, was anybody's guess, and our taciturn pilot would tell me no more. When the lights of Tulcea had faded behind us, he started up a small outboard motor that effectively precluded any further conversation. He also switched on a halogen beam affixed to the prow. The black water breaking before us looked like oil, and we were soon enclosed by the ghostly, liquid horizon of swaying reeds. We motored on for the rest of the night, cutting engine and lights whenever the docklights of some village or fishing station hove into view. In this manner, as I guessed, we made progress of some forty miles before dawn broke, gray and bleak, over the delta.

We pulled off the river onto a canal, and from then on we stayed off the main waterways, pointing and repointing through a network of channels cut into the marshes. We used only the sails, and whenever the sounds of a motor came to us over the water, we pulled into the reeds until the vessel passed. Mostly, they were barges laden with reeds, but occasionally they were hunters in motorized dinghies, shotguns at the ready, prowling the marshes for heron. The day wore on monotonously, and sometime after noon a light drizzle began to fall. The Conglomeros lay on the planking, entirely covered by the blanket; I whispered or sang to it continuously, and suppressed the occasional foray of a limb from beneath its cover. The pilot must have assumed it was a political refugee, and made no attempt to look beneath the blanket. The rain whistled eerily through the reeds, and the otherwise silent and gloomy aspect of the marshes began to tell on my nerves. I nearly fell out of the boat when a flock of snow-white egrets exploded from the reeds off the port bow.

A gray, viscous dusk fell, but the drizzle persisted, chilling me to the bone. When it grew too dark to see, the pilot switched on the beam, which cast rainbow patterns through the rain and mist as it swept back and forth across the prow. At some point in the middle of the night I became aware that the rustle of the reeds had entirely receded, and the pilot confirmed my suspicion that we were back on the main river. The wind picked up, and the boat creaked gently as it swayed. Every so often, I thought I could detect another vessel creaking in sympathy behind us, but the night was too black to see anything and the pilot did not seem to hear what I did. I attributed it to hallucination brought on by nerves and fatigue, or perhaps to some strange echo off the now-distant banks. On we sailed into the night.

Gradually I became aware of a glowing light on the horizon, some city forgotten in the marshes. As we rounded a bend in the river, the town came into view. The pilot extinguished the beam and tacked to starboard, and soon we were in the shadow of the opposite bank, allowing as much distance as possible between the town and our boat. "Sfintu Gheorghe," our pilot whispered, pointing at the docks. "Much *graniceri*," by which I supposed he meant Coast Guard or some other military force. Still, we passed the town without raising any alarms and had soon put it behind us, though we continued to cling close to the banks where the reeds provided some camouflage. Again, over the soft hiss of falling rain, I thought I heard the creaking of planks and the flapping of sails that were not ours. But hallucination or not, these sounds were soon overwhelmed by one that grew steadily more pervasive—the low boom of breaking surf. We had come to the sea. I breathed a sigh of relief as I saw the first breakers up ahead and heard the lonely knelling of a channel buoy. We made for the open waters.

The night was suddenly rent by a piercing wail, and the darkness imploded under bludgeons of blinding light. I turned to see two launches speeding toward us from the direction of the city, sirens blaring, searchlights sweeping across the broad expanse of water, flails of spume spraying from their bladelike prows. They were making straight for our boat and would be upon us momentarily. "Down, down!" hissed the pilot, and we both flattened ourselves on the floor, though I knew it would be of no use. I heard the sharp report of warning shots being fired, and waited, my face half-submerged in stinging bilge, for our vessel to be accosted and our arrests effected. The sirens grew louder and louder, and the rain lashed my face pitilessly.

Just as suddenly as they had begun, the sirens were silenced and the searchlights seemed to veer off. I could hear the sounds of men shouting angrily, orders being issued, the clash of hull against hull, but the launches' engines died to a low idle, and they were drawing no closer. I thought it was a trick to lure us into the open from our sheltered spot beneath the overhanging reeds, and I made no movement. But still, as I held my breath and waited, the voices came no nearer. Had the launches foundered or rammed one another? I peeked warily over the edge of the gunwale.

The launches had come to a complete halt about two hundred yards behind us, near the reeds. They lay to, parallel to one another, their prows pointing directly toward us. Sandwiched between them was a small ketch very similar to our own, its sails lowered. All of this was clearly visible in the light of the searches, which were directed down and onto the ketch. The decks of the launches were lined with helmeted soldiers, their rifles trained on the captive vessel. Some officers had boarded it, and were rummaging around, selecting various objects and throwing them into large boxes held by their adjutants. There was some minor scuffling, from which two civilians emerged, pulled to their feet by the officers, their hands cuffed behind their backs. A rope ladder was lowered from one of the launches, and the civilians were hauled by their collars onto its deck. Though I could not make out their faces at this distance, one was clearly a local fisherman; the other seemed rather out of place on the river—he wore a long gray mackintosh and was very short. As he was being dragged below deck, he turned for a moment and looked over his shoulder in the direction of our boat. In that brief instant, I saw under the fierce glare of the searchlight the black patch that covered his left eye. The engines revved, the prow of the launch lifted out of the water, and it turned in a wide arc back toward Sfîntu Gheorghe. A few minutes later, the ketch fastened by a rope to its bow, the other launch pulled away. Silence moved in once more to claim the night, broken only by the clap of waves on our hull and the tender, lisping rain.

The pilot eventually roused himself from the floor, and sat staring out across the water in wide-eyed disbelief. He looked at me and shook his head. I shrugged—what more could we do but give thanks? The pilot whispered a short prayer while I sang a sweet, tuneless lullaby to the shivering creature cowering beneath the blanket. Then the pilot swung us out into the current, the keel bobbing like a cork in the choppy estuary, the salt spray whipping across the bow, and we sailed on into the choppy black waters of the deep Black Sea.

I flew back to New York from Athens, breezing unmolested through customs at either end. I went home, did my Bible lesson, and slept for fourteen hours.

Physically and emotionally drained though I was, I had no time to waste on self-indulgent recuperation. I was up bright and early the next morning. My first stop was Christie's, where I left the silver brooch for appraisal. Then I took the next available train out of town, riding north along the Hudson to Poughkeepsie, where a taxi drove me to the nearest car dealership. I chose a "family car" with tinted windows, four-wheel drive, and a rear bench that could be folded down to create a large cargo space. Within the hour I was driving across the Rhinecliff bridge and heading into the heart of the Catskill mountains, where I found a quiet little inn in Phoenicia and half a dozen accommodating real-estate agents in Woodstock.

I spent the next week looking at houses.

I made my preferences and means clearly understood, so not much time was squandered on window shopping. Finally, I selected an old Dutch stone farmhouse situated on sixty acres of what had once been arable land but was now covered in fine, second-growth mixed woodlands, well secluded on a hilltop and accessible only by private road. The asking price was a little beyond what I had anticipated paying, but an offer of cash made the owners amenable to negotiation, and the house was mine, along with most of its furnishings. With the eventual sale of the silver brooch in auction, I would recoup half of my outlay on the house, and my finances, though not what they had once been, remained healthy. All papers signed, I returned to New York with several weeks to spare before the arrival of the *Ismet Inonu*. This gave me plenty of time to mull and fret over recent events, and as the day of reckoning inched nearer, all my fears and guilt grew and crystallized and blotted out all logic and consolation. I often have a dream in which the memory of a long-forgotten murder I have committed sometime in the past suddenly returns to haunt me. These weeks felt like that dream, nightmarishly prolonged.

I recalled that awful night on the sailboat and how quickly our relief at reaching the sea had turned to terror as we lurched and swayed in the towering swells. But somehow, through the ink-black night and the stinging spray and the howling gale, our pilot brought us to our rendezvous with a small tanker anchored, to my best estimate, some ten miles offshore. Under cover of dark, we were hustled along its decks and down its narrow, dimly lit metal stairways and catwalks into some hellish cargo hold, blacker even than the night outside and reeking of rancid oil and dead rats. We shivered there for several hours in our wet clothing until a sailor, speaking what I took to be Bulgarian and smelling even worse than our place of confinement, brought us each a cup of thin broth with a few potatoes floating in it. That broth was horrible, putrid, but I drank it down gratefully, while the Conglomeros picked morosely at the vegetables. For the next few days, all we got was more of the same, along with hunks of relatively edible black bread. We evacuated our bladders and bowels in the far corner of the hold, but the constant pitching and tossing of the ship ensured that we were never long separated from the fruits of our labors. I felt rather inclined to complain—after all, I was not some boat person, I had paid more than handsomely for this journey—but there was no one who spoke English to whom I might voice my indignation. Besides, we were incognito, to say the least, and entirely at the Bulgarians' mercy.

Finally, the engines slowed to an idle and then stopped altogether. After hours of banging, crashing, and shouting overhead, someone came for us. With the Conglomeros still wrapped in its filthy blanket, we were herded first up and then down into what appeared to be a bonded warehouse on a dock. To my persistent entreaties, a Turkish customs officer, with a waxed handlebar moustache and pressed uniform—obviously the man who had been bribed to let us through—finally informed me that we were in Istanbul. He also told me, in impeccable English, that we must be showered and prepared to leave in ten minutes. Too dazed to question or resist, we were shown into a vast, ornately tiled shower room, surrealistically annexed to the warehouse, where I washed myself and the numb, helpless Conglomeros with lavender-scented Turkish soap. I slipped back into my stinking rags and draped the creature entirely under its blanket, like some very large and underprivileged child at Halloween.

When we were ready, we were shepherded into a dark corner of the warehouse, where the customs official—his back turned to us at my request—explained the arrangements. I was to receive a Turkish stamp in my passport and a ticket to New York on Olympic via Athens. My "friend" was to be sealed inside a packing crate and shipped to Brooklyn by freighter. When I protested vehemently, the customs official assured me that people traveled this way all the time, that it was perfectly safe, and that the stowaway would be provided with all the necessities to ensure that his trip was as carefree and comfortable as possible, given the circumstances. And then, as he pointed out tactfully, we had no choice in the matter. The problem, of course, was that the Conglomeros was not a human being; despite its native intelligence and my assurances, I was not convinced that it understood what was in store.

I asked for a few moments alone with my "friend," and these I was granted. The Conglomeros, clearly happier now that it was clean, was nevertheless frightened and confused. It clung to me with all eight arms, clasping me within its enfolding embrace until I could hardly breathe. Its chests heaved and fat, glycerine tears streamed from its tightly shut eyes. It whimpered pathetically, like a puppy. And how could I now persuade it into its coffinlike enclosure? And yet I did. Calling upon all my reserves of courage and self-mastery, I somehow coaxed the creature into letting me go and stepping into the crate. I smiled a lot and burbled over with baby talk—"bye-bye," "don't cwy, my wittle bitty baby," "see you soon," and so on—but the creature, only slightly doubled over in its confinement, did not seem entirely convinced. It tried to smile back and to echo my sentiments of confidence—"bobby-bobby," it said, and "Lips, Arrow, lips!" (meaning "Kiss me, Aaron")—but it was only an act for my benefit. Finally, unable to bear the creature's sorrowful gaze any longer, I placed the lid on the crate and called for the longshoremen. The creature went quiet at the sound of their approaching boots, but when the first nail went in, the hammerblow echoing hollowly through the warehouse, it let out a startled cry that grew to a steady wail as the expressionless workers went on with their task. I turned and walked briskly across the floor toward the waiting customs man, but not fast enough to escape hearing, above the deafening racket of hammers, the regularly spaced cries of "Lips, Arrow, lips!"

Now, at five o'clock on a frigid November morning, I stood outside the gates of the Red Hook container terminal, watching a crane unload aluminum containers from the cargo hull of the *Ismet Inonu.* After I had waited three or four hours, the crane pulled up a small wooden crate and deposited it off to the side of the pyramid of containers. I honked my horn, and a longshoreman opened the gates for me, after first checking my name and accepting a large-denomination banknote for his trouble. I drove into the compound and pulled the car over to the wooden crate; the crane operator, having descended from his perch, helped me lift it into the back, for which he too received handsome remuneration. I was back at the stone house by four.

I was overcome with nauseated anxiety as I applied a crowbar to the lid of the crate, right there in the driveway. As the lid fell to the ground, my worst fears seemed to be realized. An overpowering stench of decay rose from the crate, and the Conglomeros lay at the bottom, impossibly contorted, encrusted in its own waste and apparently beyond communication. It was a truly pathetic sight, and I was unable to contain the sobs that rose in my throat. What could I do but blame myself for this tragedy? I should have been able to predict such an end, and somehow managed to preclude it. Under the guise of protection, I had been serving my own selfish ambition, and the wretched corpse of this once-proud and guileless beast was my trophy. The wretched corpse began to stir.

Incapable of lifting it from its hideous confinement, I hurriedly dismantled the crate. As the last panel fell away, the Conglomeros, still insensible, collapsed to the ground and groaned piteously. I ran indoors, filled a bucket with cold water, and returned to my unconscious ward. I sprinkled some water on its face and wiped away the grime that clogged its mouth and nostrils. It trembled violently and opened its eyes, rolling them in wild delirium. I spoke to it, but it did not respond in any way to my voice. I ran to the shed, found a wheelbarrow; somehow, I managed to raise the creature's limp form into the vehicle, and so half-rolled, half-dragged it indoors, its arms and legs bumping against the hard earth as if they were no more than lengths of lifeless hemp.

I bathed the Conglomeros in warm, soapless water, massaging its limbs and afterward rubbing it down with baby oil. Not being a doctor, nor, obviously, in a position to summon one, I improvised on the assumption that simple comfort and rest were the most desirable remedies. I prepared a nest of down quilts and blankets on the floor of the living room, a few feet from the fireplace in which I kindled a large fire. I settled the Conglomeros, as helpless as a baby, into its bed and decanted a glass of warm sweetened rum down its throat. It was soon asleep, and I sat and watched it through the night, keeping the fire ablaze and the radio tuned to a classical station. Toward dawn I fell into a light slumber on the sofa.

I was somewhat disoriented when I awoke, and confused by the unfamiliar surroundings—for a moment, I had forgotten where I was. But I was brought to my senses by the sound of a limpid voice. " 'Ello, Arrow," it said cheerily, and as I turned, my eyes fell upon a remarkable sight. From its rumpled bed the Conglomeros stared up at me, extending a tender smile, its cheeks flush with color, its great green eyes clear and lucid. Its many limbs extruding from beneath the covers seemed to glow with strength and youthful vigor. The extraordinary recuperative powers which the Conglomeros had displayed in its Carpathian home had once again worked their magic on its eviscerated body, as if the ordeal by steamer had never occurred, and I could but marvel. " 'Ello, monster," I said, and bent to kiss its bald pate, eliciting a sparkling laugh from the supine beast. It reached out with five or six hands and held me in close embrace, showering my face with wet kisses from lips that had regained all their usual moist and supple resiliency. My heart swelled with instinctive, almost paternal love for this ingenuous creature—as, indeed, whose wouldn't? A few brief hours in its company would melt the reserve of the most vicious banker or calculating politician, and I was able in that moment to foresee a lifetime of loneliness expunged, of emptiness abrogated and happiness fulfilled.

The Conglomeros was mine at last, in all its miraculous and sidereal being!

▲▲▲▲

Before implementing the plans that had developed in my mind since our storm-chased crossing of the Black Sea, I spent a few weeks getting to know my new companion and habituating it to my company. Since we remained strictly isolated at the house or on the grounds, I cannot say whether the creature's apparent and immediate attachment to me was a personal response or merely the result of its uniquely trusting and affectionate nature. But I do remember those weeks as an endless display of unconditional affection as wholehearted on my part as on the Conglomeros's. Despite the deepening chill of winter, I shed all my clothing in an effort to put the creature at its ease, but the hugs and kisses we shared in those early days were as devoid of concupiscence as the romping of master and puppy. We ran naked through the fallen leaves, testing one another's endurance, and mine was naturally inferior in every respect. Not only was the Conglomeros able to move as swiftly and silently as a deer—it could climb and swing like a monkey, swim like a bear, and pick up heavy stones that I was barely able to budge. But all of these feats it performed only at my instigation and for my edification, happily but with some confusion as to their utility. The creature was equally content to stroll quietly through the woods, sing with the birds that flocked about its head, or sit still for hours as I palpated its limbs and trunks in my clumsy attempts to understand its anatomy. In other words, it was consistently and, at first, wordlessly happy during its every waking moment and at night, when mysterious smiles and squeals of joy accompanied its untroubled sleep.

The creature was less comfortable indoors than out, and I often awoke in the morning to find it roaming the house, its nostrils flaring like tents in a gale, sniffing with curiosity and bewilderment at every object it encountered. It could spend an hour staring motionless and with apparent serenity at the ceiling, its three bodies reclining side by side, arms effortlessly intertwined, each neck seeming to stretch like that of an ostrich to accommodate the posture. Then it would abruptly leap to its feet and, for no discernible motive and in response to no discernible stimulus, pounce and smother me in its tight embrace and moist kisses. It was in such circumstances that I discovered its tiny ears—no more than fleshy holes, really—concealed beneath the "armpits" of the creature's antennal arms.

I soon found that its food preference was raw vegetables, especially the roots, such as carrots and turnips, and leafy varieties like lettuce and spinach. Its teeth—I counted thirty-six of them—were blunt, but its jaw enormously powerful, and the creature was easily able to grind down five pounds of food at one sitting, so that I found myself compelled to shop further and further afield in order to avoid attracting undue attention at the local supermarket. I observed the Conglomeros as it ate—the pulp went down a different throat with every swallow, and in this way each trunk was given equal nourishment. Sometime later, as we tramped through the woods, the creature would stop in its tracks, squat down on all six haunches, and deposit three like-sized piles of steaming, odorless waste which, after inspection, were buried under pyramids of fallen leaves.

But such observations give little sense of the creature's intangible mystique, nor of the joy experienced in being loved by such a creature, a joy I confess beyond my limited capacities for lyricism. It is in the first week of newfound love, or in the smile a baby reserves for its mother, or in the instinct that draws the blind kitten to the waiting teat, that others may look for its inspiration. I found it in the Conglomeros, in the creature's grace unfettered by memory, in its beauty unencumbered by self-consciousness, in its innocence unbounded by the awareness of mystery. In "Double Vivification" Brauner said it best: "This living object is my strength and my triumph."

Not that the creature did not have its quirks—endearing for the most part—but these did not really emerge until my program of education was under way. For this was my intention—to make the Conglomeros more human, so that I might understand and appreciate it all the better. When I think of those scientific experiments designed to teach apes or dolphins to communicate with us, I recognize my own impulse in that regard—whether erroneous or not, my assumption was that learning would free the creature to express itself. But what I never saw until it was too late was the evidence before my eyes that it was precisely its freedom from language that enabled the Conglomeros at every moment and with every action to expose the full beauty of its soul.

Thus, the winter months were spent in an ecstasy of basic education—both the Conglomeros's and mine. Which one of us learned more, ensconced in our cozy hideaway as the

snows deepened around us, would be difficult to say. I devoted myself night and day to the creature's comfort and
enlightenment, leaving it only for provisioning runs into
town, whence I would hurry back to find it looking through
a picture book, or staring out a window, or happily repeating
its vocabulary lists by the crackling fire. Never once did it
give me any cause to fear an attempted escape, nor even the
least hint that it was aware of being held captive. Indeed, it
took to me and its new life with evident pleasure and determination, as if it were fulfilling a duty in the natural order.
Gradually I was able to relax my precautionary measures,
such as locking it in the house when I left or strapping a
leash around its neck and radio transmitter to its wrist on
our strolls through the woods.

I started, naturally enough, with the English language. As
I have intimated, the Conglomeros showed an enormous aptitude for learning vocabulary, and rarely was I compelled
to repeat a word. We went through the house, object by object, detail by detail, and outward into the natural world and
inward, into the world of the mind. At first, for instance, a
lamp was just a "lamp." Then it became a composite object—a collection of bulbs, switches, plugs, shades, cords,
and so on. Then it was metamorphosed into a function—the
production of light, which was semantically and symboli-
cally linked with the sun. Finally, it was energized into abstraction by the concept of electricity. In this way did the
Conglomeros come to understand the word "lamp"—a pla-
tonic ideal, and I could tell by the way its eyes shone when it
said "lamp" and connected the word to the object that in
some way it understood the word better than I did. So, too,
did we move from nouns to verbs, I demonstrating "to run,"
"to eat," "to wash." "Running" was just running at first, but
it was also "moving," "jumping," "walking," and later "fleeing," "chasing," "greeting," so that when the creature ran
out of the house to meet me after a shopping expedition, it

understood that in the same motion it was greeting me, chasing me, racing me, fleeing me—"running." "Run, run, run!" it would yawp gleefully, bounding toward me, arms open, a vast, innocent grin of satisfaction beaming across its face; a week later, it was "I run!" then "I am running!" Finally, at the door, "I will run!", on the lawn, "I am running!", and in my arms, covering my face with kisses: "I was running!" And so it progressed with all its new vocabulary. In a way I find difficult to recall without a tear of nostalgia springing to my eyes, the Conglomeros took to language the way a tadpole takes to limbs—naturally, effortlessly, joyfully. These lessons, and the relish and eagerness which the beast brought to them, afforded me so much pleasure that I was almost disappointed when, after several months, the Conglomeros seemed to have gained mastery over the world of words. "Isn't it wonderful," said the Conglomeros to me one day, "that there is a word for everything you can want to say?" It was all so fast, and all too brief.

What did take a long time, however, and a good deal of ingenuity, was the implanting of the seed of abstract thought. "Tree" was easy, "growth" somewhat harder, "life" almost impossible. Likewise, the germination of "smile" into "happiness" into "freedom." I couldn't be sure of doing it right, but the last thing I wanted was for the Conglomeros to learn about "justice," for instance, from the American Constitution or from the television—which, in any case, I had carefully locked away in the attic. And so, abstract concepts proved a challenge that I met in the same way as I had taught the physical world, only in reverse—just as "lamp" grew from the concrete to the abstract in all its particulars, so did "freedom" grow from the abstract to the particular. "Freedom," I said, opening the front door and stepping out. "Freedom," I said, selecting a book at random from the shelf. "Freedom," I said, turning cartwheels on the lawn. "Freedom," I said, pointing to a swallow wheeling

across the sky. Of course, the Conglomeros was bewildered
at first because, as I discovered, at least one abstract concept
is almost always required to describe another, so that when
I said, "It is all these things, but more, an infinite number,"
I had to explain "infinite," and start from scratch.

"I think I see," the Conglomeros said to me, pointing out
various objects in the room. "Is this table abstract? No, you
can eat on it. Is this chair abstract? No, you can sit on it. Is
this fire abstract? No, you . . . you can . . ."

"You can warm your hands on it."

"Can you put it in a box?"

"Well . . ."

"And your book? You said that makes you feel warm. It
doesn't make me feel warm. Is your book abstract?"

"Not exactly. It . . ."

"Is it made of fire?"

"No, it . . ."

"I'm warm. Am I a book? Am I abstract?"

As I said, it was not a simple task. Nevertheless, with patience and a judicious selection of examples, I gradually
managed to convince the creature that I was serious about
abstraction, that it mattered. Perhaps that was my first mistake.

I also taught it to read, which was easy once it understood
the concept of symbols. But I was very cautious in my choice
of reading materials—it was of the greatest importance to
me that the Conglomeros should not be tainted with social-
ized knowledge. To protect it from the corruptions of mankind while imbuing it with the exaltations of humanity—this
was the thin line I trod. Because books allow men who are
not wise to teach wisdom, I felt I could provide all the appurtenances of wisdom without imparting the capacity to
abuse them. And because the Conglomeros was not human,
and uncrippled by the genetic defects of greed, envy, lust, or
shame, I felt that knowledge could not hurt it. I am not a

philosopher, nor did I carefully reason my way into a comfortable nominalism or epistemology. I merely loved the Conglomeros because of its beauty, its simplicity, its gentleness. It didn't talk a lot in those days—only when there was something important to say. I wanted it to remain simple and gentle, but I also wanted it to have the capacity to describe itself to me, which I supposed to be the basis of all intelligence. For the fact of the matter is, the more I learned about the Conglomeros, the more I realized how little I had to teach it, and how much it had to teach me.

Take, for instance, our daily walks in the woods. I bundled up, the Conglomeros naked as always, we would trudge through the snow or the frozen mud, discussing this or that, usually trivial matters but important to the creature's education. No sooner were we out the door, however, than birds of all description would begin flocking about the Conglomeros—cardinals, nuthatches, starlings, crows, singing to us from the branches or perching on our heads and shoulders. The other creatures of the forest behaved likewise—squirrels ran up to our feet, chattering merrily, whole families of deer blocked our path and followed in our wake, rabbits, once even a small brown bear ambled up to be scratched between the ears.

"Rush hour," the creature would call it, laughing as it recalled a picture of a freeway it had seen in a magazine.

"That's silly," I answered. "Animals don't have rush hour."

"Yes they do, Aaron," the Conglomeros remonstrated gently. "Look at the animals who live in the woods. In the morning they are busy, they are happy; when the sun is high, they feel tired; in the evening they are busy again, they are getting ready for the night and for sleep. People are just like animals. They have rush hours too. Rush, rush, rush."

"I suppose you're right," I could only say in wonderment.

Naturally, I was startled and overjoyed at first, but soon I

came to realize that not only did the Conglomeros understand and attract these creatures, it actually communicated
with them. What they said to one another, or how they said
it, remained a mystery to me, and my companion made it
clear that their conversations could not be translated. In a
painting of a figurative Conglomeros surrounded by birds,
Brauner had called this gift the "Impersonal Subjectivity of
Love," and now I could see why. However, as if in consolation for my lack of understanding, the Conglomeros would
feed me an enigma. "You know," it might say to me, "in the
times of darkness, light was decanted like wine"; or, "Dark
matter is the weight of unborn souls." Where such thoughts
came from, what experience had engendered them or why
they would spring to mind at any particular moment, I was
never to learn. Even so, the experience was remarkable, and
I was filled with a greater love and a greater awe for my
friend than I could ever have believed possible.

Nights, we would sit by the blazing fire as the snow fell
outside, and talk or read or simply watch the flames on the
hearth. It was at such times especially that I tried to draw the
creature out of itself, to coax it into revealing its past to me.
I wanted to know all the things it is natural to want to know:
where the creature came from, what were its parents, how
many years it had lived, were there any siblings, what had
been its experiences. I had my own theories, of course. The
way I saw it, the Conglomeros was the last representative—or one of the last—of an ancient species of woodland
creature that had once roamed the primordial forests of Europe and Asia. Where such a beast might fit in the Linnaean
hierarchy is anybody's guess—even calling it a vertebrate
mammal would be a stretch of the supporting evidence—
but one thing is certain: The way that early sightings of man-
atees by European sailors gave rise to the mermaid legend,
so, too, had the occasional fleeting glimpse of a Conglomeros fleeing through the brush or foraging in the wild berry

patch engendered myths of satyrs, sileni, and nixes among the Hellenes and sylvan tribes of ancient Europe. The Conglomeros's ancestors had inhabited the outermost margins of human civilization and, while probably never very numerous, were one of the first species to be brought to the edge of extinction by human expansion.

But all of this was pure speculation on my part; for all I really knew, the creature was an alien from Mars or an actual demiurge from Olympus. The Conglomeros itself was no help at all: It knew nothing of ancestors, history, or life spans.

As for its supposed ability to tell the future, I was never able to confirm my original theory. If I asked the creature to foretell some future event, it merely looked at me as if I were mad; no more did it have any recollection of ever having possessed such a talent. Though this was a great disappointment to me, and confusing in light of my theory's dependence on that ability, I was compelled as in every similar avenue of exploration to give it up as a dead end. Perhaps, I conjectured, the Conglomeros had indeed been prophetic at some point and had lost the skill the way some children are said to outgrow a juvenile ability to read minds.

I was also deeply curious about its memories of Victor Brauner, and how it had befallen that this gentle beast had so hideously enriched and then destroyed the artist's life. To direct questioning the Conglomeros was wholly unresponsive, and often withdrew into a quiet sulk if I persisted, hugging its knees, its tiny arms folded moodily across its brow, the only display of ill humor I ever saw it make in those early, happier days. I ascribed its reticence to some atavistic sense of privacy, or else to a painful legacy that it was reluctant to exhume; and so I took a more subtle approach, veiling my questions in the guise of the daily exercises which I set it. And yet, invariably and to my growing consternation, these were the exercises which the creature was unable to perform. It gradually became clear that the Conglomeros had essentially no recollection of its past, no sense of its origins, no understanding of its place or purpose in the natural world, and no concept of birth or mortality. Answers such as "I have always been" or even a mere "I am," offered in the most ingenuous ignorance of irony, only served to confuse and irritate me, since I was looking for information that could be exploited in a practical manner. And when we would occasionally seem to be making some headway— when, for instance, I brought our conversation round to the subject of Creation, with the creature's own genesis in mind—it would suddenly go off on some abstract non sequitur and leave my chain of inference dangling. "You see," the beast would say solemnly, staring into the flames, "it is in the nature of the universe that . . ." "Yes, yes," I would break in, "that's all very well, but what is really important is that you . . . ," and the Conglomeros would grow very quiet, its great eyes dim, and it would say no more. Such scenes were often repeated, and I was able to learn virtually nothing about the past of my enigmatic ward. The name "Victor," or any amount of prompting about a one-eyed lover in the distant past, or any suggestion even that the creature had once been endowed with a facility for prophecy that it did not now possess—in fact, the merest possibility that it had sustained any continuous human contact before our meeting—left the creature bewildered and unable to account for itself. It did not even have a name, nor had it ever considered the necessity for one—"Conglomeros," apparently, was merely a personal coinage of Brauner's. The most I could learn was that its traditional diet consisted of fiddleheads in the spring, fruit and berries in the summer, and nuts and wild grains in the autumn, while the winter was set aside for hibernation. Such information, the reader may realize, hardly satisfied my ravenous curiosity, but there was little I could do in the face of such intransigence. Whether these lapses were the result of some illness or trauma, or simply in the nature of the beast, was not within my power to determine, and so I resigned myself to study by observation, which in itself was fruitful and rewarding enough.

▲▲▲▲

After the great and perilous adventure of my journey to Romania and abduction of the Conglomeros, the story of its education may seem anticlimactic to my readers, and if that should be the case it is due solely to my deficiencies as a narrator. For there was nothing so stimulating or so moving as those close winter months, by which my search and our flight paled in the comparison of their capacities to terrify and elate. Not that the creature ever gave me cause to fear for my own safety—never that. Rather, what was both terrifying and exalting to me—a sensation which our constant contact never fully succeeded in dispelling—was the mere existence of this miraculous being, its proximity to me, and the enormous sway I held over it. For it had given itself to me mind and soul, clung to me and hung on my words as on those of a messiah, evinced in me a trust and an affection diluted or mitigated by none of the caution one is accustomed and expects to find in a lover. Like a Dr. Frankenstein, I had it in my power to re-create this creature in my own image if I so desired, or in any image I cared to imagine, for it had willingly relinquished to me its *tabula rasa,* as pure and unblemished as that of a newborn babe. It was not a responsibility I relished, but one I had taken upon myself and could not now abjure. I felt like the environmentalist who owns a large tract of pristine wilderness in the suburbs of a prosperous city: The temptations to exploit it were manifold and seductive, but the duty to preserve and protect it was more apparent and imperative still to any mind cursed with ethical vigor.

And so it was that I kept my monster carefully hidden from

the world, and the world carefully hidden from my monster. I developed the habit of driving into the village on Sundays for a week's worth of *The New York Times* that I arranged to be held for me, but on no account would I allow the beast to peruse the news unsupervised. Instead, I assiduously abstracted only those articles that might prove beneficial to our course of study, which aimed at avoiding as much as possible the corrupting universe of human political and social endeavor. Articles on scientific breakthroughs, natural disasters, archeology, linguistics, art, and the like—in short, anything that tended to skirt the issues of such everyday human activities as lying, cheating, boasting and killing—I found acceptable and adequate intellectual stimuli to our conversations.

"What's a 'brothel'?" the creature asked me one day as it flipped through a magazine.

"It's a place people go to have fun."

"Like Disneyland?"

"Sort of."

"Is Disneyland a church?"

"No. Why do you ask?"

"It says here that a man goes to a brothel to be humilated."

"Humiliated."

"Humiliated. Isn't that why people go to church?"

Not all our conversations went as well as this. On occasion, however, and with the deluded aim of quashing any inchoate curiosity about the human condition, I would permit discussion of articles about insider trading, the corruption of democracy by businessmen and military personnel, or the senility of world leaders, being sure to place them in their proper perspective as moral stories. In this way, I thought, the Conglomeros gradually seemed to acquire a certain sophistication of thought unsullied by prurience and worldly self-interest. Such was my goal, and as the winter months ground on and our isolation deepened on our hilltop, my trepidation about my own abilities gave way to quiet satisfaction at our progress. Indeed, and though I say this to my eternal shame, so apparently successful was my course of study, and so confident was I in the precautionary measures I had taken in that regard, that I even arranged a selected viewing schedule of certain public television programs. At first, none of these liberalities seemed to promote any ill effects, but I kept a sharp watch for signs of incipient intellectual consumerism and moral decay.

I might go on at great length about the Conglomeros's education, for that winter was the happiest and most fulfilling time of my entire life, and never again will I see its like. Suffice it to say that from a wild, uncouth beast, the Conglomeros under my supervision was well on its way to becoming a charming, eloquent, and altogether ingenuous companion, without sacrificing any of its congenital purity of soul, its trust in the potentially infinite benevolence of the human spirit, or its sweet good nature. Of course, mythology, experience, and history have shown that this cannot be accomplished in human child-rearing, but I naturally had good cause to believe that the Conglomeros, not being human and thus unendowed at birth with the burden of a "personality," would adapt perfectly to the persona I had envisioned for it—a sort of Adam-before-the-fall. Having come to believe that the creature's inability to recall and therefore to benefit from its experience was the basis of its innocence, I assumed that my program was incapable of harming it. In any event, all signs to date seemed to indicate my success—the creature was evolving into a creation.

I suppose all creators eventually fall in love with their creations, and I was no exception. Of course, I should have seen trouble on the way, and intercepted it—but trouble only plays itself in the role of sneak thief, and in any other part is no trouble at all. And in life, unlike in books, you need do more than bend down to tie your shoelace at the right moment in order to preempt a world of woe, as I have learned. Yet, how could I have foreseen, I who was the very driving force, the whiphand, always looking forward? And my beast, even before myself who was its drover, its friend, its teacher, its lover—if it could not see, how might I be expected to? And all these metaphors for such a simple idea, as if life itself were a contemporary metaphor for something else. Trouble hit me from behind. People like me, with cancer in our souls, are always the first to suspect and the last to know.

And when I say "love," I mean it in the most radical sense. Unlike most modern romances, which tend to bloom in the humus of satiated lust, this was a love sprung from the virgin soil of mutual awe and self-deprecation. Speaking for myself, I would have loved the Conglomeros even if it hadn't been a monster. And, in case I have not said enough, who could blame me? It was a beast of perfection.

I will admit, however, that it required a lust to help me recognize the true nature of my love for the Conglomeros. When it was yet wordless, the creature elicited from me the purest outpouring of respect, admiration, and compassion, much as that to which anyone is inspired by the grace and nobility of a wild animal living in its own animal sphere. And as our time together increased and the creature learned to express itself, I naturally felt my love mutate and grow, paternal certainly, yet free of parental ego and ennobled, I might even say, by a certain tremulous spiritual desire, the way a soul is said to yearn to reunite with its source. It was, I imagined, what Victor had meant by "Propulsionary Love." These were my feelings for the Conglomeros, or so I believed—surely nothing to be ashamed of, and if once the reader could have seen that creature in all the beguiling, breathtaking innocence of its early days in my care, I feel certain that I would claim his sympathy and envy.

But as the months passed and winter closed in about us, it was with a burning sense of shame that I came to recognize that such feelings, while ingenuous and disinterested in themselves, were but evolutionary stages toward the development of one more sophisticated, yet more ignoble, that I feared to name—sophisticated only because too confounding on the heels of such instinctive, almost atavistic impulses of solicitude; ignoble because I was becoming less able to distinguish between the Conglomeros I had first encountered and the one I was busily re-creating in my own image. Was this Victor's "Objective Subjectivities"? How much of myself did I love in the other? I suppose this is a dilemma shared by all lovers, yet it is a no less pitiful one for that. Given that I knew Victor to have fallen in love with the Conglomeros, and being fully aware of what it had done to him, I should say that, indeed, it was all the more pitiful. It was, I believe, around this time that images of his "Anatomy of Desire" sketches began to haunt my dreams, and that I began to understand for the first time something of what he must have gone through.

And how had Victor Brauner fallen in love with a monster? Was it in watching the creature perform a simple act, such as eating a carrot, its eyes sparkling all the while, shining in the pure pleasure of being alive? Was it in being gently awakened by the caress of eight silken hands, morning after morning? Was it in eliciting that warm gurgle of laughter that was always so ready to spring forth and envelop him in its inexplicable affirmation of the universe's good intentions? Was it in the childlike questions and the fragile, crystalline aphorisms that strayed unsolicited from the creature's lips in that sourceless, ageless little voice? Was it in the tenderness it evinced for all living things, or its seeming ability to communicate with them, himself included, at a level of compassion and intelligence to melt the iciest heart? Was it in the way its pink tongue fluttered in its mouth and its pink lips pouted and its pink skin glowed in the firelight when it slept? Was it in watching, after a run through the woods in a bleak winter's dusk, how its pink nipples puckered and its little breasts heaved and a trickle of perspiration traced a pink line the length of its abdomen, to lose itself in the downy triangle of blond, almost invisible curls? Or was it late one night by the glow of the dying embers when the Conglomeros said, "I love you, Victor," meaning what a dog means when it unleashes its most uncritical stare upon its master, and Victor, despite everything he knew of the creature and every ugly impulse he had ever examined within himself, chose to deceive himself into a willful misinterpretation of the declaration, such that his "I love you too" promised to fulfill a thousand undeclared aspirations that never had and never could have been implied?

I don't know. It might have happened like that. But I do know that when I presented myself naked to the Conglomeros before the fireplace later that evening, its eyes roved frankly and unashamedly over my body, not in the least lustful but inquisitive. I do know that when I covered one of its breasts with my hand and gently squeezed it, the Conglomeros sighed with unmistakable passion, seemingly unsure of my intentions, as if that passion were something alien and unrecognized. And I do know that when I drew it to the blankets on the floor, I taught the Conglomeros to recognize that passion.

We made love day and night thereafter, and my love for the creature grew. There was no doubt in my mind—the Conglomeros knew the desire of Eve, not only as the first time for itself but as the first of all creatures to know it. The love it offered was simple and unadorned, robust and not at all petty. It was also innocent like a child's, but so far from being corruptible, I believed, that it never occurred to me then to question my motives or to profess my attachment in words further than I had already done. Even now, I do not think the Conglomeros understood at that time how our love might in any way be a deviation from mundanity or bear reference to higher feeling. And as for any unanswered questions about how a human being makes love to a creature possessing eight arms, six legs, two penises, and one vagina—may they remain unanswered.

And so, all unawares, we had begun to act out what was to prove the final, short-lived stage of our happiness together. By day, we walked, we talked, we read and discussed our reading, we made love. By night, we sat by the fire, examining and spinning out the day's lessons, and we made love. At that time, the Conglomeros had still asked me no questions and I still had told it no lies. It accepted all my explanations as the truth, since it had as yet no conception of falsehood, while within the parameters I had defined for myself in describing human nature and history, I said nothing outside my limited understanding of the truth. Can the reader see how, in an entire lifetime, a single conversation held under such conditions could approximate the very paragon of happiness on earth? It seems so clear to me now, in morbid retrospect, how I might have worked to preserve the situation as it was then. But in my youthful folly, buoyed by my success and my love and newfound serenity, I fell prey to the commonest of human fallacies—that it is a derelict heart that refuses to aspire and a stagnant intellect that refuses to expand. I was not satisfied with what I had, and our happiness that was potentially immortal died of postnatal complications.

The end of innocence is always abrupt and intuitive, and I remember the end of ours with painful accuracy. It came without warning one night in late February as a snowstorm raged outside our warm and secluded refuge. Nothing could have prepared me for the shock and the horror of it, nor could anything have cushioned its blow. Like a flash flood or a falling icicle, it slashed into the very heart of my serenity

and smashed it beyond repair; yet, at the same time, it was over before it had begun. For as we made love that night before a blazing oak fire, and the Conglomeros tenderly encircled me with its many limbs and welcomed me deep within its body, and the warmth of the flames and the heat of passion licked me into a hallucination of paradise, I distinctly heard, hidden amongst the sighs and groans of my lover's erotic vocabulary, riding on the back of a butterfly moan, the name "Victor."

We both froze in midstroke, as if to the sound of gunfire in the distance. My tumescence evaporated, and the Conglomeros began to tremble uncontrollably, clawing at the quilts and carpets with its many fingers, beads of perspiration popping on its brow. Its eyes bulged from their sockets, unseeing, in a paroxysm of terror, tears trickling down its cheeks. Its three chests heaved in unison, wildly sucking in breath as if in the final moments of asphyxiation. The tiny arms on its head reached out for me and, though I was unaware of it at the time, their nails raked deep abrasions in the back of my neck. Then it cried out piteously, its eyes rolled upward, and the Conglomeros fell into a dead faint, while I lay paralyzed above it.

What were my thoughts at that moment? I cannot remember now whether my understanding of the event came to me then and there in one spontaneous flash, or whether it developed gradually, in retrospect, over the following days. I do know, however, that what a man may feel when his phallus is taken and mistaken for that of another is clearly defined by psychology and popular literature: shock, anger, recrimination, shame, horror, disgust, or even sympathy— but my reaction was none such. I was simply and exclusively terrified, for I had recognized the true nature of that blurted "Victor"—it was far more than the belated understanding that Victor had actually slept as I had with the creature, that not only was I not the first but that I had missed or misinter-

preted all the blatant signals in his artwork pointing toward that fact. I admit, my pride may have been a little injured at the thought of Victor's having preceded me in the creature's embrace, but far, far worse was the fact that the creature had recalled that event. The Conglomeros had never re- membered any incident from the past; that was what made it pure, ingenuous—itself. But now, what I had witnessed this evening was a grotesque, hideous birthing, the birth of a real monster, finally and inevitably, which I had fathered. For, in recalling its past for the first time ever, the Conglom- eros had crossed the threshold into humanity.

What had I done? How had all my careful planning come to this, which it had been specifically designed and executed to avoid? One moment the Conglomeros was an animal, or an angel, or something in between, anything other than what it was a moment later—a human being. One moment, the very embodiment of perfection, the next, monster. The way a man is said to see his entire life pass before him in the moment before death, I now saw all of Victor Brauner's paintings parade past, mocking my shallow efforts to under- stand his message. Now that it was too late, I saw them for what they obviously were—frantic warnings posted to divert the unwary from the dangerous course which the artist him- self had taken. How could I have been so blind? Now that I understood it, his message to me down the decades was clear and eloquent. The source of his torment was not a loss of love but a rape of innocence.

My overwrought imagination filled next with visions of the unfortunate events in Eden—was this how it had hap- pened? A well-intentioned Satan simply trying to improve on a perfect situation? Or the history of the world, for that matter—every change a change for the worse? A place where every evil is perpetuated but no good, once destroyed, can be resuscitated? I don't mean to descend to banal phi- losophizing—perhaps the reader finds it all very adoles-

cent—but how many of us are familiar with the apocalyptic thoughts that are born from personal experience and responsibility? These, and worse, *were* the thoughts that tormented me throughout that long dreary night while the fire slowly died in the grate, as I sat vigil over the unconscious form of my friend and paced fretfully with the wind howling in the chimney and the storm beating against the only glowing window in that entire barren wilderness. And—woe unto me!—every one of my darkest fears, momentarily dispelled though it was by the coming of the dawn, was gradually to be realized, as we shall shortly see.

And yet, I somehow managed to allow the gray light of dawn to soothe me, to assuage my trouble, and even to carry into the darkest recesses of my burden a rekindled ember of hope. Perhaps all was not lost. Through the night, I watched as the deep, rigid creases etched into the Conglomeros's face in its moment of agony were slowly dissolved in sleep, until, by the time it had begun to stir and toss and sigh in its preawakening, the creature looked no different than on any other night. I thought of its earlier, apparently miraculous recoveries, and the same process seemed to be at work on its current distress. Whatever it may have been, and despite the delicate and feeble appearance of its bodies and limbs, the Conglomeros was not fragile. I myself had witnessed it pull through two dreadful traumas—and who knows how many it had survived before them?—and this one had certainly been far less dangerous. Perhaps it would leave no more trace of itself than the others had. The way one awakens from a nightmare, or accepts as permanent the temporary recovery of a loved one from a fatal illness, I allowed such thoughts to comfort. And indeed, when the Conglomeros opened its beautiful eyes, and they shone on me as they had always done, and it smiled on me as it had always done, and the gentle splash of its laughter washed me as it had always done, and it stretched out its tiny arms to pull my head down for a kiss, as it had always done, the last vestiges of my nocturnal torment were dispelled. But still . . .

"Tell me," I whispered, "tell me about Victor."

The Conglomeros blinked, clearly uncomprehending. "Victor?"

"Yes, Victor," I urged. "You said his name last night."

"Last night? Victor? I said Victor?"

"Don't you remember?"

"Victor, Victor, Victor," the Conglomeros sang, arching its backs. "I don't know what it is, a Victor. No, Victor. Yes, Victor: one who wins. You are Victor!"

"Who is Victor? Victor, think, Victor!"

"You, you, you are Victor!" and the Conglomeros pulled me down on top of itself, and the love we made seemed as sweet as it had always been, since time began.

I fell into a light sleep and had a dream. I dreamed that I awoke in the same position I was then lying in, near the fireplace. The Conglomeros was leaning over me, a troubled look on its brow.

"I have an important question for you, Aaron," it said in a voice not at all like its own. "An important question."

"Yes?"

"Is love an emotion or an affective state?"

"What?"

"I said, is love an emotion or an affective state?" The creature was quite in earnest.

"I don't know what you're talking about. Go back to sleep." And, in my dream, I rolled over, and that was all I can remember about it. I'm not sure, even, why I remember that much.

▲▲▲▲

Over the next few weeks, I observed the Conglomeros with particular intensity for any indication of a sea change. I'm not sure what I expected to see. When a vast, pristine continent is first polluted, the physical change is essentially invisible. But, in fact, the alteration is catastrophic and ineluctable: One spent cartridge hidden in the tall grass, one slave ship sunken off the coast, one sermon pronounced under a tent in the deep woods, however ephemeral the manifestations of pollution may be, have changed that continent forever. It is only as such manifestations accumulate and fester, communicating themselves like a long-forgotten insult back to their perpetrators, that they become noticeable. And so it was with the Conglomeros.

At first there were no symptoms whatever to be noticed, or at least, such as they were, I may have chosen unconsciously to ignore them. We continued with our lessons, and if the Conglomeros exhibited a vague lassitude at our repetitions which it had not shown in the past, I made allowances for the creature's recuperation. We persisted in our enforced, somewhat febrile isolation from the world, and if the Conglomeros evinced a newborn tendency to boredom and restlessness, I characterized that as a natural nostalgia for the open spaces of its native home. The passion of our lovemaking endured unabated, and if the Conglomeros showed more curiosity for untried positions and variety than it had been wont to do, and a greater proclivity for employing limbs and extremities that had remained hitherto passive, I said to my heart that this was the healthy reaction of a healthy mind exposed to new stimuli. But I was fooling myself, and soon the evidence of an inward revolution of the Conglomeros's psyche began to impose itself on my reluctant senses, in manner such that it could no longer be ignored or dismissed. The Conglomeros was changing daily, before my very eyes, and I despaired of a solution to halt the process.

I remember one evening with particular dread. Having just made love, we were basking naked in the glow of the firelight. I was watching the play of light on the creature's skin, marveling at the variety of shadows cast by its limbs.

The Conglomeros had its eyes closed, and was running one of its tiny hands through my hair. Suddenly, the creature sighed deeply, not a satisfied but a wistful breath, and rolled away from me. Concerned, I leaned over and nuzzled its cheek with my lips.

"Is something the matter?" I whispered.

"No," said the Conglomeros, but I could hear the pout in its voice.

"Are you sure?"

But the Conglomeros just sighed again, this time in irritation.

"Come, come," I persisted. "You know you must tell me everything."

"Nothing's the matter."

"Yes, there is. I can tell," I said, and placed my hand on the nearest shoulder.

"Oh, honestly," the creature huffed, yanking the shoulder from my touch. "It's just postcoital *tristesse*. Do you mind?"

I sat up abruptly. "Postcoital *tristesse*?"

"Yes. Now won't you just let me be?"

"Let you be? Let you be?" I leapt to my feet. "What do you mean, postcoital *tristesse*? Where did you ever hear of such a thing?"

The Conglomeros rolled it eyes, and looked up at me with something approximating scorn, a look I had never seen on its face before.

"What?" it spat. "Who taught me to read? You did. You wanted me to see the world, to learn and to read about it, and I did read about it. I read about feeling sad after making love because happiness is so fleeting. I've seen it happen to you. Now I know what it's called: postcoital *tristesse*."

"But you," I pleaded, "you never had it before."

"Listen, my sweet," the Conglomeros said, its tone softening. "*Omni animal post-coitum triste est.* Why should I be any different?"

"I can't believe this!" I shrieked. "But you're not a . . ."

"Not a what?"

"Nothing, my love."

I lay back down on the blanket, encircling the creature in my arms, absorbing the deep pulse of heat and the light grassy smell of its bodies. "I'm sorry I made such a fuss," I sighed.

"Me too."

The very next night, the Conglomeros asked whether it had been good for me, too. And when, the night after that, it asked me for a cigarette, I merely told it that cigarettes cause cancer, then turned my back and wept softly, while a new snowstorm swept down from the north.

Sex and love, love and sex—over the weeks, the Conglomeros became more and more obsessed, while I fretted. It seemed to me at that point that there had always been sex between us, and the best kind of sex there is. But now, as I have intimated, the sex was changing. While it had gained, perhaps, in inventiveness, intensity, frequency, it had lost something—it had lost its *purity*. Gone, and quickly, were the languid hours when we had been wholly of one mind and one body, when our love was spontaneous, unself-conscious, when we spoke neither before, during, nor after and yet communicated and understood one another at a level far beyond words. Now, the Conglomeros talked about it at length, beforehand, as if to arouse itself. Now, during the act, the Conglomeros was constantly guiding my hands, my fingers, my tongue, as if I were a puppet, as if I were incapable on my own of finding the vibrant chord. Where once there had been one uninterrupted crescendo ending in an explosion of percussion and strings, now there were constant midstroke breaks as in a game of musical chairs or like someone unable to fall asleep in an unfamiliar bed. And afterward, there was always some little activity—a postmortem of the event, a poetry reading, a monologue on love and fulfillment, or a snack—as if something were required to round out or complete an exercise that, until recently, had been complete and entirely sufficient unto itself. To most people, having never known anything but the dissatisfactions of a stunted human sexuality, those things might represent the evidence of a satisfactory or even enviable lovelife. But to me, they were merely the sad proof that perfection, once shattered, can only be imperfectly restored, like the fragments of a Grecian urn one sees in a museum, a parody of the original held together by expanses of gray plaster.

And talk! I had believed that the basis of consciousness was the ability to describe oneself, and so I had taught the creature to speak, to think, to rationalize. But whereas before the change it had always avoided talking about things that it seemed to understand perfectly nonetheless, now it spoke about them endlessly, analyzing them, and itself, and me, and its own rational processes; and the apparent understanding was somehow diminished thereby. And the more it analyzed, the less it seemed to understand—a characteristic which reinforced my conviction that the Conglomeros had crossed the threshold into humanity.

Its favorite topic, by far, was love.

"I love them, and they love me—but why?" said the Conglomeros of the birds and woodland beasts that continued to surround us on our daily walks.

"Why ask why?" I pleaded. "Isn't it enough that they do?"

"It should be, but it isn't." The Conglomeros grabbed a woodpecker that had perched on its shoulder, and held the little bird up to its face. "Why do you love me, my friend?" The woodpecker cocked its head and peeped, and the answer, for the moment, seemed to satisfy the Conglomeros. The woodpecker flew into a nearby tree, and I noticed that, though it followed us to our doorway, it remained thereafter at a distance.

The Conglomeros, as was its new habit, prolonged its peroration indoors, and I grew weary. I picked up a book and flung myself into an armchair.

"You see, this is what I want to know," the Conglomeros went on, sitting at my feet. "In the absence of light there is darkness, in the absence of noise there is silence, in the absence of heat there is cold, in the absence of water there is desert, in the absence of life there is death—but what is there in the absence of love? Hatred? No, you see, it's something much worse: It is the absence of love—there's the horror of it, there is no opposite, no, ah, what do you call it?"

"Dialectic?"

"Yes, there is no dialectic, and yet people live with it every day—don't you think that is what makes them go mad? Don't you think that is what makes them behave the way they do? You see, it is in the nature of love that . . ."

"Please, can't you see I'm trying to read?" I said irritably.

"Sorry."

I know it was wrong of me to lose my patience, but it was much more out of frustration and guilt than anger. After all, I *loved* the Conglomeros, certainly more than anything or anyone I had ever loved, yet I was powerless before the creeping human condition that was engulfing it thanks to my own meddling. I knew then the anguish of passing on a dread disease to a lover, but I still refused to believe that its progress was inevitably fatal. For the condition was yet in its earliest stages, and I do not mean to give the impression that, within the brief period I have described, nothing remained of the sweet, miraculous Conglomeros I had first known. Far from it: Anyone happening upon us at that time would have encountered, still, a beast of marvelous beauty and stunning innocence, with a boundless capacity for trust, love, and wisdom. But to me, even one tiny flaw in the perfection I had known was ample justification of my grief. And still, as I have said, I believed that it remained somehow within my power to reverse the process, that an antidote of some kind was only a matter of time and trial in the finding.

Furthermore, it was not only the change in the Conglomeros that elicited my anxiety. One day in deep winter, taking our habitual stroll through the woods, like Robinson Crusoe I came across a telltale footprint that I instinctively understood was a new threat to our insular safety. This print, of course, was in the snow and had been made by a foot shod in a heavy boot. I tested it against my own foot, which proved much larger. I enlisted the Conglomeros, with its keen sense of smell, but though it got down on all twelves and sniffed as diligently as any bloodhound, it could tell me nothing save that the sole was made of synthetic materials. A meticulous search of the surrounding area turned up no more prints, and I was forced to conclude either that we had a one-legged intruder or that the other prints had been covered over by recent snowfalls and that therefore the threat was not immediate. My land was bounded on all sides by estates of a similar size and a few redneck homesteads, and the boundaries in some places were difficult to distinguish. A few footprints in the snow, deep within the woods, might simply have been left by one of my neighbors in inadvertent trespass. Also, I had been warned by the real-estate broker that, in these backwoods, it was sometimes a problem keeping the locals from poaching on your land, though the hunting season had finished months earlier. Regardless of the reasons, the intrusion was very troubling to me, and in the following days the creature and I scoured the woods for additional signs of our intruder. Our paranoia went unrewarded by a single sighting on any of our subsequent walks.

But in early March, a week or so after the "Victor" incident, the situation developed alarming indications. On several occasions, I found clear evidence that someone had been prowling around the house and had attempted, on at least one of those occasions, to peek through one of my windows. By the footprints in the mud, identical to the first we had found, I judged it to be just one prowler, and always the same one—a boy, probably, or a smallish man.

My immediate assumption, biased though it may have been, was that the prowler was a local scouting for potential homes to burglarize. Like many areas in the region, the town's prosperity was based exclusively on the recent influx of weekend homeowners from New York City, a prosperity that bypassed the local residents unless they chose to sell their land to developers. A natural consequence of the locals' resentment and frustration had been a dramatic increase in burglaries, though essentially limited to homes which, unlike mine, were empty throughout the week. As I and my companion were extremely reclusive, I assumed that some teenage ne'er-do-well had been checking out my habits for an opportune moment to plunder my treasures.

I wasn't overly concerned that my secret might be discovered: Thick curtains covered all our windows at all times, and, the house being atop a hill, there was no convenient vantage point from which we could be spied upon at a distance. Still, it was logical and prudent to suppose that my presence was known about town, and even that I might have someone living with me. The recluse on the hill would certainly be a target for gossip and curiosity, and curiosity was something it was essential for me to discourage.

The next time I drove into town for provisions, I mentioned the footprints to Walter, one of the young bucks who served behind the counter at the general store. I casually let him know that I owned a gun and was not afraid to use it, and hoped that the message would reach the appropriate ear. But the very next day I found fresh footprints in my rose-beds, and though I stayed up all of Monday night, rifle in lap, I failed to see any hint of my intruder.

In the meantime, I was desperately trying to do something for the Conglomeros, who was becoming more eccentric with every passing day. I was awakened from a nap one day by a strange and unidentifiable noise coming from the kitchen. Creeping to the kitchen door, I beheld a horrific sight: On the counter lay an open package of sliced ham; the Conglomeros was peeling off one slice at a time and rolling it into tubes, which it folded and stuffed whole into its mouth. Every attempt made the creature gag, and the sink was piled with half-chewed gobs of meat, but still the Conglomeros persisted. Without a word, I marched into the kitchen and flung the ham into the wastebasket, while the Conglomeros looked on shamefaced.

On another occasion, as we walked in the woods, the creature suddenly ran off into a copse, returning a moment later. In its six large hands, which it had formed into a kind of large, spherical cage, it held a squirrel, which it rattled around within the cage like a pea in a whistle. Though the squirrel refused to bite, it was clearly terrified. I swiped at the cage of fingers, and the squirrel fled.

Another time, I awoke in the middle of the night to find the Conglomeros gone. I had searched the house frantically, to no avail, when my ear was caught by a high-pitched hum emanating from the attic. There, I found the Conglomeros absorbed in an episode of *The Twilight Zone* on the television. I had expressly forbidden it to watch any television without my supervision, but I had never expected my injunction to require enforcement. Was this the first time it had disobeyed me, I demanded to know. The Conglomeros answered that it was, but it would not look me in the eye.

God knows I did not enjoy my role as disciplinarian; I despised it, in fact, and myself for having to play it. I had started out wanting to protect the Conglomeros from humanity, and now found myself compelled to protect it from itself. And, as

I have said, I still thought it within my power to reverse the deterioration of the creature's psyche, or its personality, or its soul, or whatever it was within the beast that was rotting away. I scoured the house for any potential corrupting influence, I got rid of all the meat, I threw out the television, I lectured on morality, I invented new word games and intellectual conundrums for us to play. But all in vain. The beast grew ever more restless, ever more dissatisfied. It was clear that my company, my instruction, my love, were not enough for it anymore. It began complaining.

"I want to get out," it whined to me. "I want to see things, meet people, see *life.*"

"But you have everything you need right here, my pet," I retorted desperately. "You have food and warmth and company. You have diversions and the countryside. You have me."

"When I lived in the mountains I had even less than that, and it was enough. But it isn't enough anymore. You were the one who taught me that, Aaron." The poor creature was unaware of the pain its words caused me.

And the prowler, though somehow eluding my vigilance, was returning with increasing frequency and boldness. I was at my wit's end.

It all came to a head, as it inevitably must, sometime near the end of March, as the tender shoots were pushing up through the mud and I was wondering how much longer I could endure my present predicament. The one thing of which I had forgotten to purge the house was the pile of old newspapers I kept by the fireplace. One day, I returned home from a provisioning run to town to find the Conglomeros reading an article on Donald and Ivana Trump in an old issue of *The New York Times.* Sickened, I ripped the offending document from its hands, gathered up the entire pile of papers, and made for the garden, where I intended to put it to flame forthwith. But I stumbled on a divot and the papers flew from my grasp, scattering across the lawn. As I kneeled to pick them up, my eye was caught by a small photograph near the back of a paper dated January 19.

The photograph showed a small, embattled-looking old man, flanked on either side by beefy secret-service types in sunglasses. The old man wore a homburg, a gray mackintosh, and a black patch over his left eye. The caption beneath the photo read "Richard Hand arriving last night at Kennedy Airport."

The title of the article ran "Romania Releases Spy Suspect." I read on.

> BUCHAREST, Jan. 18—The Romanian government announced today that it was dropping all charges against Richard Hand, an American arrested in Romania last October on unspecified charges of espionage.
>
> Two hours after the announcement, issued by the Romanian Foreign Ministry, Mr. Hand was boarded on a Pan Am flight at Bucharest's Otopeni Airport and flown to New York City, where he was greeted by officials of the State Department.
>
> Mr. Hand, a retired professor of art history who has taught at Yale, Dartmouth, and other American universities, was arrested in the early morning of October 14, 19—, on board a small fishing boat sailing in restricted waters of the delta of the Danube River. Until today, Mr. Hand has been held for questioning at the Bucharest headquarters of the *Securitate*, the Romanian Secret Service.
>
> Also arrested at that time was a local fisherman serving as Mr. Hand's guide.
>
> Though Mr. Hand has always maintained his innocence, the reasons for his presence on a fishing boat in the dangerous and strictly guarded waters of the Danube delta remain unclear. A State Department spokesman in Washington said that Mr. Hand was traveling on a nor-

mal tourist visa at the time of his arrest, and that he had
visited Romania as a tourist "a number of times" before
his last trip.

In accordance with its longstanding policy, the Central
Intelligence Agency will neither deny nor confirm any
knowledge of Mr. Hand.

The Romanian government has offered no explanation for dropping its charges against Mr. Hand, who had
no comment for reporters on his arrival in New York,
other than that he had been "treated well" by the Romanian authorities and was "glad to be home."

Nauseated with panic, I tore the article from the page and
ran into the house, where I found the Conglomeros brooding by the cold hearth. To my questioning, it urgently denied
recognizing Richard Hand, and I was certain the denial was
sincere. But I was equally certain that I had identified the
prowler. How he had found us, or what he wanted, was a
matter of speculation, but that it was connected with the
Conglomeros was a foregone conclusion. Revenge against
me was one strong possibility; kidnapping the Conglomeros
for his own mysterious but no doubt malevolent purposes
was another. Whether he was dangerous to me or my ward
I couldn't say, but having followed me this far, he was obviously a man to be reckoned with and one who should be
steered as far from the Conglomeros as possible. Given the
creature's already unstable condition, any further interfer-
ence with its development could prove disastrous.

"Do you see this man?" I said, holding the photo up to the
creature's face. The Conglomeros nodded, wide-eyed.

"Take a good look. I want you to avoid him at all costs. He
is very dangerous to you."

"To me? Why?" The Conglomeros began to tremble.

"Because . . . because he is a man."

"You're a man."

"I'm different. He's dangerous because he's like other

men. He wants something from you. He won't love you like
I do."

"I don't understand."

"Listen, listen to me." I sat down by the frightened beast,
now shivering like a lost fawn. "You must remember what
I'm going to say to you. It's very important. Okay?" It nodded.

"All humans are dangerous, all of us. You must stay away
from humans, you must shun them, for nothing will harm
you the way a man will. If they come for you, you must run;
if they trap you, you must escape; if they come from above,
you must dig; if they come from below, you must fly; if they
speak to you, do not listen; if they offer you gifts, do not accept; if they smile, frown; if they laugh, growl; and when
they corner you, do not hesitate to kill them. The tiger knows
it has teeth, the bear knows it has strength, the eagle knows
it has talons—but man does not know he carries disease,
and that is why he is fatal, even to those he loves. Every time
a man steps out he carries a whole arsenal of lethal weapons
with him, weapons so deadly he need not even aim them to
wreak bloody havoc on the world. Every man is a walking
Pandemonium, he can cast a shadow on a moonless night
and cause fruit to shrivel on the branch, ice to melt in winter, flesh to sear, fire to pale, and love to desiccate. All these
things man does just in being born. Do you understand me?
Do you?"

"No," said the Conglomeros.

I sighed, defeated. "Well, I suppose you'd have to be human to understand."

The Conglomeros stared at me, troubled, its fingers drumming across the top of its head, as I had often seen it do when
agitated and perplexed. It began to speak, then checked itself, began and stopped again, as if in convulsions. Finally, it
seemed to master itself—it drew in a deep breath and its
fingers ceased their drumming.

"What does it take to be human, then?" it asked.

So there it was—that question. It had only been a matter of time in the coming, as inevitable as "Where do I come from?" on a child's lips. I should have been prepared for it; if I had been I might perhaps have come up with something to stand my creature in good stead in its struggle toward humanity. But I hadn't, and was compelled to cast around desperately for an appropriate and meaningful response. In so doing, for some reason I recalled an anecdote I had read in college. I remembered the story of an anthropologist pursuing his studies among the natives of the Brazilian rain forest, living with a singularly ferocious and independent tribe that had so far resisted all encroachments of civilization. Once, the anthropologist had to fly to Caracas for supplies, and asked the chief of the tribe to accompany him. The chief was stonily unimpressed by the automobile, the radios, the airplane; but he could not contain his profound amazement at the length of the runway. "Where did you find such a large stone?" he inquired. Now, the anthropologist should have understood that the chief had exposed a great vulnerability with that question, but instead of reaping the benefits of his momentary advantage, the anthropologist coolly explained the process of pouring concrete and laying tarmac. The Indian therefore assumed that, in accordance with the customs of his own tribe, the scientist was merely exaggerating the truth so as to aggrandize himself in the eyes of his guest, and so the advantage was lost. But I had always thought that if the anthropologist had been a tactician of some sharp wit, he might have said, "Our god made it for us." The chieftain, confounded, would have returned to his village with stories of the incredible strength of the white man's god; soon, the entire tribe would be trembling in abject submission, and the anthropologist would be working from a position of strength in his efforts to help it.

"What does it take to be human?"

Now, I found myself in a position similar to that of the anthropologist. Unlike the anthropologist, however, I could not afford to pass up the opportunity to impose my will. The Conglomeros needed help, and badly, and experience had shown me that the time for the Socratic method, for gentle patience and tender instruction, had passed. Every other resource had been exhausted: Now was the time for desperate measures. Now was the time to invoke my gods.

"What does it take to be human?"

If I were to give in answer my own approximation of the truth, something like "You need to love and to receive love, you need courage and humility and the generosity to use them," there was every danger that the creature would take me at my word, thus prolonging our relationship on a footing of mutual parity. Needless to say, I could not allow such a thing to happen. Now, willy-nilly, the moment had come to assert my ascendancy. Right or wrong, I saw my opening and took it: For the first time, I lied to the Conglomeros.

"To live a human life," I told the Conglomeros, improvising as I went along, "you must put cancer in your soul, you must be as simple as you are sweet—love all men until they get in your way, and believe that the discipline necessary to restrain your hand from killing is the same discipline necessary to kill when required. Understand?"

The Conglomeros, bewildered, scratched its thighs and shook its head.

"You must put cancer in your soul," I continued, warming to the task. "The truly cancerous are few and far between, but they rule the world. Should you ever meet one, my friend, I suggest you put yourself with unwavering trust into his hands, because his power to manipulate is immense, and he creates or destroys with equal relish. I am such a man, and this is a gift I offer to you—cancer. That is what it takes to be human, in a nutshell. Humanity, no more, no less. Endeavor, enterprise, logic, progress, history, aspiration—those are all but as weeds to the gardener. Understand?"

The Conglomeros, trembling now and close to tears, shook its head again. It fidgeted with all its forty fingers, stretching and turning its limbs, blinking its great doe eyes in perplexity. Though it was perhaps too early to tell, it appeared that I had achieved the effect desired, which caused me great joy and great sorrow. Joy, because the creature was enslaved by its trust in me (or so I thought), and the chains of lies and inference that I had woven would be too strong for it to break. It had only been a small lie, but humanity would henceforth be a closed book to the creature, or better yet, a closed city, dark and ominous and impenetrable. Only I could guide it, and the Conglomeros would relinquish all powers of discernment and wisdom to my willing, benevolent instruction. Sorrow, because I had lied, and because blitheness had fled the creature forever. Finally, after some thought, the Conglomeros looked at me, its eyes wider than ever in awe.

"And how will you teach me to be human?" it whimpered.

I took two of its hands in mine, and stared the creature in the eyes. "Is this what you really want? Do you really want to be human?" The creature nodded dumbly.

"Then we must go to New York City. New York City is the place to learn to be human. Would you like that?"

The Conglomeros returned my gaze steadily, and behind its eyes, among all the confused and frightened thoughts, I saw something die. The creature nodded again.

"I should like that very much."

▲▲▲▲

The very next morning, I found an envelope with my name on it, slipped under the front door. Inside was a message: "Mr. X.," it said. "You must give up the beast to me. It is very,

very urgent that you do so. Sincerely, R. Hand." I made a few telephone calls, and within three days we were ready to leave for New York City. It wasn't so bad, really, I reasoned. We could hide more easily there, and I would have a greater variety of stimuli at my disposal for the Conglomeros's education. And if the creature had to spend more time indoors, and live even more secretively, and be subjected to even further disciplinary measures, it might even do it some good. After all, I was no Caligula, threatening to torture my beloved as a means of understanding my own devotion. No, I convinced myself, this was for the creature's own good entirely. No, a lie is something that hurts, and this was therefore no lie, since I was incapable of doing the Conglomeros harm, for I loved it. No, this was altogether the best move to make.

And, no, it wasn't the end of the world at all. It was only spring.

Despite all the difficulties of setting up a home in New York City, I wanted our lives and work to be consistent with what had gone before. It was important, I felt, that the Conglomeros should sense no divergence, no change of rules in the normal course of events. When a child is sent off to school for the first time, it understands that a threshold has been reached, and the knowledge it acquires thereby is necessarily self-conscious; it was precisely that growing self-consciousness in my companion that I sought to stifle in bringing it to the city. It should be, or appear to be, a seamless transition, and in that way, I hoped, it would be more within my power to mold the shape of things to my liking.

But the nature of our move unfortunately necessitated the grossest and most grotesque compromises in our lifestyle. One does not simply move into a large city and cohabit with a monster, and hope to be allowed to live in the normal expectations of peace and privacy, not even in New York. Steps had to be taken to ensure our complete anonymity.

The first problem to be solved was that of domicile. At first, I was inclined to move us back to my old apartment—which was then sitting empty—on the Lower East Side, where poverty tends to make the populace more tolerant of eccentricity and where physical disabilities are a fairly common encounter, besides the fact that indigence is itself a reliable guarantor of anonymity. But the more I considered it, the more flaws I discovered in the plan: First of all, it is difficult to secure adequate privacy in a tenement, where there are no elevators and the walls are paper thin; then, too, the public places are usually ablare with the sounds of radios, drug dealers, and the general hubbub of street life, and that was not an atmosphere in which to educate the Conglomeros; further, I would have to park the car on the street, which meant that we might be forced to walk several blocks to reach it, the surest way to precipitate public discovery of the Conglomeros. And besides, I was rich.

Instead, I took a furnished two-bedroom sublet on Fifth Avenue in the Seventies, which provided the invaluable advantages of a doorman, a parking lot in the basement, and the natural discretion traditional among the wealthy. The proximity of the park just across the avenue would allow for early-morning or late-night strolls without attracting undue attention. It was all arranged through a broker beforehand—all I had to do was pick up the key and move in with my companion, whom I described in the application as my disabled mother. We took residence late one night with the least amount of fuss and a minimum amount of baggage.

The next problem was the appearance of the Conglomeros, which, needless to say, required no uncertain skill to dissemble, nor an inadequate disguise to fashion. To cover the creature's head, I purchased a long, blond wig: The Conglomeros learned somewhat begrudgingly to fold its tentacular arms across the top of its skull, beneath the wig, while the flowing locks, properly draped, concealed the convergence of its three separate necks at the occiput. A floppy, broad-brimmed hat and a pair of Ray-Bans completed the picture of a slightly hydrocephalic but essentially human eccentric.

The three bodies could be adequately hidden beneath an oversized raincoat, but there remained the egregious protrusion of six feet below its calf-length hem. The Conglomeros had to be taught to walk on two legs instead of six, and we spent hours practicing in our new living room. We tried a variety of different positions, finally settling on the one that was both the most comfortable for the creature and the least distorting of its profile. It involved a kind of double piggyback, in which the female body rode the back of one male torso, and itself carried the other, whose arms were slipped into the sleeves of the raincoat. If you imagine a dog walking on its front paws, with its body bent double and hind legs wrapped around its chest, you can begin to understand the contortions involved in the trick. The effect, all in all, was of an obese hunchbacked old lady, and indeed the two supporting legs, shod in black tights and ankle boots, buckled so heavily beneath their burden that the creature required a walking stick. Watching the grotesque Guignol of the Conglomeros shuffling back and forth across the carpet in its outfit, and groaning with the pain, I was moved to tears by the realization of how far we had come since Romania. How could I help comparing the hideous parody of humanity before me now with that graceful, naked beast I had seen loping through the Carpathian woods only six months earlier? But there was no turning back now, I said to myself as I sniffed back my tears, and I assured my suffering friend that it would rarely be called upon to perform this excruciating trick. But how to avoid it?

The telephone rang.

"Mr. X.," came a soft, Germanic voice, "this is Richard Hand. Please, do not hang up, I must . . ."

I hung up and immediately called the phone company to give me a new, unlisted number. Not that it mattered: If Hand had been able to find me in so short a time he had to know where I lived, and moving again so soon was out of the question, given the Conglomeros's excitable condition. I would have to deal with Hand in person, though what he wanted or how I would fend him off, I couldn't begin to anticipate.

"Walk!" I told the Conglomeros, who had slumped onto the floor, limbs splayed. "You have to learn to do it right."

But in the end, unable to endure the sight of the creature's pain, I bought a collapsible wheelchair; thenceforward, most of its perambulations about the metropolis were undertaken in that, a concession for which it was truly grateful.

In the elevator, we often ran into our neighbors, the men dressed in tartan scarves and woolen overcoats with satin lapels, the women in furs. I could tell we made them uncomfortable, they didn't like us much—rich people are usually attractive and we weren't. But it was precisely the fact that they disapproved of us that made them more friendly, as if they needed to prove their broad-mindedness. Anyway, they were very discreet, they never stared at the Conglomeros for fear of giving offense, and chatted vapidly to me as we ascended or descended. I had to discourage the Conglomeros from talking too much in public, since that always made the ill-fitting sunglasses slip down its nose, revealing its enormous eyes. So my neighbors soon stopped addressing the creature altogether, asking after my mother's health to me, even in "mama's" presence. I liked it that way: The last thing I wanted to encourage was some misguided invitation to dinner, not that that was likely.

Thus did I construct our new existence, and the Conglomeros settled into our domestic arrangement with some trepidation but with evident alacrity. It was only during the first few few nights that the sounds of the city kept it awake, wide-eyed and trembling in our king-size bed; likewise, it was soon accustomed to the relatively cramped conditions of our new home, which barely allowed it to swing its long and many limbs as it was wont to do in spontaneous expressions of *joie de vivre.* It showed no resentment at being forced to hide in the bedroom whenever a delivery boy or tradesman appeared, nor at having to forgo its daily exercise and the company of the woodland fauna—since, even in the dead of night, I felt that the risk of exposure was too great to allow it ever to remove the least accessory of its disguise in public. At first, too, the creature reacted alarmingly to the city air, developing a painful hacking cough and dry, bloodshot eyes; but those symptoms soon passed when it learned to breathe in shallow breaths. Still, despite these and other minor irritants, I never heard the Conglomeros utter a word of complaint or protest in those spring months, and in any case the many delights that city life had to offer seemed to compensate amply for the sacrifice and inconvenience.

For we had things to do, places to go, people to see! We were all set for a new beginning! After a great deal of soul-searching, and some consultation with my student, I had drawn up a curriculum of sorts, and the Conglomeros, newly malleable, acquiesced to all my dicta, which I never imposed arbitrarily but framed in the form of suggestions.

It was only natural, I think, that this new phase in the Conglomeros's instruction should have been an education in the arts. There were many advantages to both me and my ward in a strict adherence to the agenda of opera, music, dance, theater, and the plastic arts that I had devised. First of all, I might as well say it, in terms of human endeavor it was really putting our best foot forward—there isn't much we've done that makes us look as good. I grant that, all stripped of social, historical, and political content as I intended to present it, that was the biggest lie of all—but then, as I have said, the truth had hitherto led only to disaster. Now was the time for artifice, and with every lesson carefully monitored and controlled, I felt sure that my creature could be coddled and manipulated onto a healthier track. In other words, despite my every precaution, the Conglomeros wanted to learn to be human—there was nothing I could do about that now, but at least I could ensure the sort of human it would become, and accordingly I chose the arts as the least dangerous catalyst for that evolution. Fool that I was, I believed that the Conglomeros would absorb only what was most beautiful, creative, and pacific in human nature, and that through art and my subtle manipulation of its not-always-optimistic messages the pernicious ubiquity of human mischief could still be circumvented or occluded.

With that in mind, it may well have been a mistake, for my student's "coming out," to take it to the Met to hear *Otello*. And yet, there we were, I in tuxedo, the Conglomeros in a beaver coat and brunette wig (which I had decided was less conspicuous than the blond), speeding down the brightly lit corridors of the Met. I had timed our arrival at the opera house to coincide with the last call before curtain, so the hallways were almost empty and the lights already dim when I maneuvered the wheelchair through the door to our private box. The Conglomeros immediately eased itself from its conveyance onto the floor, leaning its chin on the balustrade and sighing with pleasure. But even in the gloom its legs protruded from beneath the fur, and I compelled it to sit conventionally, which required two seats.

Before the opera, I had described the story to the Conglomeros, and we followed in a bilingual libretto. As I had described it, Otello, like every other human, is driven by love to kill the thing he loves most, and Iago is a hero for assisting him to fulfill his destiny. The story is the story of Everyman, with the exception that it is not every man who is lucky enough to have an Iago to point the way. In this way I hoped to deemphasize the pervasive evil lurking in the human soul—a concept that the Conglomeros could not have grasped in any case—but to avoid representing Iago as an egregious evildoer and thus as an archetype of human potential in the creature's budding consciousness. I thought myself very clever.

It turned out to be a rather uninspired production. Our Otello was listless, our Iago insipid, and the sets far too busy. But my companion did not seem to notice the defects, and for that matter, once Desdemona made her appearance, nor did I, for she was magnificent. By the end of the first-act duet the Conglomeros was enthralled, and we spent the intermission discussing the color of the soprano's eyes, which were so big and so blue as to seem almost violet in the gloom of the theater. But for me, the highlight of the performance came in the fourth act, when a real tear, glinting in the light, rolled down her cheeks as she sang the "Willow Song." Enraptured as I was, I found myself distracted by a low moan to my right, and turned to see the Conglomeros engulfed in a torrent of weeping, covering its eyes with its tentacular arms, which had somehow slipped from beneath the wig. Its blubbering grew louder by the second. The sunglasses and hat were on the floor, the wig was all askew, and people in the neighboring boxes were beginning to look our way. And still the tears kept flowing, the blubbering gave way to wailing, and finally I had to wheel the Conglomeros from the box, having first readjusted its disguise. The creature, its entire frame racked with wrenching sobs, did not stop crying until I took it to bed, all the time whimpering a tidal flow of half-finished sentences: "I never . . . I *never* knew . . . *so* beautiful . . . I *know* her . . . I *feel* her . . . never . . ." It was a great triumph for me, a vindication, for once, of all my careful planning. The next day we bought the record and learned the "Willow Song" by heart. In its lilting, girlish voice, the Conglomeros sang quite touchingly, with particularly moving emphasis on the line *Io per amarlo e per morir.*"

"But why?" the creature demanded one morning as I wheeled it through the park. The daffodils were already pushing up around the boat basin. "Why do people have to die?"

"I don't know," I said. "Everything has to die. You lived in the woods, you must have seen it every day. Everything has to die."

"Yes, *plants and animals,*" the Conglomeros insisted. "But it shouldn't happen to *people.* They're too wonderful. They're too beautiful."

In conformity with my new approach, rather than dispute this clearly misguided assertion or declare the simple truth, I preferred to exploit the vulnerability exposed by such ignorance.

"Well, you see," I said, "it's a burden we all share. It's a sign, it helps us recognize one another."

A sparrow alighted on the Conglomeros's shoulder and was promptly brushed away.

"I don't understand."

"Some people believe it's a choice we made long ago, that we had the chance to be immortal and gave it up. It's a long story."

"Tell me."

"It's a lot like Otello and Desdemona, actually. You see, a long, long time ago, there was a man called Victor—Victor Frankenstein. He was a great scientist, a doctor, and he invented a serum to make men invulnerable to disease and age. He said: 'What glory would attend the discovery, if I could banish disease from the human frame, and render man invulnerable to any but a violent death!' And he became famous for his serum, and gave it away free to anyone who wanted it. Soon, everyone in the world could look forward to nearly endless life passed in the soundest of physical and mental health. But what happened was that when people stopped dying they stopped recognizing each other. You see, unlike other animals, humans can foresee their own deaths, and it gives them this certain way of shuffling along, a stoop in the shoulder, a distinctive odor, a kind of stutter in the voice. When those were gone they didn't know what was what or who was who. All crowded together, they started killing each other off like flies. Soon, violence grew to such an extent that it accounted for more deaths than old age, syphilis, tuberculosis, and the plague had ever done in all history. Frankenstein was blamed for this, and he was maligned, hounded, persecuted, and eventually stoned to death by a mob of peasants. His theories were discredited, and within a few short years all his work had been overturned. And now, no one writes fairy tales that end with 'and they lived happily ever after,' since no one ever does."

By now we had reached the top of the long, sweeping path above the boat basin, and I was panting with the exertion. I stopped for a breath.

"And you're happy for that?" the Conglomeros asked, perplexed.

"Sure, who wouldn't be?" I puffed.

"But that's nothing like Otello and Desdemona. He killed her for love."

"Same thing."

"Really?" The creature was truly confused. "But you love me, and you do me no harm."

"That's because this is the modern world, and we know a lot more about love now than they used to. In Otello's day, they didn't understand a thing. They used to have to write guide books to explain these things: how to love, who to love, when to love, how to love a man, how to love a woman, how to love your children, how to love your pets, why you love bad people, why good people are afraid to love, why lovers are afraid to be bad. And on and on. Some guy even wrote a book called *When Bad Things Happen to Good People.* Can you imagine? They were so confused! Of course, nowadays you don't have to explain these things—we're civilized, we *understand,* and you'll understand. Love is where you find it and bad things *only* happen to good people. It's pretty simple, really. I can't see why people had to have these things explained to them."

There was a long silence as the Conglomeros took in what I had said. Then it reached up to my neck, pulled me down, and planted a big kiss on my lips. "But you explain things so well! I see it all now! You take such good care of me!"

"I do," I exulted. It was true, just like the old days: This living object *was* my strength and my triumph. With a bounce in my step, I wheeled my friend toward the Seventy-second Street exit from the park.

But my exaltation was exceedingly short-lived. As we were almost out of the park, we passed a row of schoolchildren in blue uniform entering it. The children stared wide-eyed at the Conglomeros, who returned their stares candidly, reaching out a hand, as it had used to do with the forest creatures, to stroke the head of a little boy; but the boy shrank back with a sharp cry of alarm. The column moved on, and as the last child stumbled away, looking over its shoulder, I noticed a bench that had been concealed. And on the bench sat Richard Hand, his right leg delicately crossed over his left knee, homburg at his side. He smiled up at me as we passed, a sad, hopeful smile. Naturally, I increased my pace. As I turned left onto Fifth Avenue, I saw Mr. Hand struggling to his feet, pulling himself up with his cane, and he seemed far frailer and much older than when I had last seen him. And indeed, by the time I saw him step onto the

sidewalk, we were already at Seventy-fourth Street and rolling along handily. It was only when we reached the awning
of our building, and the doorman held the door open for us,
that I recalled my resolve to confront Richard Hand and put
a definite end to the persecution. Well, I reasoned, he knew
where we lived, he could pay us a call.

The Conglomeros, blithely unaware of my thoughts and
concerns, bounded from the confines of the wheelchair,
flung all its clothing and paraphernalia to the floor, and
scampered to the kitchen. It reappeared a moment later in
the doorway, carrot in mouth, leaning seductively against
the frame, a hand on each of its cocked hips, its little breasts
thrust forward. "Take me," the creature said huskily, but
soon dissolved into giggles and cantered into the bedroom,
leaving the door open that I might see it splayed lewdly
across the unmade bed. "Take me, you beast, take me!" it
laughed. The intercom buzzed.

"There's a Mr. Hand to see you," came the doorman's
voice over the handset.

"Show him up."

To the Conglomeros, still spread-eagled and toying impa-
tiently with itself, I said: "Stay in here and don't make a
sound." I gathered up the wig, the sunglasses, the hat, and
the raincoat, flung them into the room, and pulled the bedroom door to with a click. I locked the door and pocketed the
key.

The doorbell rang a minute later, and I gestured Richard
Hand into the apartment. The brief impression I had had of
him in the park was justified: Though he remained immac-
ulately groomed in his well-brushed hat and gray mackintosh, his time in prison had clearly taken its toll. And though
I had only spoken to him once before, I seemed to remember
a sparkle in his eye that was now gone. His hand trembled
on the pommel of his cane as he lowered himself onto the

sofa, and his head bobbled a bit, as if on a spring. Still, when he spoke, there was undeniable strength and conviction in his voice.

"Mr. X.," he said to me, measuring his words, "allow me, please, to dispose with civilities . . ."

"Certainly. Would you care for some tea? Some coffee?"

"Thank you, sir, no. I know you have the creature and, for the instant, I am the only one who knows. And I am come here to tell you, as I have been for six months trying to tell you, that you must return it at once to its home, before you do the creature irreparable damage."

At that moment, the handle of the bedroom door rattled lightly, but I was the only one to notice. Richard Hand went on without pausing.

"I know the nature of the Conglomeros much better than you do, and I assure you that, despite appearances, it is a fragile thing, easily harmed. I am begging you to do as I say; god knows what you have done already." He had spoken as if from a prepared speech, and now he was short of breath, panting, his eyes lowered. "Please," he panted, "you must do it."

I must say, I felt terribly sad for him, as anybody would have—the pathetic old man was almost in tears. It was clear to me, as I considered my response, that whatever his motives, he was at least sincere in them. But that meant nothing to me, and I was not about to be swayed by maudlin sentiment—I was sincere, too, and my motives lofty and noble, and my responsibility very real and ongoing. Who was he that I should succumb to such exhortations, just because of the sorry vision he presented? What could he know that I didn't, I who had lived with the creature for six months, and he whose face it did not even recognize? The door rattled again, much louder this time, and Hand, adjusting his hearing aid, glanced in its direction.

"Mr. Hand," I began gently, slightly condescending perhaps, as I sat next to him on the sofa in an effort to distract him from the door, which was now rattling continuously. "You know, you haven't really given me any reason to trust you, sir, now have you? You lied to me in Romania, you sneak about after me like a thief, you follow me through the streets, and you are a man I should listen to? Have you ever spoken to the creature? Do you know what it wants?"

"No," said Richard Hand, almost inaudibly, "I have never . . ."

"Well, I do, sir," I went on, gaining courage. The noise emanating from the bedroom door was an insistent tapping that rose steadily in volume as I spoke ever louder in competition with it. "I have taken care of the creature, I have taught it to express its desires, I know what it wants. Shall I tell you what it wants, sir? It wants me, it wants the life I have shown it, it wants to live as . . ."

Suddenly, and as if timed to maximize my humiliation, the door jamb split, the bedroom door was flung open, and the Conglomeros stuck its head out, fully disguised in wig, hat, and sunglasses. But the smoked lenses, large and gaudy as they were, ill concealed the great gleaming tears that coursed down the creature's face. It just stood there, staring at each of us in turn, and whimpered. Richard Hand gasped, horrified, and before I could control the impulse, I shouted: "I thought I told you to stay in the bedroom!" The Conglomeros leapt back into the shadows and closed the door, but the damage had been done. When I turned to my guest, his face was buried in his hands.

"Please," I told him. "Let me explain. You don't understand what . . ."

"I have understood everything." His voice, despite being muffled through his fingers, was cold and sharp as steel.

"It isn't what . . ."

"It is! It is exactly what, Mr. X.!" Richard Hand leaped to his feet, all his fragility and resignation subsumed in overwhelming rage. Spittle flew from his lips, and he sputtered and choked apoplectically on his own words. His face turned a livid scarlet and he seemed in great danger of biting off his tongue. He brandished his walking stick and stamped his feet, just as I had seen him do in Paris! "You are abusing this creature, sir, abusing it most shamefully! By what right have you . . . ? It is not a pet! A plaything! A zoo animal! How is it you . . . ? Desires . . . ! Trust . . . ! Yes . . . in my sacred trust . . . ! Forty years, sir, forty years . . . ! And you come along . . . *you* know . . . a scandal, a tragedy . . . ! I . . . it is my trust to give to you . . . ! And you steal, you steal . . . ! No, sir, you are a scoundrel!" So saying, he collapsed breathless into the sofa.

Astounded as I was, at once moved, amused, and disgusted by this onslaught, and utterly bewildered as to its meaning, there had been something about his speech that had struck me as particularly mysterious and compelling. I sat down by the wheezing old fellow and placed a compassionate arm around his shoulder. His eyes rolled in his head like those of a terrified cow.

"Mr. Hand," I said. "I think perhaps I can understand why you are so upset with me. You think I have kidnapped the creature and brought it here against its will. Is that right?"

Unable to speak, the old man nodded and choked.

"And you believe I am keeping it a prisoner here, so to speak, for my own pleasure?"

Another nod and a wheeze.

"And that I am corrupting it?"

Nod and hack.

"Well, allow me to assure you that you are quite mistaken. The Conglomeros is here with me entirely of its own free will, and my entire life is consecrated to its comfort, edification, and well-being. What you saw is merely the conse-

quence of a recent, insignificant illness, from which the creature is almost fully recovered. Otherwise, it is perfectly happy, perhaps happier than it has ever been, and if I may say so, quite devoted to me. I hope that satisfies your fears?"

The old man choked and wheezed and hacked and hiccoughed.

"And now," I pressed on, "please allow me to ask you a few questions. What is your interest in the creature? What gives your claim to it greater weight than mine? And just what did you mean by 'sacred trust' and 'forty years'? Please, take your time."

We waited several minutes while the old man recovered his composure and his breath. I brought him a glass of water.

"Yes," he finally managed to gasp out. "You see, you are the newcomer, not I. I have known the creature almost forty years."

"But you said you'd never even spoken to it."

"That is true. Nevertheless, for forty years I have been watching and studying and protecting the creature, as I promised once to do. And only now have I failed." He sighed miserably, wringing his wrinkled hands.

"Promised? To whom?" But I already knew.

"Young man, I will tell you this story, yes, so you do not think I am crazy. It was during the war, 1940. I was living in Vichy France, in Nice, where I was teaching. This was before the Jews were deported, and I was a courier for the Resistance, which was just beginning. I was traveling often between Nice and Lyon, to the university, and I passed messages along the way. Often, I stopped in a safe house in the mountains, a place called Gap, because it was about halfway.

"Once when I stayed there, there was another Resistance fighter. They were hiding him in the cellar, and he was very sick. He had a high fever, he had just come from a long, a terrible journey across Europe. They thought he would die. He was missing an eye, like me, so I took an interest in him. On my way back from Lyon, I brought some medicine, and the medicine saved his life. After that, whenever I stopped in Gap, I saw him getting stronger and stronger, and we became friends. When he was better—but he never fully recovered, despite a hospital stay in Marseille—he remained in Gap because he was a painter and he wanted to be left in peace. His name was Victor Brauner.

"Many times, I was very curious about this journey he had made across Europe, but never would he tell me. It was his big secret, so naturally I did not press him. But it was very suddenly so, one night with a cognac or two inside him, that he told me. He was never returning to Romania, he said, he knew he would never again see his home. Something heavy weighed on his mind, he needed to trust a person and I was that person. He had a story to tell me and a great favor to ask. Tell the story, I said, ask the favor. He told the story.

"He told me about the fabulous creature in the woods of the Carpathian mountains, how as a boy he had seen it in the woods and it told his fortune and no one ever heard about this creature from him. And as he grew up, he began to think that he imagined the creature, that it never existed, but he had dreams of it, dreams where he saw his eye flowing down his cheek in blood. And when he returned to fight the Fascists in Romania, these dreams it was that led him back to the woods and to the same creature, the Conglomeros.

"To make a story brief, he was enamored of the creature. Every week he takes time from his work for the Communists, he rides a bus to the mountains, he meets his creature, they walk, they talk, he leaves. Soon it is not one day but two, not two days but three. His comrades start to wonder what it is he is doing. They are suspicious: Is he a traitor? Where is he going, that he should disappear this long? They follow him, he escapes, that is all the proof they need. When next he returns to Bucharest, there is confrontation, they evict him from the party.

"And this is all he wants. Politics forgotten now, Victor moves up into the mountains, where he is living with his beloved Conglomeros for more than a year. He is happy, oh so happy his heart is bursting. Everything they do, they do together: eat, breathe, swim, sleep, laugh, love. Can it be that such joy goes on forever? No, for soon Victor notices changes—little changes at first, nothings, he ignores. But then he cannot ignore, he sees what is happening: The creature is becoming *him*! It is gradually absorbing all his personality like a sponge, like a mirror, like an empty soul the creature reflects all that is in him, good and bad, conscious and unconscious. It is not attractive. And Victor sees himself in the creature, for the first time in his life he really *sees* himself as few ever do, and what he sees is so ugly he is driven almost mad! Can this be him? He thought himself a good person, average at least, but he recognizes the portrait so it must be accurate! And in the meantime, all that was most beautiful in the Conglomeros, all he loved it for, is being lost.

"So what to do? He loves, and cannot leave. But if he stays he destroys what he loves. Ach, dilemma! But it is also 1938, Communists everywhere are being killed in Romania. This decides him: To save his loved one, he will go. He returns to France, he loses his eye, and paints the greatest work of his career, his so-called 'Twilight Period.' But it does not last: He cannot live without the Conglomeros, and he decides to damn his consequences. The war begins, he somehow reaches Ceahlau, and what does he find? Like an elastic band, the creature has reverted to its primitive state! Like when first he saw it! It does not remember! Nothing! No love! Like it never happened! He would stay, Victor would, to start again, but now the war is just across the river. He returns once more to France, by train, on foot, by boat: a most dangerous journey. And this is where I see him first, in Gap, only one week after his return. A sorry sight, a man who wants to die but is afraid."

He paused here to catch his breath, and to wipe away a tear that was glistening in the corner of his good eye.

"I must say, Mr. Hand, every time I see you, you have a riveting story to tell me."

"It is all true, yes. At first, when he told me, I was thinking 'This man must be a drunk.' It is a crazy story about such a monster. But then he showed me drawings, and photographs even, and I knew it was true."

"And the promise?"

"The promise? Ach, the promise. I promised to kill anyone who harms the Conglomeros."

"..."

"No, this is just my joke, excuse me! My promise to Victor Brauner was to see the creature whenever possible, to make sure it was healthy, and happy, and living. At first, you know, I make this promise, I do not think to keep. And then prison, I forgot about promises. But after the war I did remember, and I went secretly, the first time, in 1946, before I moved to America. I spent a month looking for the creature, but when once I found it—oh! I have gone every year, just to watch. I stay far away, I do not interfere—this, too, Victor asked of me. And then, I would report all's well to Victor. And when poor Victor died, I continued to go. I think, for sure, this is my last year. I cannot protect the creature any longer."

By now I was pacing up and down. I must admit that I had grown impatient with the old fellow, with his wistful sadness, his wizened old features begging for sympathy and understanding, his façade of wisdom and gentleness—frankly, they made me a little sick. Because, in the end, I knew he only wanted what anyone who knew the Conglomeros—anyone except me—would want: control over the creature, to make it their own. I believed him sincere, as I have said, but then I was sincere too and my motives, at least, were altruistic. This gnarled old dandy could take a flying leap with his superior airs, as far as I was concerned. Still, diplomacy was in order, given his potential for troublemaking.

"Mr. Hand—sir," I said, "please try very hard to understand this: The Conglomeros no longer needs any protection. It is under *my* protection. My very responsible protection. No harm can come to it."

The old man stood up—it was clear to him that I wasn't about to crumble under his pressure. "And you, sir," he said, "must surely see that it is from your kind of protection exactly that the creature needs protecting."

"I am not Victor Brauner."

"But you are a man! That is enough! All men are dangerous to the . . ."

"I think we have nothing left to discuss, Mr. Hand. I tell you I am honorable, you insist I am not. Why don't we just leave it at that and go our separate ways? I'll see you to the door."

Head bowed, the old man allowed me to escort him to the door. As he was leaving, he handed me his calling card, ornately printed with raised wax. "If you need me, sir, or want my advice, please do not hesitate to use it," he said.

"I sure won't," I said. I swung the door to behind him.

"Ah, please, one last thing," he interjected just as it was about to close.

"Yes?"

"I have a message for you, from a friend."

"A message for me?"

"From Ion Gusti, you remember? He says he hopes you are well and happy, and asks you please to remember to send him John Updike's books."

"Ion? Ha! Where did you see him?"

"In prison, he was in the cell next to mine. We became friends. A coincidence, no? Of course, he will be there much longer than I was. Helping spies to leave the country, it is a serious offense in Romania. Well, good day to you!"

I closed the door slowly, deep in troubled thought about my responsibility for Ion's troubles. Naturally, I felt sick at heart for what had happened—who wouldn't?—and in mitigation I could not even claim that Ion had known what he was getting himself into. It was no wonder, under the circumstances, that Richard Hand had little faith in my goodwill or gave little credence to my protestations. On the other hand, that he should employ my guilt as a bludgeon, and strike with no other purpose than the pleasure of wounding me, was in and of itself ample persuasion of his own malice and a confirmation of my instinctual distrust. He was just a spiteful old man thwarted in his aspirations, irresponsibly wielding every weapon—compassion, love, loyalty, the whole gamut of the generous emotions—to weaken my resolve to defend the innocence and integrity of my beloved ward.

Thoughts of the Conglomeros brought me to my senses, and I rushed into the bedroom, where I found my dear monster sprawled naked on the bed, sobbing into a pillow and kicking its six legs like a child in a tantrum. I sat at the edge of the bed and stroked its downy skull; at first, the tentacular arms slapped my hands away, but gradually the creature succumbed to my ministrations, its sobs subsided in intensity, and its frantic limbs relaxed. Finally, the creature spoke while I massaged its necks, though it kept its face turned away from me.

"I heard everything you said."

As I comforted my beloved with sweet nothings and pet names, I described the workings of Richard Hand's devious mind. Some people, I explained, were willing to go to any lengths to achieve what they wanted; to that end, they sometimes said things that weren't true. We called this "lying." It was the terrible disease I had once warned the creature against, and it was dangerously contagious. Richard Hand suffered from it, and that is why he had invented that terrible story about a man who had never existed. Fortunately, I myself was immune to the disease and so was able to recognize its symptoms in others. Thus, in my zealous effort to protect the Conglomeros from lying, I had shut it away and locked the door. It was only my great and protective love that had made me seem cruel—love was like that.

"Really?" The creature's eyes were as big as grapefruit.

"Sure, you can't help it: You love, you hurt. It's like the animals in the zoo: We love them so much we lock them up. Like children. But they forgive us, they love us, and we forgive them, we help them, we guide them. That's the nature of love."

"Yes . . . I remember . . . once . . . something . . . it was the universe . . ."

"Leave the universe to take care of itself, my pet," I said, kneading the creature's buttocks, lightly grazing the tops of its thighs with my fingertips. "There's just you and me now, and I forgive you and I love you."

"Yes," said the Conglomeros, closing its eyes with pleasure as my hand pursued its explorations. "Yes, do forgive me. I don't know why I'm like this, maybe because I love you so much. Yes, because I love you so much, that's right, yes, because I love . . . yes, that's right . . ."

"And later," I whispered, licking its fingertips, "we can visit the Bronx Zoo . . ."

▲▲▲▲

We did visit the Bronx Zoo, and later that week the Botanical Garden in full bloom, but neither excursion was a very great success. In general, accustomed as it had become to city life, the Conglomeros seemed to have lost much of its patience for wild things, which in turn had lost all their interest in the Conglomeros. They no longer flocked to it; indeed, some of the higher vertebrates slunk moodily into the corners of their cages when the Conglomeros peeked through their bars, giggling. I was glad to note, however, that my friend was not upset by their aversion—in fact, seemed amused or barely conscious of it. Still, by the end of both trips the Conglomeros was listless and bored, bouncing in its chair and fidgeting with its paraphernalia, and we were both relieved to get home, take off our clothes, put Verdi on the turntable and go to bed. Sometimes we ordered in a pizza, which the Conglomeros had taken a liking to and which I, against my better judgment, allowed it to enjoy. Its favorite topping, I remember, was eggplant.

No, nature was no longer a determining characteristic, and as the weeks of spring passed on, I noticed with ever-increasing satisfaction the ongoing evolution of the Conglomeros's personality. Bringing the creature to New York had been a last-ditch act of desperation, one fraught with countless and unforeseeable dangers; given my decidedly limited successes to that point I had had no compelling grounds for optimism. And yet, as we settled into our new lives and grew to accept the limitations intrinsic to the situation, it seemed to my astonished gratification as if the manifestation of my every hope for the creature's intellectual and cultural development was only a matter of time. Yes, I had to hand it to myself: I had done us proud. This was undoubtedly my more successful version of Brauner's "Triumph of the Favorite." I gave no further thought to Richard Hand and his dire predictions.

The strange thing is that the closest approximation to the consummate human being, as defined by the Conglomeros at the evolutionary stage it had then reached, is a New Yorker. Of course, by that I mean a certain type of New Yorker, and I do not wish to imply that my ward became a typical one. How could it? At that time, the Conglomeros was no more capable of evincing suspicion, greed, calculation,

destructive and self-destructive tendencies, spleen, obsessive or compulsive mannerisms, double standards, or
treachery than a baby; on the other hand, such affects are
not necessarily exclusive to New Yorkers. No, the creature
was still about as guileless, generous, and trusting as it had
ever been, but it was becoming culturally literate, which
seemed to me at the time like reasonable compensation for
the mistakes made earlier in its education. And, like any
good New Yorker, the Conglomeros, under my tutelage,
happily spent its days and nights in pursuit of great truths in
the greater cultural institutions of the greatest city in the
world.

The opera season was essentially over, but there were still
more than enough activities with which to fill every waking
minute of every day. I had several summer dresses especially made for my beloved, and we soon became a regular
sight at the art museums, I in my newly acquired double-
breasted linen suits, the Conglomeros in its Laura Ashley
prints, red beehive wig, and butterfly shades. I admit we had
become a bit smug and begun to attract unnecessary attention, but that was only a function of the confidence attained
in the ease of deception: After all, people were naturally going to see a hideously deformed old woman in my wheelchair over a three-bodied monster with arms for ears, and
so they did. Still, even I had to admit it to be priceless when
the Museum of Modern Art put on a surrealist retrospective,
and the Conglomeros was able to sit there, surrounded by a
skeptical and erudite opening-day crowd, and scrutinize
Victor Brauner's sketch "Beware Appearances" at close
quarters. At such time I was visited with the same, soul-
shattering thrill I had when first I saw the beast, a sense of
the miraculous rarely felt after puberty.

The Conglomeros took in everything it saw and heard
with the uncritical eye of a child, and was thus able to make
comparative studies and cross-references that were as-

tounding in their novel perspectives and perspicacity. I am unable to reproduce the logic with which it persuaded me of the similarities between a Mycenaean urn and a Warhol, or between a medieval papal bull on usury and the works of certain young contemporary novelists, and yet the logic was irrefutable. Better yet, the creature absorbed everything I had to say on any topic and was able to repeat it for me, almost verbatim, back in our apartment that night. After a postmodern poetry reading, for instance, or a SoHo vernissage, or a visit to Rye Playland, I expatiated and propounded at will, and the visions of the world thus conjured were integrated wholesale into the Conglomeros's consciousness. Mostly they were technical or historical, but often they were somewhat fantastical, too. At some later date, the Conglomeros would trot out one of these theories and apply it, with no sense of irony, to the most diverse of uses. For instance, in one day alone I heard the creature apply the theory of the internal combustion engine to the historical progression of art, the preference of arrowroot over cornstarch in the thickening of Oriental sauces, and the latest trend toward minimalism in fiction, and there was no instance in which I could honestly claim the theory misapplied. Such, I gloated, are the advantages of culture, and congratulated myself one more time. The Conglomeros, too, was beginning to be mightily pleased with itself.

We also greatly enjoyed the movies, but I found when trying to make appropriate selections that the presence of unsuitable material—violence and any kind of general dishonesty or betrayal, most especially—was difficult to determine in advance. The ratings were no help, since a film that was horrifically gory might receive a low rating because there was no sex or swearing in it. Eventually, then, we stopped going to the films altogether, staying at home and watching old musicals on the VCR instead. When it came to protecting my lover from human nature, even Frank Capra was too earthbound for my tastes. On the other hand, we had a fine time at the Museum of Broadcasting, where we sat through hilarious hours of old science fiction movies and *Mister Ed* reruns.

Occasionally, I would catch a glimpse of Richard Hand following us about the city. He was neither particularly subtle, nor, I felt, particularly threatening. He was just keeping an eye on us, I believed, living up to a promise made to a friend many years dead. It was rather sad, his being all alone day after day while we amused ourselves, and there were times when I was tempted to ask him to join us, though I resisted. Once, however, we were in a position to help him. We were strolling through the park one Sunday when we were passed by a group of ireful and threatening teenagers. A minute later we heard calls for help and scuffling behind us, and without thinking I turned the wheelchair around and sped toward the spot. There, surrounded by the four teenagers variously armed with pipes or stilettos, was the tiny defiant figure of Richard Hand, clutching his crushed homburg and swearing at his attackers. At the sound of the wheelchair, the boys turned toward us and advanced. When they were almost within reach, the Conglomeros leaped from its chair, casting aside all its clothing and accessories. Though it had no roar and no sharp teeth to speak of, the creature drawn up to its full height, all eight arms outstretched and bodies quivering, was indeed a sight too much for the boys, who dropped their weapons and ran. Richard Hand, after a moment, thanked us with a stiff bow and made off in the opposite direction. The monster and I laughed, though I was quietly bemused by its capacity to menace or even to appear menacing, which I had not known it to possess. We made straight for home and spent the rest of the day in bed.

Lovers that we were, we enjoyed the wide realm of other pleasures that New York has to offer in the springtime. We spent entire afternoons on the Staten Island ferry, descending to the lower deck with the cyclists so that the Conglomeros could enjoy the spray blowing across its face; the Empire State Building, with its crisp breezes, was another favorite. We explored the antiques fair at the Armory and the construction sites at the Battery; we lingered for hours over cappuccino and zuppa inglese in the garden of a quiet West Side café; we strolled the Brooklyn Heights promenade and the Coney Island boardwalk; we rode the merry-go-round in Central Park (the Conglomeros insisted, despite the pain of straddling the horse) and took a skiff onto the lake; and, one perfect April night, with the stars twinkling and the foghorns of outbound cruise ships blaring, we made love out on Pier 84.

In short, as April wafted into May and May bloomed into June, it seemed as if all were well with us. The Conglomeros was happy again and obedient to me, a loving companion and friend, bright, cheerful, and growing. Certainly, it was not the same creature it had been eight months earlier, but if it had lost certain worthy attributes in its development, it had incontestably gained others. Still, the doom foretold by Hand and Brauner seemed farther away than ever—there was no sign or suggestion of the creature "becoming me," of its adopting my character and foibles in any way. Deep down, it was the same Conglomeros it had always been, I kept telling myself. That in my willful blindness I ignored the loss of its abilities to predict the future, to communicate with animals, to speak with convincing assurance about the nature of the universe, or at least that I pretended their loss to be somehow mitigated by its newfound capacity to criticize modern art, julienne vegetables, or coordinate fashion accessories, remains to my eternal shame. And whether disaster might have been avoided had events taken another turn, it is impossible to know and bootless to speculate, though I doubt it. Whereas in the early days I had been preparing the recipe for disaster on an open flame, now I was simply simmering it. But the time would come just as inexorably when I would have to swallow it, and all unknown to me, that time was nearly at hand.

▲▲▲▲

In 1945, Victor Brauner painted "Face to Face with Destiny," in which destiny is depicted as a vicious, sharp-fanged cat. It was on a Friday evening, in front of the Russian Tea Room, that destiny finally caught up with me, though I didn't recognize it in its disguise at the time. We were on our way to Carnegie Hall when I heard someone calling me by my old college nickname.

"Hey, Achey!" came a voice I knew immediately. "Achey, wait up! Achey!"

I kept moving. The Conglomeros, oblivious, went on with its exegesis of the Book of Job. I braced myself, and a moment later came the tap on my shoulder.

It was Dave Fluegelman, my freshman-year roommate. We had been close friends all through school, and when we graduated, he had moved in with Sarah and me on the Lower East Side. When Sarah and I picked up to go traveling, Dave had looked after our apartment; after our travels, Sarah stayed in England, while I returned to New York and lived with Dave for a while, until he moved in with his girlfriend. Then Sarah died, and I hadn't seen any of my old friends for nearly three years, until tonight.

He was on his bicycle, and dressed almost exactly as I had last seen him, in his spandex shorts and "Cyclic Nucleotides" T-shirt, a messenger's bag slung across his back. He hadn't changed much, either—still skinny as a rake, still prematurely balding, still covered in a thin film of grime and perspiration. He hugged me to his chest.

"Achey, I can't believe it!" he cried, pushing me away for a better look, then pulling me in for a second embrace. "It's really you, isn't it! Where the hell've you been?"

"Hello, Dave," I said.

Dave gave me a brief synopsis of his recent life—the meager recording contracts, the sublease minidramas, the concert tours in obscure midwestern college towns, the girl-friends won and lost, and so on. He also offered me his sincere condolences on Sarah's death and lamented his inability to attend the funeral. We talked over the old days a little, but Dave was distracted by his overwhelming and ill-concealed curiosity about the grotesque figure in the wheel-chair. Finally, he asked me what I had been up to.

"Oh, you know, bit of this, bit of that." I was really very eager to be on my way. I loved Dave for the sake of old times, the way people do, but right then, with the Conglomeros on my hands, I was nothing but uncomfortable and anxious.

"Say, who's this?" Dave, unable to contain himself any longer, pretended only then to have noticed the creature. He stuck out his hand, and the Conglomeros shook it willingly.

"I'm Connie," it said in a babydoll voice with a slight Latino accent. "I'm Achey's special friend from Romania." Dave and I both looked at the seated figure with admiration.

"You in New York for a while?"

"That depends on Achey," said the creature with a broad leer behind its shades. I had never seen it put on such a performance, but, then again, I had never introduced my ward to anyone else. It was only now that that fact struck me for the first time, with troubling clarity. Dave continued to gape.

"Well, that's good," he said in awe. "Then we'll get to see you again."

"I sure hope so."

"I don't think we'll be . . . ," I began abruptly.

"How about tomorrow night?" Dave asked, looking at his

watch. "I'm playing down at the Specula. Why don't you come by?"

"Well, I . . ."

"Come on, you know you'll love it. What about you, Connie, you ready for the downtown arts scene?"

"Yes, I am."

"All right then, be there at a quarter to eight. But listen, I've got to go . . . so you'll be there, Ache?"

"Yes, yes, I'll be there."

"Good. See you tomorrow then. See ya, Connie."

"See ya, Dave."

And he was gone down Fifty-seventh Street.

Later that night, I argued a little with the Conglomeros, but the creature was adamant: The East Village was one neighborhood we had yet to explore, and the creature resented my having kept it a secret. I had had my reasons, among them a powerful reluctance to run into a host of old friends, lovers, and other reminders of my past life. We discussed the situation in depth, but the conclusion was foregone.

The next evening found us on East Ninth Street, outside the performance space where Dave was scheduled to play. The "space" had probably been a coal cellar at one time, and was accessible only by a flight of stairs hidden beneath a pair of metal doors embedded in the sidewalk. One small room underground, fitting perhaps thirty people at the most, and yet it was the focal point of the downtown music-improvisation scene. The place had once been an anarchist laboratory called the "Speculation Theater," but the anarchists had lost their lease and somebody had stolen the T-I-O-N from the lintel above the stairs. Thus had been born the Specula Bunker, where most of my musical friends had had their debuts. On weeknights, the place was for rent for thirty dollars a night. I enlisted help in easing the wheelchair down the stairs.

The little cavern was full of people, many of whom I knew from college or from the bars Sarah and I had once frequented. I responded with some coolness to their fraternal greetings, but found as I attempted to maneuver the wheelchair through the crowd that I was unable to resist being drawn into conversation with long-lost friends I barely remembered. Incapable of dissembling my indifference, however, and anxious to avoid repeated interrogation about my wife, I was a poor participant in the charade, and soon retired with my ward to a corner.

Of course, the grotesque figure cut by the Conglomeros, hunched over in a wheelchair in the corner of a crowded cellar and masked in sunglasses and a floppy hat, aroused an enormous prurience in the crowd. We were approached by many who were clearly impressed by the eccentricity of its appearance—which happened to echo the kitschy retro look then popular in the East Village—and thereby assumed that the monster was someone to know. Unfortunately, these were people who knew or had once known me too, and I couldn't pass the Conglomeros off as my mother to them. I introduced the creature as my friend Connie who didn't talk much—she was known as "La Grande Silencieuse" amongst certain circles in France, I joked. I ignored the conspiratorial, questioning glances and the chummy appeals to ancient friendships for information. "She's just a friend," I would say coldly, and that was generally all the discouragement most of them required. Eventually, we were left alone, and the music began.

Dave was the first to play, punctuating the melodic phrases of his improvised violin solos with atonal squawks and electronic screeches purposely fed back. It was intended as a challenge to the audience, and I suppose that to some the challenge was to remain in their seats, but I enjoyed it. The sound of Dave's violin also brought me back to the last time I had heard it, back to the days when Sarah's occasional snorts of heroin were still few and far between, and it made me happy to picture her that way, without bitterness. And the Conglomeros's eyes were so wide that they rose above the frame of its Ray-Bans. When it was over, we all clapped politely, thoughtfully.

The next act was a skeletal guitarist with a shaved head who sang political songs about philistinism while banging on his electric guitar with drumsticks and mechanical toys. Then it was time for a break, and most of the audience ascended to smoke cigarettes on the sidewalk. Dave remained with us in our corner.

"So, what do you think?" he asked the Conglomeros. There was a long pause.

"It's remarkable," the Conglomeros finally whispered, throwing me a glance I did not quite understand. There was another long pause as we absorbed the answer.

"That it is," Dave said. "Peter used to play with Henry Frask. He's getting ready to sign a contract with . . ."

We were distracted by an altercation that had begun across the room. A young couple were having a fight, leaning into each other and hissing breathily. Only the obscenities reached our corner intact, but from their rising frequency we could tell the argument was reaching its climax. Finally, quivering with rage, the girl stamped her foot, spat "You fucking shit!", burst into tears, and stormed up the stairs.

A complete silence fell on the room, while her companion looked sheepish and her sobs reached us from the sidewalk above. I happened to look down at the Conglomeros at that moment, and was astounded to see a rapturous smile spreading across its face.

"Listen! Hush!" it whispered, raising an index finger. "Ah! D'you hear!"

"Shh!" I sputtered.

The creature's smile took on an almost religious serenity.

"There's nothing like it, is there?" it said. "The sound of a blue-eyed woman crying!"

The young man involved in the argument, having over-heard the creature's remarks, slunk from the room in shame, while Dave and I blushed and smirked in embar-rassment at the ingenuous gaffe. There was, however, an-other person who seemed to have taken note of the exchange and to be according it an inordinate amount of interest. Across the room—a tall, sallow blond woman hang-ing on his elbow—was a tall sallow blond man whose thin-ning hair was pulled tightly back across his head and tied in a ponytail. He wore stovepipe jeans and a seersucker jacket over a white T-shirt, and was staring intently at the Con-glomeros while pulling on a joint. His high, sharp cheek-bones, slanted profile, and tiny eyes made him look like a viper, and I turned to Dave for information.

"That's Forrest Schaeffer," Dave said in a whisper. "He's a music critic for the *Voice*. He also runs some sort of reading series out of his apartment. I went there once, it was really weird, some sort of religious cult or something."

"Does he always stare like that?"

"Looks like he's got the eye for Connie."

I sat through the second half of the evening—a gawky banjo player in a polyester suit singing obscene country-and-western ballads—acutely and uncomfortably aware of Schaeffer's piercing gaze. He seemed somehow to be sizing the creature up, with the self-assured and knowing smile of a slaveowner assessing a prospective purchase. The Con-glomeros, in turn, had noticed his behavior early on, and since the sweet thing would always hold a gaze for as long as it was returned, they spent the entire half-hour staring at each other. When the music was over, I tried to enlist Dave into helping me up the stairs with the wheelchair, but it was too late. Forrest Schaeffer was up and pushing his way through to us before the last note was plucked.

"Shit-hot blasting gear, man," he said in mock Californian, lighting up a new joint and offering it around, his eyes locked on my companion and an unctuous smile frozen on his paper-thin lips. "What's up, Dave?" he said, still looking at the Conglomeros, who stared back unabashed.

"Not much," Dave said, accepting the joint. He made the introductions.

"Forrest Schaeffer. How are you?" said the young man, extending his hand to the Conglomeros, who shook it silently. He pulled back his lips in a skeletal smile that revealed yellow teeth and bleeding gums. Retrieving his joint from Dave with his left hand, he continued to hold on to the Conglomeros's with his right, and might have stayed there all night had the tall, sallow blond woman not taken him by the elbow and whined something into his ear. Whatever it was she said, he frowned and turned away from her, but the connection between him and the Conglomeros had been broken. But before leaving, he extracted a rolled-up sheaf of papers from his back pocket, peeled off a couple of sheets and handed them to us.

"Listen," he said conspiratorially. "I've got this little group going, we meet twice a month. You guys should come. It's tomorrow night."

"What is it?" I asked, glancing over the flyer. It had a typeset letterhead that read "Institute of Dialectical Variablism," with an address and phone number, and handwritten across the otherwise blank page, "Art and Politics: Threat or Menace? Sunday, June 17, 7:00 P.M." The blonde tugged more insistently at Schaeffer's elbow.

"I don't have time to explain it right now, but why don't you read this?" He pulled a dog-eared paperback from inside his jacket and chucked it in the Conglomeros's lap as the blonde steered him toward the exit. Halfway up the stairs, he turned and called out, "That's my only copy, so bring it with you tomorrow." And then he was gone.

Dave helped me wheel the Conglomeros up the stairs, and we exchanged awkward good-byes and promises. On the drive home, the creature was strangely silent, staring moodily out the side window or at its own reflection in the black pane—I'm not sure which. That night, we made love reflexively, an almost cursory action, and I sensed in the creature a pensive reticence that I was at a loss to define and loath to infringe. I rolled over and fell into a light sleep, only to awaken sometime in the middle of the night to find the bedside lamp still on and the creature awake and reading. I inquired.

"It's the *Manifesto of Dialectical Variablism,*" the Conglomeros told me.

"What's it say?"

"I'm not sure," the creature murmured thoughtfully. "I think it says that God is in all of us."

"Novel concept," I grunted, and returned to my unsuspecting, dreamless slumbers. But it was an awakening in every sense of the word when, upon opening my eyes to the bright sunlight filtering through the blinds, I found my companion still engrossed in the same spiral-bound volume. Its great eyes were wide in awe, and seemed to have receded into their orbits as if into the depths of glaucous meditation. Without looking up from the book, the creature answered my questions by saying that it was on its third reading, and had not slept.

"Give me that," I said irritably, snatching the book from its grasp and turning to a page at random. It was typewritten and photocopied, and this is the paragraph upon which my gaze fell:

Thus, we must tear down the old monuments to Truth and herald the impulse to untruth. Since we hold such Truths to be subjective, any pretense of objectivity is, *a priori,* a mendacious fallacy; and yet the Western traditions of monotheism and philosophy are founded on that pretense. For thousands of years have we listened to liars claiming to have found the Truth, and their mendacity is compounded by maliciousness when they pretend to have passed it on to others. Received knowledge, objective, logical, transcendental and voluntaristic idealisms, metaphysical dualism, formal, efficient, final and material causes—these are the buttresses of a specious teleology that . . .

"But this is absolute garbage," I said, throwing the paperback to the floor. The Conglomeros leaned over the side of the bed, picked up the volume, and began smoothing down its crumpled pages.

"How can you say that, Aaron?" The creature's tone was sad and hurt. "You haven't even read it. A lot of it seems very . . . familiar to me."

"I don't need to read it, I can tell . . ." I began, but was interrupted by the ringing of the telephone. I took the call in the living room. It was Forrest Schaeffer, asking to speak to "Connie."

"We were just talking about your *book*," I said, hoping he would catch my somewhat sneering emphasis on the last word. "Connie is very taken with it."

"Is that so?" I could tell that he sensed the challenge in my voice. "That's great. I was just wondering if we could all have brunch together, maybe we could talk about it then."

"Well, *I* haven't read it yet, so . . ."

At that moment, the bedroom extension was picked up, and I heard the Latino Kewpie voice that "Connie" seemed lately to have adopted as "her" public persona. Ignoring all my attempts to intervene, the creature arranged to have brunch with Forrest Schaeffer that very morning at a popular Cajun restaurant downtown. As they worked out the details there was an anticipatory enthusiasm to both of their voices—like that of two people who, having briefly met at a party, are tremulously setting up their first date—that didn't sit at all well with me, and when the line went dead without so much as an acknowledgment to me from Schaeffer, I slammed down the receiver and stormed into the bedroom, where the creature was sitting up in bed, absentmindedly toying with all three of its genital organs, a vague, dreamy smile hovering above its lips.

"What the hell was that all about?" I shouted.

"That was about brunch," said the Conglomeros, only slightly fazed by my anger.

"We don't eat brunch."

"Just because we haven't doesn't mean we can't. I don't understand why you're so upset."

"It's that guy. How can you like him?" I sat on the bed.

"What's wrong with him?" asked the Conglomeros, stroking my cheek.

"He's so . . . slimy, so devious. He's a schemer, you can tell." I rubbed concentric circles on the creature's belly.

"I don't understand."

And it was true, of course: How could it understand? Though I had often spoke of lies and self-serving people, I had never taught the creature to recognize the signs of underhandedness and deceit; for me, in fact, such rhetoric had merely been an improvised and expedient abstraction, evoked less as practical advice than as preemptive exhortation. The way a mother warns her child against strangers without wanting ever to believe that the day could come when such admonishing would require the child's active implementation, so too had I never considered that the day might come when the creature—my child, my lover—might crave independence. Whatever my instinctive suspicion of Forrest Schaeffer and his motives, that day hadn't come yet, as far as I was concerned.

"He's not like me," I said softly. "He's not cancerous, he

doesn't know what's good for you; and neither do you, for that matter. Not like I do."

"I'm only having brunch with him," said the Conglomeros. "Please, don't," brushing my hand from its breast.

"I just don't want you to get involved with this guy, that's all."

For the first time, a grimace of irritation crossed the creature's face, and it pushed me away with all eight hands. "You know, you're just like an internal combustion engine—whenever you start turning, you . . ."

"Okay, we'll have brunch."

At brunch, what with the wheelchair and the crowd in the little shoebox of a restaurant, we were wedged in rather too closely to one another for my comfort. But "Connie" didn't seem to mind at all: Behind those dark glasses, I could tell that "she" was enthralled.

Forrest Schaeffer did most of the talking, and most of that was about himself. He was hard to get a handle on: While he came across (to me, at least) as vulpine and self-serving, there was an unmistakable foundation of sincerity to his cant. He told us about his elaboration of the theories of Dialectical Variablism following an extended binge of suicidal intoxication, about his establishment of the "Institute," about his aspirations for the group and his frustrations at being unable to expand its membership. He spoke about Dialectical Variablism as "the philosophy of consolation without hope through the applied science of self-deception." It was an alternative to both religion and art, he said, designed especially for those who have plumbed the depths of cynicism and found them boring. The beauty of Variablism was that, no matter what you did or who you were, you could apply it to any solution in life and it would make you a happier person—to that extent, he claimed, it was a neo-Platonic rather than an Aristotelian ideal. All you had to do was convince yourself that your life and actions have value and meaning, even if you know in your heart that nothing at all has any value in this world. In other words, Variablism took up where existentialism left off—bringing the self into existence not through the exercise of freedom but through the science of self-deception. Or something to that effect.

It all sounded like rubbish to me, and I know that the Conglomeros could not have understood much of it, being alien to the concept of cynicism. Still, his words seemed somehow to strike a sensitive cord deep within the creature, and even I had to admit that there was something compelling about the speaker, a passion and eloquence he showed only for that one topic. Schaeffer was always to remain an enigma to me, and the closest I was ever to get to understanding him was in the attraction he held for others through the power of his enervated zealotry. Whenever he declaimed, his eyes flashed, his thin lips became engorged with blood, his hands gesticulated and his ponytail swung wildly. To me, he seemed the consummate evangelist, and to that extent I thought I understood the fascination he held for the Conglomeros, who had been educated on my more dispassionate appraisal of the phenomena of life. I myself was not taken in, but I was able to observe his theory in actual practice—he had truly deceived himself into believing the sophomoric tripe he was spewing. Besides, as he demonstrated, his theories on "consolation" were based in part on his own dire need in that regard.

"You see these?" he said, showing us his raw and bloody gums. "I'm losing my teeth one by one. The doctors can't do a thing about it. I'll be getting porcelain choppers pretty soon."

"What's wrong with them?"

"Well, it's kind of complicated, but basically it's a kind of cancer. My gums are cancerous."

The Conglomeros threw me a bold, triumphant glance,

and I knew then that I had perhaps made a bed I should have preferred not to lie in.

"You're cancerous, are you?" the creature asked.

"Well, yes, kind of . . ."

"I've never met another cancerous person before. I knew it from the moment I saw you."

"You did?"

"Yes, you are a very rare and special people."

"Well, not so rare . . ."

"Yes, rare!" The Conglomeros banged the table with its fists. "Look at all these people: How many of them do you suppose are cancerous?"

"Well . . . I . . ."

"Or look at the coffee!"

"The coffee?"

"Yes, think of all the different kinds of humans in the world whose work went into putting this coffee on the table! Millions, and not one of them cancerous! All the people who picked the coffee, the people who transport it, the people who make the trucks to transport it, the people who roast it, the people who make the machines to roast it, the people who dig mud, the people who transport the mud, the people who make the mud into cups, the people who milk the cows, the people who breed the cows, the people who make rubber nipples for the milking machines, the . . ."

"Wow," Schaeffer said in awe and wonder under his breath.

"Connie, I think you'd better calm down," I said tensely. The creature's voice was getting louder by the moment and people were beginning to look in our direction.

"No, keep going, it's great."

". . . people who grow the . . ."

"Don't tell her to keep going, she's getting hysterical!"

"She's just hitting her stride!"

". . . made the little paper bags, the people who . . ."

"Connie, knock it off now!"

"Shut up, can't you see she's . . ."

"No, *you* shut up!" I leapt to my feet, my hands curled in tight fists, at which Schaeffer stared in contempt and disgust. By now the entire restaurant had fallen silent, and we could hear the bacon frying in the kitchen. The Conglomeros, its diatribe cut short, hung its head. I pushed myself from the table and strode into the bathroom, where I paced the floor in a torment of self-recrimination. What had prompted the violence of my reaction? How had things gotten out of hand so quickly? The Conglomeros had often gone off on such tangential flights of fancy in the past without provoking the slightest objection from me. But now . . . was it Schaeffer's goading that had merely brought out my contrariness, or was it rather the unwitting inspiration he had provided that aroused this dark streak of envious insecurity in me? In all my years of marriage and through several instances of infidelity I had never been a jealous man. What was it about Schaeffer—something so familiar striving to make itself recognized by me—that was so quick to raise my ire and anxiety? I looked at my image in the cracked mirror, and saw the trembling hands, the high color, the veins bulging in my neck. Splashing my face with cold water, I took several deep breaths and opened the door, but Schaeffer and the Conglomeros were gone. I found them outside, amiably chatting about Salvador Dali as if nothing had happened. All things considered, and in a sincere effort to repress my nauseated wrath, I attempted a conciliatory approach.

"Listen," I said, putting an arm around Schaeffer's shoulder. "I'm sorry I got upset. It's just that you can see that Connie isn't in the best of health, she mustn't be excited."

"She's all right. Look at her, she's fine. You ought to loosen up a bit is all, let her have some fun. She has a magnificent imagination."

I gripped his shoulder tightly and looked him in the eye.

"You may be right, Forrest," I said, "but in the end I'm the one who's responsible for her, and I've been taking care of her a long time."

"It looks to me like she can take care of herself."

"Let's go, Connie." I had begun pushing the wheelchair toward Lafayette Street when the creature motioned for me to stop, and called to Forrest. When he approached, the Conglomeros grabbed him around the neck and pulled his face to its puckered lips. It was very much the kind of kiss I had used to get unbidden, and the blood rushed to my head. Again, I had to control my bile, telling myself that the creature could mean no harm in that innocent kiss, since it was incapable of malice. Forrest squatted at the wheelchair's side.

"See you tonight, Connie?" he said affectionately.

"I don't think that would be a good idea," I said.

"I'd like that, Forrest," the Conglomeros said.

We had another argument when we got home that afternoon, the worst by far that we had ever had. I daresay it roughly paralleled the argument between a teenage girl and her father, except that in our case, of course, there was nothing perverse about the sexual undertones. The issue at stake was a simple one: I wanted the Conglomeros to stay at home, I wanted to protect it from those who would harm, cheat, corrupt, and abuse it, unscrupulous opportunists and charlatans; the creature, in turn, felt it had earned the right to be trusted with other people—what hurt me so deeply was that it wanted to be with them at all, when it had everything it needed with me. And what of its debt to me? Could that, like my love, be so lightly set aside? But the creature insisted that it loved me more than anything, and why should Forrest be any threat to me at all? In the end, of course, I was right about Forrest, but wrong about everything else; and, in the end, we went to the meeting that night.

The "Institute," it turned out, was Forrest Schaeffer's studio on East Twelfth Street. The apartment was on the fourth floor, and it was truly horrible to watch the Conglomeros's pain as it negotiated the stairs on two legs, while I carried the wheelchair behind it. We were the last to arrive, and Forrest introduced us to the dozen or so "members" sitting about the room on chairs, tables, the bed or the floor. "Connie," in particular, was glowingly praised as a "brilliant and witty representative from Eastern Europe" and a "potential Iron Curtain evangelist."

The first event of the evening was a debate on "The Tools of Production," to be carried out along Variablist lines. By that token, the purpose of the debate was to use opposing viewpoints to reach the same conclusion, thus breaking down the illusion of objective logic and promoting the elaboration of subjective value structures. The winner of the debate was the one deemed to have reached the preordained conclusion by the most circuitous route of logic. The debaters tonight represented the capitalist and communist viewpoints, and the conclusion they were both required to reach was that "tools are an invention of the other side to enslave the workers." The Conglomeros sat wide-eyed, drinking it all in.

The communist argued that tools do not make work easier, they just make work. He waffled on for a quarter of an hour or so, while I observed Schaeffer observing the Conglomeros with the slit-eyed, viperish expression I had seen him wear the evening before. What it was that he saw in the creature, or wanted from it, was far beyond me to fathom, but he made me most uneasy nonetheless. The Conglomeros, meanwhile, was striving in bewilderment to make sense of the purpose and content of the debate, and was wholly oblivious to the intense scrutiny to which it was being subjected. It sat hunchbacked in its wheelchair, unconsciously shifting back and forth in its search for a comfortable position that it would never find in that narrow,

ungainly perch. Finally, the communist began his summa-
tion. "In short, tools make work, and work makes slaves,"
he concluded passionately. "What comfort is it to the slave
that, thanks to the printing press, he can now make books he
can't read? What comfort is it to the slave that, thanks to the
forge, he can now make metal ships he'll never sail in? No,
tools and technology are clearly the invention of capitalism
to enslave the masses." He was roundly applauded as he
resumed his seat by the washbasin.

The capitalist got up and argued that tools and technology
make all the products of labor of the same quality, and thus
deprive the skilled craftsman of his ability to excel. He, too,
rambled interminably before reaching his conclusion,
though Schaeffer and I seemed to be the only ones in the
room not deeply absorbed in the intricacies of his argument.
"We all work the same, we all use the same products," he
exhorted. "We become robots, machines ourselves. No,
tools are clearly the invention of Marxism to enslave the
masses." He acknowledged the cheers and retired to the
window ledge. Voting followed, and the capitalist won by a
handy majority.

"But they both came to the same conclusion," the Conglomeros whispered.

"Yes, isn't that strange?" I whispered back. "Shall we go
now?"

But, even had my companion been willing, it was too late,
for at that moment Forrest Schaeffer arose and cleared his
throat. In his hand he held a thick sheaf of papers, obviously
the text to the keynote "Art and Politics: Threat or Menace?"
speech. He swept the room imperiously with his piercing
gaze until there was absolute silence, and cleared his throat
again.

"Dialectical Variablism will help us to define the century
ahead. In the past, what people called the 'new'—in art, in
politics, in philosophy, in ethics—was limited to a novelty of

style or content. What has remained constant is the motor of that evolution, and that motor is—the truth. Variablism, however, tells us that our motors must change if we are to redefine our lives and our art. We must tear down the old monuments to Truth, and herald the impulse to Untruth!

"You want to talk about Morality, God, Love, the Universe? Fine! But for god's sake, lie about them! Lie to yourself! You know you can do it! You're just as likely to hit on the truth, anyway, than if you tried to tell the truth about them. The world is full of people who claim to be good, to be truthful, to have found the right way to live. They're wrong if they say they found it, and malicious to boot if they pretend to have passed it on. The Western tradition lies in that pretense—it's the only link common to centuries of . . ."

"Let's get out of here," I said, turning to my companion. But the Conglomeros didn't hear me: It was staring intently at the speaker, its eyes sparkling, its mouth half-open, the tip of its pink tongue protruding from one corner. I closed my eyes.

The speech went on for another half-hour, but I had stopped listening already, giving myself over to a deep brood. What could the Conglomeros hear in such twaddle to interest it? If it had ever heard me talk in that manner, I should now deserve to have it desert me ignominiously. But my instruction—not to mention its own innate, visceral sense of the universe—should have raised it far above this kitchen-table philosophizing, to the point where it could look down on abominations like Forrest Schaeffer and see them for what they really were. If I had said or done something to disenchant the creature, I might perhaps be made to understand this infatuation, this desertion; but I loved the creature more now than I had ever done, and had been treating it with infinite solicitude, generosity, and permissiveness. Or, finally, if this Schaeffer fellow had had something new and interesting to say, something that could by rights or by fantasy appeal to a Conglomeros more intimately than any of our intimacies over the last eight months, then I might even have been tempted—who knows?—to consign my lover to his care; but, it seemed to me, his pronouncements were trite and without any redeeming insight, his ideas unoriginal, and his physique . . . well. And yet, twist and turn as I might, the evidence remained in plain view: As its guru prattled on, the Conglomeros sat there, unblinking, with a look of such soulful devotion as to put a puppy dog to shame.

What was I missing, what subtle clue was right before my eyes that could possibly explain this unfortunate turn of events? I searched my memory in vain for a painting by Victor Brauner to help me through this difficult moment. But I was at least to catch a grosser hint of Schaeffer's motives when, from the depths of my melancholy meditation, I heard him mention the movement's need for a leader, a "charismatic evangelist" to take Variablism's word out into the world, and saw him direct a most meaningful look at my companion. If that was his intention—to groom Connie for the leadership of the institute—it would make a certain amount of sense: It was impossible to resist her open, joyous and intuitive approach to anything she encountered. But was that all that drew him to her? With the same perplexity with which I regarded the Conglomeros's fascination for Schaeffer, I was now compelled to ask myself what it was that Schaeffer saw in the Conglomeros—something that I, who was its constant companion, its mentor, and the guardian of its secret, had failed to intuit. Like a child overhearing the veiled sexual innuendo and euphemisms of an adult conversation, I was shamed by my inability to decipher the coded messages that passed between my lover and my nemesis that night. And like that child, my eventual mastery of that language would leave me none the wiser and none the happier. When the meeting broke up, Schaeffer asked my darling out for coffee, and because I was Connie's ride home, I was suffered to tag along. They spent hours over cappuccino in De Roberti's while I read the newspaper cover to cover. It was the most humiliating evening of my life.

Why should I drag it out? The reader has surely surmised that the situation was to deteriorate rapidly over the following weeks. What could I do? Lock the creature in our room, like some monstrous Lolita? Yes, I could have done that, and as a matter of fact I tried it on several occasions, but it proved finally an unsatisfying means for me to exert my moral prerogatives, or what few of them remained intact by that time. And, on a purely ethical level, I could hardly justify depriving the creature of that very independence for which I had unwittingly groomed it. No, things were changing, and despite my unremitting harangues, pleadings, scoldings, and attempted seductions, they had very soon moved beyond my capacities or supposed emotional jurisdiction to contain them. And why should I now impose a retrospective, psychological, or sociopathic analysis on what was happening? Let me give it its real name: This was the age-old battle for the affections of a loved one, and I was losing.

The days of art museums, opera, theater, poetry readings, and walks in the park went hard and fast by the wayside. Now, the Conglomeros asked for nothing better than to spend the entirety of every day with Schaeffer, whose days were free thanks to his evening work as music critic. At first, with commendable fortitude, I refused to ally myself with their unnatural relationship, and told the creature point-blank that if it wanted to go downtown every day it would have to find alternate means of transportation. Since tooling around town in a wheelchair by itself was out of the question, the Conglomeros was forced to adopt the painful two-legged walk on its sorties, and the daily sight of my beloved in such agony was more than I could endure. Relenting, I resumed my chauffeuring duties, dropping it off on Twelfth

Street in the morning and picking it up again at five-thirty every afternoon. How they spent their days I did not presume to inquire, nor did the Conglomeros offer much information in that regard. Our evenings were spent in desultory fashion—eating a silent meal at the kitchen table, perhaps watching a video that neither of us found entertaining, and were going to bed early to spend nights that, more and more, became devoted exclusively to sleep, and when they weren't probably should have been.

In all fairness, I must admit that it was mostly I who tainted the atmosphere of our relationship with gloom—the Conglomeros made sincere and prolonged efforts to sustain the ease and familiarity of our earlier days together since, in its mind, there was nothing wrong with a shared allegiance and thus no grounds for claims of victory or defeat—there simply was no competition. But I, naturally enough, and despite recognizing the comfort and validity of such an argument, could not muster such blithe insouciance, and I only had myself to blame, which made me feel even worse. I had taught the Conglomeros to behave and think as an independent human being, and now it was doing so: Only, as I kept thinking, there were so many ways of being independent— why did it have to choose this one? I was angry, humiliated, and confused; and I was in pain, so who could blame me for being morose and ever so slightly resentful in the presence of the ingrate who was causing me to suffer so dreadfully? This was the pain that Brauner had felt and depicted in "Coexistence," in which a woman is seen squirming within the belly of a beast, which has been transformed into an imprisoning cage. I daresay it is not as uncommon a pain as I imagined it at the time to be.

The changes wrought in the Conglomeros's character by its new companionship were, to me, distressing and immediately noticeable. They were all changes for the worse, and

I began to give some credence to Richard Hand's theory of transference. For one thing, the creature insisted on being called "Connie" now, where before it had always been content with terms of endearment. Now, whenever I let slip a "my pet" or "my dear beast," the Conglomeros would become indignant, fold its tentacular arms resolutely across its brow, and pronounce self-righteously, "My name is Connie." And I actually began to think of this new Conglomeros as "Connie." It wasn't the Conglomeros behaving this way, it wasn't the Conglomeros spitting on all my good intentions, it wasn't the Conglomeros breaking my heart—it was Connie, the six-legged monster.

And gradually, too, a condescending lilt crept into its voice that I had never heard before, a lecturing, pontifical tone. There was no reason to be so glum, Connie would tell me of a night in her adopted Latino accent. It was easy to wallow in my misery, why didn't I get out more, enjoy life? I might as well, she harangued, since I wasn't changing anything by moping. A whole person is a person who can integrate pain into his daily life and be the happier for it. Now, take someone like Forrest . . . I would leave the room, or turn on the television set.

It all happened so quickly I don't suppose I even considered that there might be larger implications. Sufficient unto the day was my own sense of shame and frustration, my jealousy and helpless rage, without torturing myself with imagined slights as well. At that point, I was just waiting for the Conglomeros to return to me; I wasn't thinking that things could get any worse than they already were . . .

"You know what Forrest told me today?" Connie said one evening as we picked through cold and half-eaten spaghetti in the dim light of the kitchen.

"No," I said. "What did he tell you?"

"He told me I was 'monstrously beautiful,' " Connie said in the prideful tone of a spoiled child.

"Did he now?"

"Isn't that pretty?"

"What's so pretty about it?" I snapped. "I tell you you're beautiful all the time."

"Yes," Connie said matter-of-factly, "but you're lying."

I dropped my cutlery in astonishment. Until recently, the creature did not even know the word "lying," so well had I protected it. And now, having taught the creature all it knew about mendacity, I was the first to be accused of it!

"Lying?" I screamed. "What do you mean, lying? Did he tell you I lied to you?"

"No, he didn't have to. It's obvious. When you say I'm beautiful, you only mean a part of me. When he says I'm beautiful, he means *all* of me. That's why he says I'm 'monstrously beautiful.' "

A horrifying thought occurred to me. "What do you mean by 'all of you'?"

"You know what I mean."

"No."

"I mean when we make love. He touches me all over. There are parts of my body you won't even acknowledge!"

"You make *love* to him?"

"That's not the point, what I'm . . ."

"Of course that's the point!" I was almost out of control, hyperventilating, my voice rising to a dizzying falsetto. "My feelings aside, don't you realize that if *he* knows what you really are, then . . ."

"I'm not ashamed of the way I am! The rest of you are just cheap imitations. You don't have enough limbs and you've only got one sex apiece! Why do you want me to be ashamed?"

"I'm not ashamed! It's just that it's so dangerous. If just *one* wrong person finds out about you, one reporter, one scientist, one . . . lawyer . . ."

"I trust him," Connie spat. "I trust him a lot more than I

trust you!" And she swept from the room, slamming the door.

I remembered how once—such a long, long time before—the Conglomeros had expressed such joy that there was a word for everything you could want to say. But I don't think there is a word for what I felt then, alone at the kitchen table in the half-light. How can a person discover, all in the space of two minutes, that he has lost someone's love, fidelity, respect, and trust, and expect to find a word that means what he's feeling? And if such a word did exist, he wouldn't want to say it, not even whisper it, not even there, where he finds himself neck-deep and sinking fast in the formless tarpit that he once called his soul. I'm not sure how long I sat there, feeling my life's blood turn to vinegar in my veins. But I do remember thinking how there was one more thing I had to know. I found Connie in the living room, curled up in a corner of the sofa, reading Bulgakov's *Heart of a Dog*. I was very rational, very subdued.

"Let me ask you this," I said. "Do you remember when I saved your life, how you . . . ?"

The creature snorted derisively without looking up. "You never saved my life," it scoffed.

"Of course I did. When I found you, you were sick, dying. I nursed you back to health."

"Don't be stupid. I wasn't sick. I was hibernating; you woke me up. *That's* what made me sick."

"Oh."

What else did I have to lose?

"Why don't you love me anymore?" I asked.

"I do love you."

"Then what do you see in him that you don't in me?"

"Nothing."

"I don't understand."

"You really don't, do you?"

"No."

"What I see in him," said Connie, putting down her book, "is that he's just like you."

"What?"

"You and he are exactly alike. That's why I love him, because he's just like you. He's even more like you than you are, but he's honest enough to admit it."

"But he's nothing like me! That guy is a joker, he's a deceiver, a confidence man! He only wants you for what he can get out of you, he doesn't love you for your own sake. He'll try to manipulate you and use you and make you serve his purposes! He'll break your heart! He's an opportunist!"

The Conglomeros, picking up its book, didn't even bother to reply, since we both knew the only answer it could have given.

▲▲▲▲

For the next few days there was a deep silence between us, and then I received a telegram from England, summoning me to my mother's deathbed. I was on a flight to London that very evening. The plane landed in the early morning, and by ten o'clock I was in a rented car and on my way to the old manor house in Sussex. An intercom system had been installed at the gates, which glided open when I announced myself. I drove up the white-gravel drive and was greeted at the door by Nurse Goodman.

"Mr. X.," she said, shaking my hand, "what a pleasant surprise, sir. Welcome to Oakshott Hall." But seeing the look on my face, she shook her head. "She's done it again, hasn't she, sir?"

"Yes, I'm afraid she has, nurse," I said sternly.

Nurse Goodman accompanied me down a long corridor of the east wing, dappled with the light streaming through windows overlooking the formal gardens. As we passed each window, I looked for my mother among the patients strolling along the paths or seated on the benches, but she was not there. Nurse Goodman knocked at number 31A and left me at the door. I went in without waiting for an answer.

My mother was sitting up in bed, reading a book, her shoulders draped with a shawl. Her hair was wild as a nest, and she seemed to have grown a little paler and a little thinner, but she was otherwise no worse than the last time I had seen her. As usual, she was smoking a cigarette through a rubber tube attached to a cigarette holder welded to an ashtray that was clamped to an arm of her wheelchair by the bed.

"Hi, Mom."

She looked up and smiled a crooked smile. She held out two shaking hands, which I took in my own and kissed.

"Hi, baby," she said. "I thought you were dead."

"*I* thought *you* were dead. You know, you really shouldn't send telegrams like that."

"How else can I get you to come more than once a year?" Her lower lip began to tremble, and she turned her head. It was precisely scenes such as this that prevented me from coming more often. I grabbed her chin and pulled her face toward me.

"You know you just have to ask and I'll come. Just ask, Mom."

"But I don't like to bother . . ."

"So you send fake telegrams?"

"Didn't it work? How'd you like them apples?"

"You're crazy," I said, and gave her a hug. She was definitely frailer than last time—my knuckles rapped hollowly on her shoulder blades—and she smelled incontinent. "How're you feeling, sweetheart?"

"I'm dying."

"So what's new? You've been dying for five years. Every time I see you you're dying."

"And so? You think a person can't take five years to die? Or ten, or twenty, if she needs it? Boy, have I got news for you, Sonny Jim." She paused momentarily. "This place is killing me, Ari," she said softly.

What could I tell her that I hadn't told her a hundred times? She knew every argument by heart, since we had the same conversation every time I visited. She knew she needed professional care, that her illness, though not in itself fatal, had advanced beyond the possibility of home treatment; she knew that the money paying for the care couldn't leave England; she knew that the care here was much better and more personal than anything she could get in an American home; she knew she had lived in England for so long that she would feel lost and out-of-place back in the States; and she knew that I couldn't take care of her, for a variety of good reasons. Still, like some well-worn litany that comforts through repetition, she insisted on trotting out the same complaint, eliciting the same answers, year after year. For her sake, I went through the routine yet again, and then I lifted her into the wheelchair and we went for a stroll around the grounds. We sat in the shade of the rhododendrons and talked about her health, my health, about the old times when the family had consisted of more than just the two of us. Later, I took her in to lunch, cutting her food and feeding her, since her hands shook too much to do it for herself. After lunch, I wheeled her back into her room for a nap, and sat in the sunshine outside her French windows until an orderly came to wake her up and change her diaper.

"You know," she said later as I sat at her bedside, "there *is* something else." Somehow, through the heaviness of her lids and the yellowish sag of her cheeks, she managed a coy look.

"I thought as much."

"I hear you got a new girl."

"You hear . . . ?"

"A young girl. A very young girl."

"I don't know what you're talking about, Mom. I don't have a girl. Who've you been talking to?"

"There." She nodded toward her dressing table, and I opened the top drawer. "The cigar box." I placed the box on her lap, and she pulled out an envelope that rustled like a tree as she handed it to me.

"Read it."

I opened the envelope, pulled out two small sheets of onion paper covered in a tiny, florid handwriting, and read.

> June 10, 198–
>
> Dear Mrs. X.,
>
> It is with a great sense of urgency that I have taken the liberty of writing to you without ever having made your acquaintance. Please believe me, Mrs. X., when I say that I would never consider taking such a liberty, or allow myself to interfere in the personal lives of others, were the situation not quite so desperate and in need of such urgent remedy.
>
> I am a friend of your son, Aaron, and it is with regard to him that I write you today. Aaron, on a recent journey abroad, made the acquaintance of my niece, and that acquaintance was renewed on the occasion of her arrival in the United States for a short visit with me. To put it bluntly, Mrs. X., the friendship between them rapidly developed into a romance, and my niece now refuses to return to her native country, preferring instead to destroy her life and prospects by remaining with your son. My pleas for reason, both to the girl and to your son, have gone unheeded, and so I write to you in the fervent hope that you will consent to wielding a mother's influence to the moderation of your son's irresponsible behavior.
>
> I have been Aaron's friend for some time, and in other circumstances have known him to be a sober, dutiful, and mature man of decision. In this instance, however,

he is beyond my powers of persuasion. The girl is very young, and still has her studies before her. She is alone in a foreign country—as she refuses to see me—and therefore entirely dependent on your son. She has led an extremely sheltered life and has no parents to guide her through her transition into adulthood. Furthermore, like most girls of her age, she is prone to making rash and ill-considered decisions. The responsible thing for your son to do, if he truly loves her, is to send her home to her school and guardians and to wait until she is mature enough to take the wisest course. I have taken certain legal consultations and find that, because the girl is not a minor in this country, I have no recourse to the law in this matter. I beg you, therefore, as a mother yourself and my last hope for my motherless niece, to do everything in your power to dissuade Aaron from the destructive and selfish path on which he is embarked.

I thank you from the bottom of my heart for your kind patience in this matter, and earnestly urge you to look favorably upon my request.

Yours sincerely,
Richard Hand
— W. 113 St., NYC 10025

I read the letter through again, shaking my head in disbelief.

"It's true, then?"

"Some of it."

"Which some?"

"Don't worry about it, Mom. It's over between us."

"You sent her away?"

"She dumped me for another guy. She's not what Richard thinks she is. Or me. The girl is a monster, she's not human."

"How bad could she be, a girl so young, so inexperienced?"

"Trust me, Mom, she's bad news. She's just . . . she's . . . she's bad . . ."

"Poor Ari. There, there . . ."

▲▲▲▲

I returned home a few days later, thoughts of revenge on Richard Hand uppermost in my mind. That he should want to keep his word to Victor Brauner was one thing, but that he should be delving into my family affairs was absolutely inexcusable. All the indignation, humiliation and heartache I had endured over the past weeks I focused on unleashing in our first interview, and on the drive home from the airport I was already beginning to feel sorry for the old geezer. But all my prepared speeches, all of my carefully sculpted and polished wrath, all thoughts of vengeance evaporated as I walked through the front door of our apartment.

The place reeked of booze, stale cigarettes, and marijuana. Every shade in the room was drawn, every window closed and, despite the heat outdoors, the air conditioning off. Empty bottles and overflowing ashtrays littered the living room, along with magazines, plates encrusted with days-old food, clothing male and female, towels; every cushion from the sofa was on the floor, as was every record from the rack and every glass and bottle from the liquor cabinet. The kitchen was no better, and the master bedroom infinitely worse.

As I flung open the door, I was met with a blast of frigid air, and there, on the bed, only partially covered by the rumpled sheets, sat the Conglomeros and Forrest Schaeffer like monarchs receiving homage, eating chocolate-chip cookies from a bag. A videotape of *E.T.: The Extra-Terrestrial* was playing on the television.

"Welcome home," the creature said, smiling sweetly. "How was your trip?"

"Get out," I said to Schaeffer.

"Forrest has moved in with us, sweetheart."

"Get out."

"He stays or I go, sweetheart."

"Fine."

▲▲▲▲

I have to admit that Richard Hand received me far more graciously than I had him; toward my own state of suffering, I might say, he was even solicitous, which was perhaps more generous than the situation warranted. In short, by his kindness and gentleness he put me to shame, and in the distressed, almost distracted state in which I arrived at his apartment that very morning, I was particularly grateful for his compassion.

He sat quietly fingering the strap of his eyepatch as I described the current state of affairs and the events leading up to them, including my own discovery of the Conglomeros's existence. At no point did he interrupt, except when the kettle boiled, though my narrative was a long one and, I realized as I told it, not entirely palatable to a sensitive heart.

When I had finished my tale, he began to pace as we moved on to a discussion of the current situation and the courses of action, if any, that were open to us. In his even-handedness, Richard Hand agreed with my assessment that Forrest Schaeffer was an even greater potential threat to the Conglomeros than I was. We also concurred in detecting an unquestionable deterioration in the creature's intellectual, moral, and emotional development, a deterioration which, as he had once intimated to me, could only be checked by removing the degenerating catalyst. Lastly, we agreed that the creature would not willingly relinquish that catalyst, and that it was thus our most solemn and unshirkable duty to act independently on its behalf in order to compel it to do so.

How to go about that was another matter entirely. Richard Hand insisted that the creature could be saved only by being returned to its native land and released to the wild, thereby allowing its primal instincts to reemerge as they had done when Victor left in 1938. I, however, tried to explain to him that the Conglomeros had diverged so far from its original, natural way of life, had been eating cooked and refined food for so long, and had become so accustomed to human company and corrruption that to fling it back on its own resources might prove fatal. I found it hard to believe that the creature could ever return to what it had once been. Hand insisted, however, that nature always reasserts itself, as witnessed by the ruins of great cities and great empires found in deepest tropical forests or in grass-grown meadows. Even New York City, he said, if left to itself would eventually return to primeval forest, as humans return to savagery when deprived of a civilizing environment. In argument, I pointed out that animals raised in captivity usually die when released abruptly to the world. I was for a gradual deprogramming, a slow reintroduction to the old way and weaning from human dependencies.

But as we argued through the afternoon, there arose a consensus between us on one inevitability: The Conglomeros would have to be forcibly removed from Schaeffer's influence, which Schaeffer might have to be forcibly restrained from exerting. In other words: kidnap. When once the creature was safely in our custody, there would be ample opportunity to decide on an appropriate course of action regarding its rehabilitation.

By the time we had reached this conclusion, dusk was already beginning to fall. Exhausted as I was by my transatlantic journey and the emotional upheavals of the day, I suggested that we interrupt our scheming and resume it on the morrow, to which Hand acceded. Knowing how I felt about Schaeffer, he was kind enough to offer me a room for the night. I declined, intending to return home just long enough to pack some clean things and reserve myself a room in some midtown hotel. But that proved unnecessary, as it happened, since on my arrival I found that the apartment had been cleaned from top to bottom and that Connie and Forrest had vanished, leaving a note thanking me for my hospitality and wishing me the best of luck in my future endeavors.

I was not to see the Conglomeros again for another six months. That is, I saw "Connie" often enough—far too often, given the circumstances—but only at a distance and rarely in person; and even in such instances, I was never but once afforded the opportunity to speak, to reason, or to plead with the creature. For, as the long, torrid summer months gave way to autumn, it gradually became clear to me that, under Forrest Schaeffer's tutelage, the Conglomeros was being groomed for the "leadership" position of which I had heard him speak and that, as I had predicted, its new mentor intended to exploit his captive toward his own ruthless ends, whatever those might entail. Attending this corruption as I must from afar, I could only look on in horrified rage and frustration.

Nor was it for lack of effort that I found myself helpless to intervene. During the first few weeks following the infamous desertion, I laid siege to my rival's apartment, bombarding it with telephone calls that were always intercepted by an answering machine smugly informing me that "Forrest and Connie can't come to the phone right now, but if you'll leave a message after the tone, we'll get right back to you"—which, needless to day, they never did. I inundated their hideaway with letters that went unanswered, telegrams, flowers, eggplant pizzas. Day after day I planted myself across the street from the front door of their tenement on Twelfth Street—all to no avail.

They were obviously well prepared to withstand my assault. There was a constant flow of Forrest's friends in and out of the apartment—I quickly learned to recognize and distinguish them from the building's legitimate inhabitants—laden with provisions and presumably reporting on my movements. Since I could not be there twenty-four hours a day, I guessed that they took the air in the evenings, and I varied my schedule accordingly but equally in vain. Furthermore, on one of the earliest of my evening vigils, I encountered the tall, sallow blond woman who had been Schaeffer's companion the night we met. She was leaving the building in tears, black freshets of mascara running down her cheeks, and informed me bitterly that it was all over between her and Schaeffer. She was only too happy to describe the lurid goings-on in the fourth-story studio—all-night indoctrination sessions, Schaeffer sitting at the foot of the wheelchair, plying Connie with visions of moral hegemony and apostolic worship; the constant background activities of acolytes bearing victuals, cleaning house, delivering and receiving messages; the bunker atmosphere heightened by lack of sleep, tantrums rabid on Schaeffer's part and hysterical on Connie's, and the abrupt interruptions occasioned by their regular withdrawals into the inner sanctum of the curtained alcove, whence would emanate the humid sighs and maniacal cackling that had finally driven the blonde from the apartment in tearful recognition of defeat. It was clear from the way she described the Conglomeros—"hunch-backed bitch" was one of her milder epithets—that she had no inkling of the creature's true physical nature, and that Schaeffer had evidently deemed it expeditious to keep the knowledge of that little anomaly to himself, for the time being. But for how long? Obviously, if and when the creature's secret was publicly revealed, the situation would pass beyond the capacity for one person, no matter how manipulative or firm of will, to control or dominate, and so it was of minor comfort to me to realize that that revelation would not be soon in coming. Schaeffer knew as well as I did what side his bread was buttered on. My comfort, however, was more than extenuated by my shame and fury in learning that not only were the two perfectly aware of my presence at their doorstep, but that this presence afforded them no end of mirth and spiteful witticisms at my expense. The blond woman told me all of this in a tone of voice that left me in no doubt that she had little sympathy to spare for my plight, and that she contemptuously regarded me as an even bigger sap than herself, with which determination, as I watched her stumble wearily off in her spike heels and black Lycra minidress, I could only concur.

Finally, however, taking up my post late one balmy night in June, I managed to surprise them returning from a stroll. I watched their progress up the street, and it shook me to the marrow: The creature hunched in its wheelchair in full disguise, Forrest blithely pushing from behind, they were engaged in conversation, the Conglomeros turning occasionally to laugh with its captor over some *bon mot* or other, and I realized with a deep pang of nostalgic recognition and regret that they looked very much as the two of us must once have looked, what seemed already a very long time ago. As they approached, I emerged from the shadows of the doorway in which I had concealed myself and planted myself directly in their path.

The sight of me before them, standing legs apart, fists clenched, trembling from head to toe and deathly pale in the glow of the streetlamps, stopped them in their tracks. The smile failed on the Conglomeros's lips and it turned its head away. Forrest Schaeffer merely rolled his eyes and tsked in exasperation. At that point I was indifferent to the image I presented, however pathetic, but the tone of my voice belied my violent posturing.

"Don't you have anything to say to me?" I whined, but the creature refused to meet my gaze. I crouched down to bring our eyes level.

"Why can't you talk to me?" I went on.

"Listen, Aaron," Schaeffer said as if he were speaking to a recalcitrant, bad-tempered child. "Just this morning Connie and I had a talk, and I told her, 'It's perfectly natural to have murderous thoughts about the ones who love you. After all, they have murderous thoughts about you.'" He smirked. "And you know what she said? She said, yes, you had once told her exactly the same thing." He flashed me one of his vampirical, bloody-mouthed grins and rolled the wheelchair around me as if I were no more than a troublesome pothole. The two of them disappeared into the building in silence, while I found myself rooted to the pavement, curiously powerless to stand up.

Later that night, I paid a visit to Richard Hand and, I am ashamed to admit, I wept in the old man's arms. I spent a fitful night on his sofa, listening to the laughter and shouting of students reveling below. In the morning, Richard Hand urged me to lift my siege—it could only alienate my quarry further, and was doing my own health and mental balance no good whatsoever. Reluctantly, I allowed myself to be persuaded, and agreed with him that practical planning and patience would be far more helpful in achieving a reconciliation or, should necessity dictate, a successful kidnapping. Richard helped me to understand, too, that my actions had played into Schaeffer's hands. My siege, forcing him as it had done to remain holed up, had given him ample leisure to formulate a plan of his own, and to poison his captive's mind against me, with what evident success I had already witnessed. And when the two of them were once more free to roam the streets at will, he was able to put that plan into action, which he did with an expediency and on a scale that left me breathless.

Having compelled myself as an exercise in self-control to avoid the East Village altogether for several weeks, the first time I heard anything about it was from Dave, one evening as we drank morosely in an Irish bar on Eighth Avenue. We were talking about our old hangouts and exploits back in the days when Sarah was still alive, and Dave, either unwittingly or by design, mentioned a café on Tenth Street that had been one of our favorite spots. It soon came out that, in recent days, he had spotted Schaeffer and the Conglomeros there on several occasions, surrounded by a small assembly consisting for the most part of the Variablist contingent. Though he had not approached the forum gathered in the café garden giving onto the street, it had been clear that "Connie" was soliloquizing in a manner that held "her" audience in rapt attention. It had reminded him, he said cautiously, of nothing so much as Plato in the groves, and for some inexplicable reason had caused the hairs to rise on his neck. I knew what he meant: Merely in listening to his incoherent account, I too felt a coldness envelop my heart.

Over the course of the next few weeks, having a good deal of free time on my hands and a great rent in my soul, both of which required filling, I began looking up some of my old friends. Though I made sincere efforts at these reunions to concentrate on their personal anecdotes and updates, I'm afraid that I alienated many of them by my constant references to Connie. Whether they felt it inappropriate for a recent widower to wax obsessive about his lover, or whether they were simply offended by my apparent indifference to their own stories, since I had been the one to insist on our meeting, few of them had the courtesy so much as to call me in thanks for the lavish dinners to which I treated them. That, however, was of no consequence to me, since in answer to my persistent questioning it turned out that a number of them still living downtown were able to report sightings of Connie holding forth, always closely shadowed by Schaeffer, in Tompkins Square, Roosevelt Park, St. Mark's churchyard, the fountain in Washington Square, various cafés, coffeehouses, and after-hours clubs—anywhere, it seemed, was an appropriate marketplace for her perorations. One of these friends, an out-of-work film editor who spent the first half-hour of our meeting enumerating the calamities of his existence, had even listened to and been won over by the creature's oratory. I gathered that the sermon, or whatever it was, had been liberally imbued with homily, parable, and reference to the "teachings" of Dialectical Variablism. Against my better judgment and Richard Hand's warnings, and aware of the pain and damage I was likely to inflict on myself, I determined to attend one of these gatherings in person. Asking around, I was informed that the most likely place to come upon it was by the bandshell in Tompkins Square, to which I took myself one sweltering afternoon in mid-August.

As the bandshell came into view, I was shocked to see a crowd of thirty or more people congregated in a tight circle in its shadow. Those near the edge were standing, while those closer to the center sat on the ground like children around a storyteller. I recognized some of the faces from my evening at Schaeffer's apartment; the rest of the listeners consisted of an altogether incongruous mixture of punks, skinheads, homeless people, some artist types, and even a few young businessmen and women from the newly converted condominium across the way. Except for the homeless, they were all young—white, black, Hispanic, Oriental. And at the hub of the circle sat the Conglomeros in full regalia, its wheelchair raised some two feet off the ground by a makeshift plywood ramp. Forrest Schaeffer stood directly behind the creature, smiling serenely as it gesticulated with its two free arms.

I approached, concealing myself behind a low bank of shrubbery, close enough to hear while yet remaining undetected. The creature's talk held the audience's undivided attention.

"... the man who, on his deathbed, recited the *Star Trek* litany and, with its terrible, dark, and foreboding split infinitive—expired.

"And so you ask me about the soul. What do I know—what do any of us know—about the soul? If you want to believe someone else's lies about the soul, there are plenty of them to choose from. Go off to your church, your synagogue, your mosque, your ashram—listen, believe, and good luck. But as a Variablist, I say that since it's all lies, why not believe the lie of your own making? Who is to say it isn't the truth, and who is to stop you making it the truth? Be as simple as you are sweet: If the carpenter builds a table and chooses to call it a bed, who's to stop him sleeping on it, if he sleeps well? And who will wake him to tell him it's not a bed?"

I couldn't listen to any more. As I crouched behind the hedge, my head reeled and my tears mingled with the sweat pouring off my brow. Such tripe, flowing from a mouth that until so recently had been a dispensary of simple, beautiful truths! And those truths, worthy of veneration as they had been, both their speaker and I had taken so unseeingly for granted—it was only now that they were lost that the creature, like every self-proclaimed prophet who has ever sought to speak the truth, was attempting to pass off their shadows for the substance. Yet, I knew why the crowd remained entranced—I, too, had been in the thrall of that mesmerizing voice and presence, though back in the days when they did not stink with corruption and burn the nostrils with iniquity.

And behold how under Schaeffer's influence the creature's degeneration had progressed far more rapidly than even I, who understood only too well its capacity to metabolize received knowledge, could ever have anticipated. I loved the Conglomeros more than life itself, since I owed it my life, but at that moment the sight of it disgusted and appalled me beyond all measure. I could have murdered Schaeffer on the spot, if I had thought that his death could have saved my beloved or reconciled the creature to me. I stumbled disoriented from the park, and returned to report to Richard Hand. Upon hearing my somewhat garbled account of the sermon in the bandshell, he concurred with my appraisal of the situation: Something had to be done, and quickly, to separate the Conglomeros from its evil taskmaster. We both acknowledged that we were now in "virgin territory," far beyond Victor Brauner's experience and capacity to guide our actions.

We began to formulate a plan of our own, and a viable one was not as easy to design as one might suppose. The actual act of kidnapping could probably be accomplished without untoward difficulty, though neither of us had ever perpetrated one ourselves. Some egregious diversion, a waiting van, and the creature could be spirited away in a matter of moments. But after that? Neither Hand nor myself could ever dare to contemplate a return to Romania, and in any case, despite Brauner's experience, I still did not believe that releasing the creature into its native home was a feasible solution. Obviously, then, it would have to be transported to my house in the country, and forcibly held until its formidable regenerative powers gradually healed and returned it to its natural state, or as near enough as its present deterioration would allow—a sort of surrealist version of *Born Free*. But Schaeffer would know immediately who had captured his meal ticket, and it would not take a private detective long to discover the location of our hideaway. The question remained, then, whether Schaeffer would attempt to regain ascendancy over the Conglomeros by persuasion, or whether he was malevolent enough to call in the police at the risk of exposing the creature's secret. Either way, the risk was too great. The only other alternative, short of actually murdering Schaeffer—an option which, I must confess, we briefly considered before discarding—was to remain perpetually on the run, driving from state to state, from shore to plain to mountain to shore and back. But that, clearly, was no way to achieve our primary goal of rehabilitating the creature that had been so cruelly abused and so ruthlessly exploited.

Like all men of moral integrity, we found ourselves foundering in a quagmire of considerations, essentially impotent against "men of action"—men who will use any means to an end—such as Schaeffer. We squabbled back and forth for weeks, trying to reach a solution that would satisfy each other as well as the ethical requirements of the instance, while Schaeffer's hold over my ward grew daily stronger and evidence of his evil designs ever more apparent and public. Almost every day, it seemed, I heard reports from Dave and those of my few remaining sympathetic friends who understood the nature (if not the cause) of my quandary—reports that described the ever-larger crowds attending the creature's "sermons," the ever-more vociferous, charismatic inflections and inflammations of the speaker, and their increasingly mystical effect on their audience. Hand and I continued to bicker, and the mounting sense of desperation and hysteria surrounding our predicament made a consensus that much harder to reach. It was only when I came across an ad in *The Village Voice* for the upcoming "Wit and Wisdom of Connie Lo Meros" at Performance Space 122 that I put my foot down: The kidnapping had to take place before the performance, before the creature's face became known to a wider public—the Conglomeros would be whisked off to my estate and held pending further deliberations. It was the desperate act of desperate men, and needless to say, it failed miserably.

The plan was gloriously simple and ill-considered. We were to drive a rented van to a vantage point on the square from which we could watch our quarry's every move. When the gathering broke up, we would be able to determine the exit toward which they were heading and direct our vehicle accordingly. By the time they reached the exit, the van would be stationed directly in front, side doors open and ramp in place. At the opportune moment, we would leap out, Hand would fall to the ground as if in pain, I would grab the Conglomeros while Schaeffer was distracted, wheel it into the van, drive off, switch van for car at my place, and head for the hills, where Hand would join us the next day.

We chose the day before the performance to execute our devious stratagem. Everything seemed to be proceeding smoothly as we pulled the van up to the southwest exit of the square on Seventh Street. But as we leapt from the van, we were horrified to see that Schaeffer and the Conglomeros were not alone—an enormous contingent of the audience, some fifty people at least, was following them like the children of Hamelin. As we stood, mouths agape, the laughing, singing crowd swept us aside and moved off down Avenue A.

After the incident of the botched kidnapping, I'm afraid to say that I rather gave up hope. And who could blame me? Like an honest man in local government, my cause seemed to be a lost one. All evidence pointed to the fact that the course of degeneration was too mature to staunch and that its parasitical source was growing daily stronger and more brazen. Even the stoical Richard Hand, always more optimistic than I, seemed to crumble, a moribund pallor rising to his sunken cheeks, an ugly, listless dejection creeping into his voice, his withered hands rioting in fits of trembling. No doubt we made a sorry sight, the two of us, in our self-indulgent depression. And now, of course, I cannot repress the thought that, had I concentrated less on my own sense of inadequacy and guilt in the business, and more on the hard necessity of saving the victim whom I had delivered into the hands of evil, the course of events might somehow have devolved differently. . . .

Be that as it may, I gave up my pursuit of the creature, though not my precious pain. Oh, yes, I followed its progress assiduously in the media and on the grapevine, I constantly asked after my beloved to those who were in contact with it, I attended some of its meetings, and I continued to love it and to dream nightly of its return—all without lifting one miserable finger to further that end. Throughout the months that followed, perhaps the worst in my entire life, I joyed only in the perverse recognition of my own culpability, the way certain deeply religious people wallow in the luxuriant stench of their own sinfulness. And I watched the rise of "Connie Lo Meros" with a sort of detached, sullen satisfaction, knowing that, whatever Schaeffer had done to bring the flower to blossom, it was I who had planted and nurtured the seedling.

And that rise was frighteningly meteoric. Of course, I did not attend the performance at P.S. 122, but rumor had it a spectacular success, and *The Village Voice* ran a two-column review the next week. The headline, juxtaposed against a close-up of the creature's face in sunglasses, wig, hat, and— oh, god!—pink lipstick, heralded "The Ugly Truth" of the creature's sermon. The article lavishly praised "Ms. Lo Meros's almost prophetic ability to rehabilitate the self-evidence of ancient truths" and her "New Testament bombast and rhetoric." (Throughout the ensuing months, media coverage would be heavily weighted with biblical reference.) It also managed to equate the performer's "spectacularly hideous appearance" with a modern reincarnation of Oedipus' Sphinx. Finally, the article concluded that the monologue had "oracled the demise of postmodernism, and perhaps of the Western postindustrial sensibility. Ms. Lo Meros may have given us an advance preview of twenty-first-century dialectics: an ugly truth, beyond any doubt, but an irreducible one for all that." Need I describe my nauseated reaction to this reading?

The review, coming at a time when several downtown monologuists were beginning to attract the attention of the commercial theatrical establishment and media, elicited widespread interest in Connie Lo Meros. She was soon performing her monologues at most of the larger downtown spaces to houses packed with her converts, while her free "sermons" made Tompkins Square a *de rigueur* stop-off for Gray Line tourist buses. The Institute of Dialectical Variablism was formally incorporated and took over the Specula Bunker as its headquarters, publishing a weekly newsletter that was distributed free and, so rumor had it, commanded very respectable rates for its advertising space. When they were not touring the West Coast or locked up with their business associates, Connie and Schaeffer could be found mingling on any night of the week at one of the trendy nightclubs of the moment, and their faces soon became regular features in the back-page photographic gossip column of New York's premier muckraking rag. It was even said that the new concrete ramp outside Jupiter had been installed specifically to accommodate Connie's wheelchair. When "Andy" suddenly ceased frequenting Panjandrum, precipitating a disastrous decline in the club's fortunes, Connie was popularly supposed to have influenced his abrupt defection. It was only a matter of time, I guessed, before she would appear in ads for "Amaretto de Connie." And her followers, the faithful, kept growing in number.

All of this, I might add, happened within the span of a few short months, and if it seems improbable, I can only hypothesize the effect modern electronic communications would have had on any number of ancient gospels. I do not care, however, to dwell at length on this period of my life. It is too painful, and besides, the whims and ephemerality of New York glory have been too exhaustively explored by others for me to be able to add anything new. In any case, we have seen such things happen often enough in recent times to obviate any obsolete reaction of amazement or dismay, which prevented neither me nor Richard Hand from expressing both with increasing acrimony.

I can remember, for instance, a day in November that ranks particularly low in the annals of my despair. It was one of those marvelously crisp, sunny days in late autumn, and I was strolling through the streets of midtown, for once almost oblivious to the weight of oppression that had hung on my shoulders since the spring. But my happy oblivion was not destined to last, for as I passed a discount electronics store I was confronted with the Conglomeros's face— Connie's face—refracted in the screens of dozens of television sets banked against the windowpane. Despite myself, I entered the store.

The creature was a guest on a local cable talk show, being interviewed by some pedantic, self-appointed guardian of avant-garde culture. Hunched as always in its wheelchair, the Conglomeros sat with Forrest Schaeffer on the podium, while the host wagged his head and squinted.

". . . the schizophrenic relationship of the artist to society," the creature was saying. "Not long ago, the artist was proud and free and bold, and society cast him out. Now, the artist is a paranoid, hysterical introvert, and society lionizes him. You see, a true individual is detested in a . . ."

> Host: "So what you're trying to say is that we all ask things from ourselves that . . . because we're unhappy . . . and society doesn't . . ."
> Conglomeros: "No, what I mean to say is, these things might all be tragic, but they are not tragedies, if you see what I mean. I . . ."
> Schaeffer: "I think what you mean is they're all tragedies, but they're not really *tragic,* is that it?"
> Conglomeros: "Yes, perhaps. Anyway, I . . ."
> Host: "Good difference, good difference."

"Sir? Are you all right?" the shop clerk asked solicitously, tapping me on the shoulder.

"Yes, I'm fine," I sniffled.

"Well, would you mind not leaning your head against the screen?"

I returned home, and later that evening I once more drenched Richard Hand's fatherly shoulder with my bitter tears.

▲▲▲▲

I don't wish to give the impression, however, that I spent those terrible months moping and feeling sorry for myself. In that, as in many regards, Richard Hand was very kind to me, and I grew to rely on him for guidance and solace. Though he himself, having failed in his mission to protect the creature from the outside world, must have been almost as grief stricken as I, he was ever ready to put a rosy complexion on the state of affairs, to reassure me of my innocence, and when all else failed, to comfort me with his silent, avuncular presence. I came to realize, too, more through his constant availability to my needs than through anything he might have told me about himself, that the comfort sought and provided in each other's company was not entirely unilateral, for he was a very lonely old man with few friends and no family, the latter having been mostly killed during the Nazi occupation or having died soon thereafter. Thus we mourned together, the measure of our sorrow borne out in the companionship in which it bound us.

But it was Richard Hand who, in September, suggested that I try to alleviate my suffering by reintegrating myself into the world of the living, by which he implied not only the contrast between self-indulgence and a useful life, but also that between the infirmities of old age and the energy of youth. In other words, he was concerned about my spending too much time with him, and he urged me to the point of redundancy to seek out new stimuli, new preoccupations, new friends, in my attempt to put the past behind me. At first, I flatly refused: His health remained fragile, though far improved since the time of his release from jail, and I felt that he needed me—my company—at least as much as I did him. But he was insistent, and went out of his way to furnish proof of his own autonomy. Finally, then, I did as he requested simply to spare him the exertion of persuading me, and later I recognized that his advice had been sound.

So it was that I returned to my volunteer work with the homeless and the elderly. I spent two afternoons a week at the senior citizens' drop-in center near Port Authority, and my weekends at a soup kitchen in a synagogue on the Upper West Side. My work in these places helped me twofold: first, in an immediate way, by preventing me from dwelling morbidly on my own problems and compelling me to concentrate on those less fortunate than I; second, and more important, by allowing me to put the events of the past year in perspective and thereby to understand and reconcile myself to the role I had played in them. For although I never at any time attempted to mitigate my own culpability in the disaster that had befallen us, I did come clearly to see that I had behaved much as any human being would have done in similar circumstances. Normally, that fact in itself would have been cripplingly depressing, but I was grasping at straws and finding comfort wherever I could. No, I realized that, just as a person grows up and begins as an adult to behave in the precise manner which he had forsworn as a child, I had gradually become the monster while the Conglomeros had grown into its potential humanity, and that this was the most natural thing for a human being to have done, as if it were a pattern grafted on our genetic makeup. Indeed, I imagined, it was the story of human history. And if I had been unable to take that final leap into irredeemable monstrosity, somebody had to be there to do it, and Forrest Schaeffer had been. In other words, if I hadn't been there to nurture the Conglomeros into the world, somebody else would eventually have had to. I do not wish to make an even greater fool of myself by delving into philosophy—there will no doubt be enough philosophers ready to do that for me—but I found these and other similar thoughts strangely comforting at the time. My nights, for the most part, were spent quietly with Richard or advancing in my Bible correspondence course.

Nor was the volunteer work my only effort at obliterating my pain. In November, shortly after the incident at the television store, Richard Hand persuaded me to pay an extended visit to my mother, and I in turn persuaded him to accompany me. It was a surprise visit, and she was suitably thrilled. We stayed at a local inn and spent each of our ten days there with her, from morning to night. She was very happy to meet Richard, and he made up a story for her about his niece having been safely restored to her guardians in Romania. At first, Richard felt the need to absent himself for a portion of the day, in consideration of an imagined need for my mother and me to be alone together. But it was soon evident that an abiding friendship, a sense of kinship perhaps, was growing between him and my mother, to the extent that, by the time we were ready to leave, I was the one who felt in the way. Indeed, he took her for several solitary strolls through the grounds of the home, and watching the two of them put me in mind yet again of the happy days when I, too, had pushed a wheelchair; I grew so thoughtful at the sight that, when they returned, they had to cajole me into a cheerful humor, and it felt like family. We all cried when the time to part was upon us, and I even promised to look into the possibilities of sending for her in New York, which promise Richard Hand heavily belabored throughout our Atlantic crossing. He didn't even wait for us to land to begin writing her what was to be the first of many, many letters, all reciprocated.

I even found myself a girlfriend of sorts. I have mentioned that, between the time that my wife left me and the time she died, I had had a lover whose gentle patience and generosity had failed to wean me from the life of vapid self-indulgence to which I had grown accustomed. Now, just when I needed it, fate threw us together again. Her name was Polly, and like me she was a volunteer at the drop-in center. Though she was naturally disinclined to approach me at first, given the callous treatment she had once received at my hands, I think that she sensed my burden of sorrow and was the kind of woman to whom such things are an attraction. And though she tried gently to wheedle my secret from me, I never spoke of the Conglomeros, and the mystery in which I shrouded my wound made me all the more urgent a target for her selfless affection. I'm afraid she fell a little in love with me again, and though I felt very tenderly toward her, and tried to be heedful of her evident sensitivity, that love was not one I was able to reciprocate. We made love sweetly, but even that was tinged with my sadness, which saddened her in turn.

One autumn evening, as we lay draped by my melancholy as if by an extra blanket, weighted even further by my sense of guilt at having abandoned Richard yet again, and exacerbated by a bottle of heavy port, my story spilled out of me. It came in a torrent deepened by a spillway of tears and accompanied, I seem to remember, by some gnashings of teeth and beatings of breast. It kept coming, all of it, until there was nothing left, neither the littlest sigh nor the least saltless tear.

Polly lay silent at my side for some time. I imagine that she felt I had told her an allegory, or at the very least a *commedia dell'arte* version of my actual tragedy. It is possible that this may have offended her. It is also possible that, despite having asked for it, she did not feel herself to be the appropriate receptacle for such a confession. Or, indeed, she may have sensed that my having chosen her as that receptacle was a not very subtle artifice for establishing a certain distance between us or for signaling that she was more of a friend than a lover to me. Whatever emotions were brewing in that preliminary silence, when she finally spoke there was an unmistakable impatience in her voice.

"So now what?" she asked. "You still love her."

"I suppose so."

"Shouldn't you be trying to win her back instead of wasting your time with me?"

I know I should have responded to the plea for reassurance that underlay her question, even if only out of compassion. But I couldn't, and the fact is, it never occurred to me to try. Instead of withdrawing the blade I had inadvertently planted, I twisted it.

"I would if I could," I whined, "but I don't know how. I don't know what she wants anymore. I used to think it was me. But the fact is, Forrest was always a mystery to me. I could never figure out what Connie saw in him, or what he wanted from her."

"What did you want from her?"

That was an easy question: Nothing, I thought, I wanted nothing but to be in her presence, to be allowed to love her. But was even that little true? What does a father want from his child? What does the child want? What does the fantasizer want from his fantasy woman, or the little girl from her prince? What does the serial killer want from his victims, or the priest from his flock, or the john from his whore, or the patient from his doctor, or the monarch from his subjects? The least I owed Polly was an honest answer.

"All I wanted was unconditional love."

"Is she a monster or a German shepherd?" Polly joked.

"No, no, it wasn't like that. I gave Connie more respect, independence, and admiration than I've ever given any human being. It's Forrest who treats her like a dog, keeping her on a leash, training her to perform, teaching her to jump at his command, manipulating her as it suits him. He's the one who does that."

"And you didn't?"

This was the second time I had been compared to Forrest Schaeffer, and I was beginning to resent the comparison. Of course, with hindsight I am willing to admit that there may have been some element of aptness to it, but at the time—and despite all that I had suffered—I could only attribute it to the sense of inadequacy felt by my accusers in the face of my moral strength, an inadequacy that prompted feelings of spite and vengefulness. Now, there was neither a spiteful nor vengeful bone in Polly's body—I know that now—but I wanted sympathy, not challenge, and comfort, not truth, so I daresay that our relationship would not have lasted long in any case, even if what transpired in December had not cut it prematurely short. Although I admired and respected Polly enormously, I seemed somehow destined to treat her cruelly and dismissively.

▲▲▲▲

A week before Christmas, as the frozen rain turned to black ice on the sidewalks overflowing with frantic shoppers, the Conglomeros returned to me. It returned of its own volition, and it returned tearfully repentant, the prodigal monster, and the fact that it did so in such a manner made me immediately ashamed of the ease with which I had abandoned all hope of such a miracle.

It was very late on Tuesday night, I recall, as I was trying to plow my way through *Moby Dick,* that the doorman buzzed to inform me that my mother was on the way up. My first thought was that, at Richard's instigation, my mother had somehow contrived to travel across the ocean by herself to pay me a surprise visit. Indeed, so sure was I of this hypothesis that when the door opened on a figure slumped in a wheelchair, it took me a moment, though but a brief one, to recognize my beloved ward. The creature just sat there, melting snow clinging to the brim of its pathetic, bedraggled sunbonnet, mascara-dyed tears coursing down its cheeks from beneath its Ray-Bans, until I recovered enough presence of mind to step aside and allow it slowly to wheel itself into the room, where it slid limply to the floor, limbs splayed every which way. I kneeled at its side, removed hat and wig, and gently stroked the great dome of its bald head. "There, there," I whispered. "It's all right, you're home now." The creature continued to weep for several minutes.

When finally the torrent abated, and I held the trembling creature tightly in my encircling arms, the story emerged. "I've left him," the Conglomeros said, and went on to describe the horrors of being Connie Lo Meros, human prophet. The creature evoked the continuous discomfort and pain of being perpetually in disguise and consigned to the wheelchair. Toward that end, Schaeffer had not even allowed the poor thing to disrobe and stretch in the privacy of his apartment, for fear of spies and yellow journalists. On the road it had been even worse, to the point where Connie had been compelled to sleep in wig and nightrobe, which was so restricting that the creature would awake with cramps in all six legs. It cited the never-ending daily cycle of interviews, press conferences, performances; meetings with managers, publicity agents, photographers, and charity hostesses; the long hours and bad food.

But worst of all had been Schaeffer himself. The creature could not find enough insults and curses to heap upon him. A slave-driving moneygrubber, an egomaniac, an insensitive, ruthless exploiter, he had turned out to be all that I had ascribed to him, and the creature was embarrassed and bitter at having allowed itself so willfully to be deceived. The philosophies of Dialectical Variablism were vacuous, facetious, self-serving, and it had only been by dint of daily indoctrinations, in conjunction with Schaeffer's enormous "personal charms," that the Conglomeros had succumbed to its false and dangerous teachings. Moreover, Schaeffer's charms themselves had proved evanescent, and he had begun not only to treat the creature with increasing callousness, but to lapse egregiously in his bedside manner, to the point where they had not made love in ten weeks and Connie suspected him of impotence (a suspicion which obviously I heard with great if dissembled satisfaction).

Furthermore, he had plans for the future involving privations and exertions even more terrible than those currently imposed. They included, as rumored, the foundation of a church with Connie as its prophet and high priest, yearly international tours modeled after the practices of the pope, and a variety of licensing agreements and franchises ranging from vegetarian restaurants to silver wheelchair pendants. But of all these plans, the one that had finally prompted the creature's desertion was the most heinous: The Conglomeros's true physicality was to be revealed to the world at a well-publicized rally to be held in the Tompkins Square bandshell. Schaeffer had gone so far as to draft sketches of the platform and of the scarlet robe that was to fall away at the triumphal revelation of Connie's naked form. The creature, fearful for its own safety and of possible reactions on the part of the government and the scientific and religious communities, had pled vigorously for the right to retain the new identity for which it had struggled and suffered for so long. But Schaeffer had insisted that such a revelation could only enhance—nay, authenticate!—Connie's status as a prophet, and that, with the host of the faithful swelling beyond all enumeration, any antagonistic agency would be powerless in the face of public support. And when he had told Connie that it would happen "whether she liked it or not," she had left, opposing to his acerbic threats a brief but decisive display of her own capacity to intimidate.

And now, here she was—"she" no longer, a Conglomeros, a glorious "it" once more—prostrate before me, begging my forgiveness and rueful of the day when the serpent had ever come between us. For the moment, all I could do was to insist that there was nothing to forgive, explaining what love means in the modern world. And we cried a little more while my heart exulted, my body clung to that precious warmth, and for one last, oblivious moment, with those eight tender arms encircling and caressing me, I was happy again. I could not express the joy I felt, I stuttered, that the creature had finally recognized its destiny as my beloved, and not as some crackpot postmodern prophet.

"What do you mean, 'crackpot postmodern prophet'?" I felt the Conglomeros's bodies stiffen beneath me, its arms disentangling from our hug.

"I thought . . ."

"You didn't think I was going to give up my preaching, did you?" The creature's voice was thin with disbelief.

"But . . . you said . . ."

"I left Forrest because he was manipulating me," it went on, "not because I doubted my calling. No, you taught me what I am. I am the prophet, and nothing can stop me from spreading the new gospel."

Later that night, when the Conglomeros, exhausted from its travails, was spread out in deep repose across the bed, I called Richard, describing the situation in a frantic whisper. He agreed with me that our friend was sorely troubled and potentially unstable, and that urgent measures were called for. He arrived first thing in the morning, and together we persuaded the creature that what it needed above all, in preparation for the tribulations ahead, was some healthful, recuperative country living, emphasizing as well the need to elude the thwarted taskmaster who would surely not be far behind. It was the latter argument, eliciting a deep shiver of panic and some palsied waving of tentacles, that won the creature over; in any case, we would have used forcible sedation if necessary to remove it to seclusion, and by noon we were settled and barricaded into our rural retreat, where the winter snows were piled in drifts almost to the windowsills.

▲▲▲▲

For Richard and me, the following weeks of "deprogramming" were marked by a fearful sense of urgent mission. Our anxieties were based on any number of well-founded concerns: that the creature, emotionally unbalanced as it was, would simply reappraise its rejection of Schaeffer and return to him; that it would recognize the nature of our plans before the program had time to take effect, and that such a recognition would provoke enough suspicion to thwart our designs; that Schaeffer would appear and attempt a re-seduction, or worse; that the creature's condition had progressed too far to be reversed, or that any attempt to effectuate such a reversal might lead to unforeseeable harm. There was also an unfounded paranoia that we were poised on the threshold of disaster, and it is precisely that paranoia which, in retrospect, seems to color and dominate my memory of those final, frenzied, snowbound weeks.

Not that frenzy or disquiet were the prevailing mood in our hideaway. On the contrary, as Richard and I invested our very souls in redeeming the creature so sorrowfully waylaid, we strove to infuse the household with an aura of hypnotic tranquillity, such that any sense of our being there for anything other than restful vacation might be allayed. In no way could the Conglomeros be allowed to suspect our intentions or motives, since one of the primary objects of our program was to cleanse the creature's psyche of all knowledge of human duplicity.

And what, precisely, were those intentions? Our plans were never specifically formulated, we were in any case entirely dubious of their potential effectiveness, and, of course, we were never given the opportunity to carry them to fruition. But given the creature's almost febrile delirium, none of that precluded the dire and immediate necessity of putting them into action. And, simply and straightforwardly, those plans were to return the Conglomeros, as nearly as circumstance and degeneration would allow, to what it had been when I first encountered it. That was the creature's only hope. I remembered having once scoffed at the concept of perfection restored like a shattered Grecian urn. Now, I would have to piece that urn back together, missing fragments or no, or I would soon have no urn at all.

We felt like Victorian doctors in a mental ward, baffled by schizophrenia and hysteria and having only the crudest theories and treatments available. Feeling our way blindly, then, our nostrum was to institute a program of subtle exercises and influences that would reverse the process of socialization that had brought the Conglomeros to its current state. Thus, instead of processed food, we would eat nothing but organic vegetables and grains, and roots and berries with the advent of spring; instead of television and literature, we would hold simple conversations and enjoy only the pleasures of nature; moral imperatives were to be replaced by instincts of survival, and, eventually, human company by animal. The idea was that, like Elsa the lion, the Conglomeros would by then be capable once more of fending for itself in the wild, and that, even were it never to be fully wild again, the memory of its life among humans would grow dimmer and less intrusive, and the creature's true, semianimal nature would be able to flourish and reassert itself. Gradually, then, we would restore the creature to an instinctual understanding of its place in the natural world, into which, in the final phase of our plan, it would be released.

We knew, however, that returning it to the Carpathians was impossible. Instead, we planned to rent a cabin somewhere in the Rockies—Idaho, Montana, or British Columbia—and expose the creature little by little to its new home. If the conditions seemed amenable and the patient adaptable, that is where it would stay while we returned to our home, perhaps never to see it again. We had no illusions that the plan was not ambitious and perhaps overly so; yet, knowing what we did about the creature's recuperative and mimetic capacities, we had every hope that what had been so carelessly wrought could, with care, be successfully unwrought. It is probably only due to thousands of years of acculturation that a similar plan cannot be implemented in human child rearing.

The first days were nightmarish. The Conglomeros ranted

its gospel while refusing the steamed rice and vegetables that were our only fare. One aspect of its humanity was a newfound sense of shame that would not allow it to go naked through the house, despite our example, which it deplored as "decadent." Like a smoker deprived of cigarettes, it wandered listlessly through the rooms searching for reading material, a television or a radio, all of which had been consigned to the conflagration. It cursed us as "prison keepers" and "abominations," and on several occasions seemed prepared to use violence to drive home its arguments. As agreed, Richard and I responded to such provocations with as few words as possible, and those were tender while eschewing sentimentality. The creature also refused pointblank to accompany us out of doors or to play or even look at the little kitten that we had bought it. It woke up in tears and terror several times each night, to which none of our comforting ministrations seemed to provide any comfort. There were even those moments we had feared most. "I don't know what I'm doing here," it would spit. "At least Forrest had some vision."

But those moments passed, and with them the worst obstacle to our plan. I knew the worst was behind us—that the fever, as it were, had broken—late one night about five days after we had arrived. We were receiving our nightly lecture on the immorality of cynicism, and the sermon was coming to its climax: "Somewhere in California," the creature pontificated, pointing a forest of fingers to the west, "a grape drops from the vine in protest against injustice. Do you do as much? Somewhere in Maine a wave laps against the shore in protest against racism. Do you do as much? Somewhere in Iowa a worm emerges from the soil in protest against illiteracy. Do you do as much? Somewhere in New Jersey, a crab louse . . ."

It stopped in midsentence, confused by the words that had sprung from its mouth. But I had recognized their import immediately: Those were not the words of *the* prophet, or of any prophet; in fact, there had been no prophecy or evangelism in the entire sermon. It was not the voice of Connie Lo Meros we were hearing, and though the voice had no identity as yet, the mere fact that the prophet seemed to have vanished was encouragement enough. While Richard and I exchanged meaningful glances, the Conglomeros let out a choking sob and fled the room.

Our experience had taught us to expect rapid progress after the initial symptoms of recovery, and indeed so it was. Those were weeks of great hope for Richard and me, and we might have savored them more than we did had we known what the immediate future held in store. As it was, we were too busy working on our plan and congratulating ourselves on its imminent success.

Now, too, I came to understand Victor Brauner's "The Meeting at 2 bis rue Perrel," which had perplexed me long before. In that painting, the Conglomeros reaching out to a passive virgin is actually reclaiming its lost innocence, a plea which Brauner—no longer "virgin" but corrupter—is unable to fulfill. But now I, triumphantly, would finally answer the call of that ancient plea!

Day by day we watched as the Conglomeros sloughed off the appurtenances of human weakness: anger, neurosis, shame, greed, pride, began slowly to melt away, revealing, as the melting snows the edelweiss, the far more simple and more beautiful entity beneath. It is a difficult process to describe, this reconstitution of innocence and childlike wisdom, since the emotions elicited in observing it are so close and personal to a man's heart. But when we dream of childhood, or when we cry to think of what has been lost, or when we joy in the inscrutability of a baby's face, those feelings bear a kinship of intensity to the ones that overwhelmed me as I watched the chrysalis of humanity disgorge its blissful monster. And as the old Conglomeros reappeared, so did I fall in love with it for a second time, to the point where doubts about returning it to nature began to trouble me and I had to turn to Richard to bolster my resolve.

Sure enough, the sermons and the Baptist self-righteousness were the first to go, followed by the sense of shame and suspicion. Naked and trusting, the creature wandered the house restlessly, craving stimulants of any kind to quell the still-ravenous human appetites that raged within. It retained a rampant libido which I was at great odds to resist, though resist I did (resistance came somewhat easier to Richard). It also craved meat, sugar, newspapers, witty repartee, and entertainment, but since none of these were available, the need for them quickly died. Within three weeks, it was happy just to snack on carrots and raw turnips, and to stare into the fire on the long evenings that Richard and I spent in loving supervision. It stopped answering to the name "Connie." Within a month, the deer were shyly poking their heads from the copses as we strode past on our daily walk, the naked creature happily oblivious to the cold. It developed a deep friendship with Victor the kitten, who returned the affection while steadfastly ignoring Richard and me. The creature's active vocabulary was also beginning to dwindle: I can remember how, not twenty days into its recovery, the Conglomeros searched its memory in vain for words like "virtue" and "American" that it had freely used only a week earlier. Gradually, too, its memory in general lost all definition and focus. "Dialectical Variablism" was soon no more than the lyrics of a song it had once known by heart, while Forrest Schaeffer was simply a fondly remembered eccentric. On the other hand, the creature's affection for Richard and me continued to grow, and the hugs and kisses we were constantly receiving bore not a trace of contrivance or disingenuousness.

This is not to say that the Conglomeros was anything close to truly resembling its former self. That, if at all achievable, was still a long way off, we knew. The creature was still very unstable, emotionally and psychically. Our very presence prevented it from ever breaking entirely with its human past, forgetting human speech, or requiring emotional sustenance, all of which would have to take place before we could even allow ourselves to consider heading west and experimenting with release. And if we ignored the occasional relapse—in which the virulent Connie Lo Meros would suddenly reappear for no apparent reason, lash us with stinging invective, and just as suddenly disappear without a trace—that, too, can be forgiven, since such episodes were rare and seemed to have no lasting effect on the creature's otherwise angelic disposition, daily reaffirmed. Yes, we were still far from "sol-rye" and hilltop caches, but we were moving in the right direction. Dizzied by the speed of our progress, and somewhat dulled with satisfaction by our vindication, Richard and I could be forgiven for anticipating the triumph of our wills and overestimating the preeminent durability of our handiwork.

For that was our mutual state of mind—hopeful and cocky—when the telephone rang one Friday morning in late January.

"Don't hang up on me if you know what's good for you," Schaeffer hissed.

"What do you want?"

"You know what I want. I want Connie back."

"You can't have it back. It doesn't want to go back."

"Listen," Forrest Schaeffer began, with the tone of exasperated condescension I had come to recognize and loathe, "have you read the papers lately? The whole country is in an uproar over the disappearance of Connie Lo Meros. A nationwide search is under way. Her followers are ready to do anything to get their hands on the people who kidnapped their prophet, and I would be only too happy to tell them where you are. Imagine a hundred angry Variablists overrunning your property."

I imagined it, and it was indeed an ugly prospect. "But there's something you don't understand," I said, trying to suppress the whine of panic that had crept into my voice. "The creature isn't the same. It's not Connie Lo Meros anymore. That's all over, forever. It's been deprogrammed. So you see, even if you did get the creature back it wouldn't do you any good at all."

"I don't believe you," Schaeffer said after a pause.

"It's true," I said, and added cockily, "Would you like a word with the creature?"

"No! I want to see her for myself in person, tomorrow, or we'll be on your doorstep by Sunday."

I had no choice but to acquiesce. "Where?"

"Here in New York."

"No, here."

"I said, New York City," and I crumpled before the menace in his voice. Eventually, after some negotiation, we came to an agreement. I wanted to meet in an open, public place in order to forestall any potential for deceit or violence, and I insisted that he be alone. Thus, we agreed to meet on Grand Army Plaza, across from the Sherry Netherland, at ten in the morning. By the time I hung up, Richard was hovering anxiously at my side.

We discussed our options. We both had the same first instinct—to jump in the car and drive and not stop until we had reached the mountains. But sober judgment quickly put that thought to rest: If Schaeffer had so easily discovered our number and address, he surely had my license plate number as well, and we would be sitting ducks for the state troopers on the interstate. And even if we were, impractically, to take the back roads and switch vehicles, Schaeffer would not let us go that easily. No, if I had found the Conglomeros in the Carpathians, Schaeffer could find it in the Rockies, and we did not want to condemn our ward to a life in flight and the even more awful prospect of recapture. For no good reason, then, we decided that we would trust Schaeffer to the extent that we would give him the opportunity to see for himself that Connie Lo Meros was no longer. If he was satisfied with that, we would be able to continue the implementation of our plan in peace of mind; if not, we would take our chances on the open road. Neither of us was very comfortable with our decision, and a deep oppression of foreboding hung over our household that night, causing the Conglomeros and Victor to whimper unconsciously in their games by the fireplace. Richard and I sat glumly at the bay window, staring out into the ink-black night, and I wondered what, if anything, he heard as he listened to the wind that howled out of the north and danced like banshees in the treetops. Our sleep, and the evil dreams that accompanied it, brought no tranquillity to our restless hearts.

We were up before dawn the next morning, and prepared ourselves in silence. Fortunately, when leaving New York I had had the foresight to bring along the bag of disguises, and from it we availed ourselves of a shaggy black wig and beard that had never been used before, such that, with the addition of a fisherman's cap and smoked granny glasses, the creature took on the appearance of a somewhat crazed war veteran in its brown herringbone overcoat. As we wheeled it into the back of the wagon, it seemed to sense the somber nature of our mission. "Where are we going?" it asked quietly, stroking the quiescent Victor curled in its lap. "New York," I said, trying to inject some cheer into my answer. "Won't that be fun?" the Conglomeros asked Victor, but Victor did not respond and the creature trembled involuntarily. Not a word was spoken as we hurtled down the thruway, but over the drone of the engine I could hear the creature softly humming the "Willow Song." Victor set up a plaintive accompaniment.

Richard drove to give me the freedom to move quickly in case of an emergency. We crossed the bridge, took the F.D.R. Drive to Ninety-sixth Street, then headed west. As we turned onto Fifth Avenue, I said to Richard in a whisper: "Remember, if there's any sign of trouble, hit the gas." He nodded, and I noticed that his hands, too, were trembling. We drove past my old apartment and were soon within sight of the Sherry Netherland.

A block before Grand Army Plaza, at Sixty-first Street, we stopped for a red light, and I saw Forrest Schaeffer up ahead, standing by the statue of Sherman and stamping his feet against the cold. Out in the open like that, he appeared to be alone; there were a few other loiterers on the plaza, but I would have recognized any of the hard-core Variablists and I saw none. Everything seemed to be in order, and Schaeffer to have upheld his end of the bargain in arriving unaccompanied. As a last-minute precaution, I tested the creature's preparedness. "Who's that?" I asked, pointing at Schaeffer through the windshield. But the creature had retreated so far into its animal nature that it merely squinted at my outstretched hand and said "Finger?" I was satisfied that we were ready to meet my nemesis and emerge victorious from the encounter.

The light changed and I turned to roll down my window so that I might talk to him without running the risk of leaving the car. But as I turned, I spied a lone figure huddling between the locked-up stands of the sidewalk book market. This person seemed to be staring intently through the tinted windows of our car, and it took us each a few moments to recognize one another. It was the morose film editor whom I had seen at the early sermons of Connie Lo Meros, and as his eyes widened in recognition, I saw him raise his fingers to his lips and let out a shrill, piercing whistle. Immediately a crowd of people began swarming out of the park a block ahead, some heading toward us while others ran to block the street. A trap!

"Go! Go!" I screamed, and Richard floored the accelerator, jamming his hand on the horn as we sped through the crowd. Fist blows rained down on the roof and windows as we drove past, and we were swamped in a tide of abuse and rage. Still, we made it through, and Richard ran the red light at Fifty-ninth Street. Our enemies followed in pursuit, and though we put some distance between us, we were forced to obey the signal at Fifty-seventh Street because of the heavy cross-traffic. When the light turned green they were less than a block away, close enough for me to see the fanatic delirium on their faces and to make me extremely fearful for my safety. The Conglomeros whimpered in the back, pathetically straining and twisting in its strapped-down wheelchair to get a glimpse of our pursuers. Victor huddled in the crook of its neck.

It seemed as if we would make our getaway easily enough, and as I exhorted Richard to make straight down Fifth Avenue and jump the lights, we put several more blocks between us and the mob, which ran heedlessly down both sidewalks. But the traffic, swollen with holiday-makers and weekend shoppers, grew steadily heavier as we approached Rockefeller Center, so that by the time we reached Fifty-second Street our lead had again been dangerously narrowed. Ahead of us, I saw only a sluggish tide of vehicles, and the sidewalks were clogged with tourists. Our capture seemed inevitable. And then I had a brainstorm.

"Turn left, turn left!" I shouted as we approached Fiftieth. "Pull up!" Temporarily concealed from our pursuers, I leapt from the car, flung open the side door, and wheeled the terrified Conglomeros out, jarring it painfully against the pavement. "Drive on!" As the car disappeared toward Madison,

I rolled the wheelchair up the ramp and into the side entrance of St. Patrick's Cathedral. Hidden behind the swinging doors, I watched the Variablists fly past, pursuing the car now empty of its quarry. My knees buckled and I sank to the floor with a sigh of relief, but was jolted to my feet a moment later as the door opened for a herd of tourists. "Let's take a rest in here," I panted, and the Conglomeros, with Victor's head poking out from the collar of the overcoat, nodded dumbly. As I guided us into the heart of the cathedral, I leaned over and whispered soothing words into the ear of the shivering creature, who, in imitation, bent down to soothe the terrified kitten. We made for a central pew, where, surrounded by the milling tourists, we might find safe haven for a moment while I considered our next move. I sat by the aisle, parking the wheelchair beside me.

The situation was certainly a desperate one. If the Variablists were to catch up with Richard, as was entirely likely, they would discover the deception and be down upon us in no time. On the other hand, if Richard had managed to evade them, the creature and I would have to make our escape from the city without him, an extremely precarious undertaking to say the least. He would undoubtedly come back to us here—eventually—but how long would we have to wait exposed like this to the public eye, every moment bringing closer the chance of discovery? And in the meantime, our harrowing experience had brought the Conglomeros to a highly agitated state of nervous excitement. Its eyes rolled wildly behind the sunglasses, and the wig and cap squirmed alarmingly over the fidgeting tentacular arms which they concealed. Victor keened pathetically.

How had we come to this? As I sat hanging my head, I inwardly bewailed every benevolent impulse that had ever sprung to my heart, for it was indubitably benevolence that had led me to entice the Conglomeros, to ravish it from its home, to educate it, to love it, and finally to corrupt it. And now it was benevolence again, the desire to save my ward from my own supposed altruism, that had brought us to the brink of disaster.

"Sorry," said a fat tourist as his camera swung into the back of the Conglomeros's head. The blow seemed to bring the creature partially to its senses.

"Where are we?" it asked tremulously.

"In a church, my love."

And what was to come next? How else would my generosity, my gentle humanism, my enlightenment, contribute to the creature's downfall? I tried to picture its future, to project it into the coming years, and I failed to see how it would ever be able to live wholly free of my influence, and by extension of every stinking, destructive, and meddling aspiration of the "human spirit." *I* had done this, no one else, and yet I had been motivated precisely by the desire to spare the creature from the taint of human contact, or so I had thought at the time. If I had not succeeded in saving the Conglomeros, who could?

"And all these people," the creature said, indicating the ever-growing multitude of gum-chewing, flashbulb-popping tourists swarming over the flagstones, chapels, and reliquaries, "are they worshipers?"

"No, my love," I cooed, "they're tourists. Now close your eyes, rest."

But perhaps it wasn't so bad. After all, I mused, just look at the remarkable progress made in mere weeks, and think of Victor Brauner's experience, of his return to a Conglomeros for whom he had become a total stranger. That was encouraging—if the creature had reverted to its former self on that occasion, why not again? Providing we got out of our current predicament, there really was no reason to despair—in fact, everything I knew about the creature should permit me to entertain great hopes for the future. The Conglomeros *would* return to the wild, it *could* recover the entirety of its miraculous nature, and I, as the guilty party, *should* be the one to restore it to all that I had stolen.

"Tourists in the temple?" the creature asked quizzically.

And not only tourists. All my optimism and cheery resolutions evaporated the instant I spied Forrest Schaeffer and several of his minions standing in the narthex and scanning the hordes with minute scrutiny. Obviously, they were not here to pray. On the other hand, while they had perhaps figured out our little ruse, it was clear from their behavior that they had not yet seen us and that they were not even certain we were here. There was still a good fifty yards between us, and the confusion of the crowd and the natural dimness of the cathedral assisting to delay our discovery, I felt confident that we could make it undetected up the nave and out the exit of the north transept onto Fifty-first Street. What we would do once outside was anyone's guess, but the current circumstances called for a cool head and quick and decisive action. The Variablists had already divided and were slowly advancing up the aisles in our direction. I stood up, my back carefully turned to our enemies, and eased the wheelchair into the pedestrian traffic of the central aisle. If I walked at a casual pace and resisted the impulse to look back, we would be safe.

"Tourists in the temple?" the Conglomeros repeated in an agitated voice tinged with ire, a voice that boded no good. I had heard this voice before, up at the stone house, whenever the creature was on the verge of one of its demented harangues. All the stress and anxiety of the day must have sparked it, and I knew from experience that there was little that could be done to forestall or mitigate its fury, once unleashed. Within a very short time, if I did not hurry, the creature would be preaching hellfire and brimstone to the tourists and bringing a world of woe crashing down upon us. I began to move faster, calling out "Watch your back!" as astonished tourists leaped aside to let us pass.

"Tourists in the temple?" Its voice, now beginning to assume the familiar Latino strain, was loud enough this time to draw some sharp glances, and we still had some distance to go to the exit. The crowds around the chancel looked to be almost impenetrable, but there was no other way to reach the exit, since the pews were too narrow for the wheelchair. I looked back, but could not distinguish any of our pursuers among the tourists. Was it possible that they had given up the cathedral as a lost cause? Victor mewed and I shushed him. I broke into a trot.

"Watch your back!" I called to an obese, blue-haired matron who had stepped directly into our path, Instamatic waving heavenward. She ignored my warning.

"Tourists in the temple!" the Conglomeros roared, and as we bore down she jumped in the nick of time. "This is a house of prayer! You will not carry cameras through the temple!" The crowd drew back in horrified anticipation of an apparent war veteran about to go berserk.

What transpired next happened so fast that I had no time to think, let alone to avert the ensuing disaster. In its increasingly evangelical wrath, the Conglomeros violently kicked out with one of its legs at the impeding crowd. This caused the fabric of its overcoat to snap taut in its lap, and little Victor, who had curled up there to sleep, was sent sailing into the pews, paws akimbo and wailing like an air-raid siren. Following the arc of its friend's flight, the creature let out a reedy "Victor!" which our pursuers, were they still present somewhere in the building, could not have failed to hear—the entire cathedral must have heard it. And indeed, there was Schaeffer, wearing a startled but grimly determined expression as he pushed his way up the nave toward us, eyes fixed on the wheelchair. But the wheelchair was now empty, for the Conglomeros had meanwhile sprung from the chair and gone scrambling through the pews in search of its wayward companion. Ducking low, I darted after it.

On its hands and knees, and having to squeeze through the narrow space between each row of pews, the Conglomeros showed its natural aptitude for speed and agility, and I soon lost it from sight. Nonetheless, given its constant cries of "Victor!" and the terror of the worshipers disturbed in their prayers by its passage, its progress was not difficult to follow. I kept up as well as I could as the creature weaved its way through the pews below eye level. In the meantime, the Variablists were closing in, endeavoring amid the growing confusion to box the creature in. One against four, there would be little I could do should they corner my beloved. And in the meantime, alerted by frightened tourists, the guards posted at the entranceways were beginning to take an interest in our strange and earnest game of cat and mouse.

The Conglomeros, as best as I could tell, was over near the altar of the Holy Face; I was by the north aisle, about thirty feet away; two Variablists were closing in from the confessionals, while two others (including Schaeffer) had us pinned down from the stations of the cross. In a moment, the Conglomeros and I would be cut off from one another. Suddenly, miraculously, my foot struck something soft and I looked down to see little Victor huddling beneath the leg of a pew. I picked him up and held him over my head. "It's Victor! I've found Victor!" I shouted at the top of my lungs. Like Venus rising from the sea, the Conglomeros slowly emerged from the pews to its full height, poised and dignified, its three slim bodies quivering gazellelike with tension. In its frantic pursuit, it had shed all its clothing. Now, a great smile of relief blooming on its face, it stretched out its tentacular arms to the mewing kitten, whose voice was the only thing to be heard—so it seemed to me—in the entire cathedral.

"Connie!" Forrest Schaeffer was dashing down the aisle toward us. The creature froze and its eyes filled with confusion and fear at the sound of its old name. It looked back at me, its gaze pleading for direction and understanding. We stood as if frozen, waiting, as if the moment possessed its own, innate resolution. But neither of us had time to make any decision, for just then a tourist, having taken a few seconds to assure herself of the reality of the monster before her, let out a shriek that filled the vacuum of our indecision and sent a wave of panic through the momentarily stunned audience. Within instants, the scene was one of vortical pandemonium as waves of people struggled toward exits that could not accommodate them, while a small phalanx of guards pushed their way in the opposite direction. I managed to sidestep into a pew to avoid being crushed and to keep close to the creature. Schaeffer was swallowed up in the chaos.

If the Conglomeros had only stayed where it was, I feel certain that disaster could have been avoided. The Variablists were nowhere to be seen and the guards were still far off. We could have waited a few minutes, then ducked under the pews, retrieved the wig, clothing, and wheelchair, and slipped quietly out a side exit. But the Conglomeros, as we all know, was a very impressionable creature. Watching the scenes of terror and panic, it was quickly terrorized and panicked too—unable to understand, of course, that it was itself the cause of alarm. When the main bronze doors of the cathedral were thrown open, and bright winter light flooded the interior and the mobs stampeded for the street, the Conglomeros was right with them, howling and flailing its arms in convincing imitation of their horror. With the frenzied monster right behind them, people tried to dodge and twist their way out of its path, but it stayed close on their heels, obeying precisely the same herding instincts. Of course, it looked like a chase. Of course, anyone who did not know the Conglomeros would see in it an abomination lusting after human flesh—a Minotaur, a Gorgon, a Scylla. And of course, when the guards drew their weapons and fired warning shots in the air that continued to echo long afterward, and when everyone threw themselves on the floor, and when the Conglomeros was left standing alone and confused, a perfect target as it turned this way and that, unaware that it was a target, not even when the guards slowly lowered their weapons, training them directly on the cowering monster—of course, when all this happened, I was too far away to intervene. The guns popped, the Conglomeros flinched and lurched but managed to flee out the main doors and down the stairs. Running after it, I almost slipped on the puddle of blood.

As I emerged into the bright sunlight, I saw the wounded monster, arms clutched to its sides, loping diagonally across Fifth Avenue as cars screeched to a halt and horrified shoppers scattered in every direction. Those who had been chased from the cathedral kept on running, so that, despite the crowds, I was alone in pursuing the creature as it disappeared down the Rockefeller Center Promenade. By the time I had rounded the corner, closely followed by several policemen, the Conglomeros was at the top of the stairs leading down to the skating rink, leaning against the handrail, its chests heaving furiously. I called to it as I ran, and it slowly turned its great head, its eyes so wide and translucent with fear that, like a physical blow, they knocked the breath out of me. And for a moment—I know, I'm sure I saw it— there flickered a light of love and compassion for me, for me alone. But then the policemen charged past and the creature jumped.

I reached the terrace above the rink and looked down. While traumatized skaters clung to the rail, the dying monster made pathetic, exhausted attempts to raise itself from the blood-stained ice. But, like a newborn foal, its failing limbs sprawled in every direction and it fell with every attempt. I ran down the steps, vaulted the barrier, and slithered across to my beloved, who by now had given up trying to move and lay panting, face pressed to the ice, beneath the statue of Prometheus. I took the creature's head into my lap and stroked its face, whispering. Its tentacular arms fluttered like butterflies about the crown of its skull, then alighted gently on my wrist. Its eyes stared, unable, I think, to see me.

"Now I see," the Conglomeros said, gasping for breath.

"What do you see, my love?"

"I see . . ."

"Who? Victor?"

"Victor . . . ? There is no Victor."

"Shh," I murmured. "Dobey-fray."

"Dobey-fray," came the hoarse, almost inaudible reply.

"Sol-rye," I said, but there was no echo.

When next I looked up, my eye was caught by a flash of gold through the thick green boughs of the Christmas tree. It was the engraving above the entrance of the RCA Building, but through my tears it recalled another spark of light, glimpsed through the trees long before in a distant land. For some reason I found myself unable to tear my gaze from the legend. "Wisdom and knowledge," proclaimed the wayward star, "shall be the stability of thy times."

That, then, is the substance of my story.

There are, of course, loose ends to tie up. As you know, I spent the three months following the Conglomeros's death in the deepest and most sinister depression. It has since taken me some four weeks to compose the tale you have just read—completed, as it were, in one sitting—and though it is now early April, the only signs of spring are the tiny crocus buds pushing up through the winter's mire. I shall soon be leaving this house forever—the real-estate agent has already communicated an offer that I shall accept. I will return to New York City, of course—to my Bible lessons, to my apartment, to my volunteer work, and even to Polly, who has apparently forgiven my desertion and must steel herself for a more subdued—though, I hope, a wiser—Aaron than she knew before. I will also return to Richard Hand, who is waiting for me, and to my mother, who will shortly be joining him. Ion, I am deeply grieved to say, still languishes in jail, and there is nothing I can do for him. Perhaps a change of leadership in his country will someday free him. I have kept little Victor with me, of course, and his playfulness and nonchalance are of great comfort to me in this solitude.

Within moments after its death, the Conglomeros's body was carted away by some city agency or other and lies, I believe, on several dissecting tables and under myriad microscopes deep within the bowels of Rockefeller University. Having claimed responsibility for the creature, I had hoped to be allowed, too, to claim its body; instead, I find myself charged on various counts of mayhem and guardianship of a dangerous animal without a permit. My trial comes up in the fall, and my lawyer assures me that I will get off with a fine. The entire affair has been miraculously hushed up—which explains the leniency of the charges against me—and no one has yet made the connection between the vanished Connie Lo Meros and the so-called "orangutan" that ran amok in central Manhattan. Forrest Schaeffer has kept his mouth shut, as shall I, it goes without saying. If this book is ever published, it will be as a work of fiction and under an assumed name, since, fictitious or not, its lessons are the same.

I want so desperately to spare the reader a self-righteous analysis of those lessons—I have learned, if nothing else, the perils of self-righteousness. You can think of me and of my actions as you will: I am beyond caring, and whatever judgment may come to your mind has occurred to me first. And yet, I would like somehow to be able to compose a fitting epitaph to the Conglomeros, and that I shall not attempt. How can you write an epitaph for someone you never knew, for something that was ever changing, ever new? It is like writing an epitaph for oneself, which, like all epitaphs, is a great mistake. The Conglomeros was not an evil, ugly thing—it was good and beautiful, and I have had such little experience in that sphere that I hesitate to comment upon it, let alone to eulogize its passing. All I can say about the death of the Conglomeros has been said a thousand times before in other contexts, and all I can suggest about the death of goodness and beauty is that you look at the world around you. I don't mean to end with the facile pessimism that it is not spring but only the end of the world, but when I think of Victor Brauner's assertion that the Conglomeros is before, after, and within Man—I can only wish that the Conglomeros were still alive.

About the Author

JESSE BROWNER is a native of New York City, where he works in the international civil service. His previous books include translations of Cocteau, Eluard, and Rilke, and, in 1992, *Céline: A Biography.* He is currently at work on his next novel, *Turnaway.*

About the Type

This book was set in Walbaum, a typeface designed in 1810 by German punch cutter J. E. Walbaum. Walbaum's type is more French than German in appearance. Like Bodoni, it is a classical typeface, yet its openness and slight irregularities give it a human, romantic quality.